Dawn of Wolves

BOOK THREE
THE KINGDOM OF MERCIA

JAYNE CASTEL

WINTER MIST
PRESS

Historical Romances by Jayne Castel

DARK AGES BRITAIN

The Kingdom of the East Angles series
Night Shadows (prequel novella)
Dark Under the Cover of Night (Book One)
Nightfall till Daybreak (Book Two)
The Deepening Night (Book Three)
The Kingdom of the East Angles: The Complete Series

The Kingdom of Mercia series
The Breaking Dawn (Book One)
Darkest before Dawn (Book Two)
Dawn of Wolves (Book Three)

The Kingdom of Northumbria series
The Whispering Wind (Book One)
Wind Song (Book Two)
Lord of the North Wind (Book Three)
The Kingdom of Northumbria: The Complete Series

DARK AGES SCOTLAND

The Warrior Brothers of Skye series
Blood Feud (Book One)
Barbarian Slave (Book Two)
Battle Eagle (Book Three)
The Warrior Brothers of Skye: The Complete Series

The Pict Wars series
Warrior's Heart (Book One)

Novellas
Winter's Promise

Epic Fantasy Romances by Jayne Castel

Light and Darkness series
Ruled by Shadows (Book One)
The Lost Swallow (Book Two)

Dawn of Wolves by Jayne Castel

Edited by Tim Burton

Cover photography courtesy of www.istockphotos.com

Maps courtesy of Wikipedia

Visit Jayne's website and blog: www.jaynecastel.com

Follow Jayne on Twitter: @JayneCastel

***

For grandad—your love for East Anglia inspired me to write these books.

***

Maps

Settlements of Angles, Saxons and Jutes in Britain in about 600

Celtic peoples
Angles
Saxons
Jutes
sea, swamp or alluvium

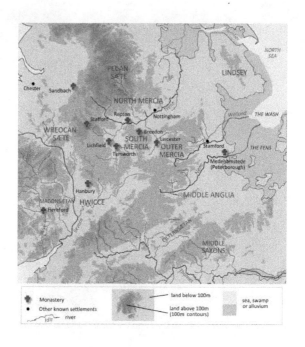

Historical background for
Dawn of Wolves

In the seventh century, England was not as we know it today. The Anglo-Saxon period lasted from the departure of the Romans, from around 430 AD, to the Norman invasion, in 1066 AD. My novels focus on the period in between the departure of the Romans, and the first Viking invasion in 793 AD—a 300 year period in which Anglo-Saxon culture flourished. The British Isles were named Britannia (a legacy of the Roman colonization) and split into rival kingdoms. For the purposes of this novel, we focus on two of them: Mercia and Kent.

Glossary of Old English
(in alphabetical order)

béagas: arm rings
Blod monath: Blood month (November)
ealdorman: earl
Ēostre: Easter
Englisc: English (language)
fæder: father
fyrd: a king's army, gathered for war
handfasted: married
heah-setl: high seat (later called a "dais") for the king and queen
hōre: whore
Hwæt?: What?
Lindisfarena: Lindisfarne Island (Holy Island)
mōder: mother
Nithhogg: a fire-breathing dragon that lived in the underworld
nón-mete: midday meal (literally "noon-meat")
Powys: Wales
thegn: a king's retainer
Thrimilce: May (month) (literally "the month of three milkings," when livestock were often so well fed on fresh spring grass that they could be milked three times a day)
thrymsas: Anglo-Saxon gold shillings
Thunor: Thor
"Wes hāl": "Greetings" in Old English
Winterfylleth: Anglo-Saxon Halloween
Woden: the Anglo-Saxon father of the gods (Odin in Viking mythology)
wyrd: fate

Cast of characters

Aeaba and Burghild: thegn's wives at Tamworth
Aethelred: Prince of Mercia
Aethelthryth of Ely: Ermenilda's aunt, Seaxburh's sister
Cyneswide: Wulfhere's mother, now a nun at Bonehill
Elfhere: Mercian warrior
Eorcenberht of Kent: Ermenilda's father, King of the Kentish
Eorcengota: Ermenilda's sister
Ermenilda: Princess of Kent/Queen of Mercia
Glaedwine: cunning man (healer)
Oswiu: King of Bernicia (Northumbria)
Paeda: Wulfhere's brother (dead)
Penda: Wulfhere's father (dead)
Seaxburh of Ely: Ermenilda's mother
Seaxwulf: monk
Tondberct of Ely: East Angle ealdorman
Wada and Alfwald: King Oswiu's stewards
Werbode: Mercian warrior, Wulfhere's chief counsellor
Wulfhere: Prince/King of Mercia
Wynflaed: Ermenilda's handmaid

Love will find a way through paths where wolves fear to prey.
—Lord Byron

Speak of the wolf and you will see its teeth.
—Unknown

Prologue
The Winter Meeting

*Cantwareburh, the Kingdom of the Kentish,
Britannia*

Winter, 657 AD

Ermenilda watched the snow fall. The delicate
flakes fluttered down from a darkening sky like
apple blossoms caught by a gust of wind. An
ermine crust covered the garden's gravel paths and
frosted the plants that had not died away over the
winter.

Damp, gelid air stung Ermenilda's throat, and her
fingers were numb, but still she lingered. As always, she
was reluctant to leave her refuge. She circuited the path
between the high hawthorn hedge and the frosted sage
and rosemary, her boots sinking deep into the snow.

Despite the cold, she had ventured out here to escape
the oppressive atmosphere of the king's hall, which was
full of greasy smoke and the reek of stale sweat.
Outdoors, the air tasted like freshly drawn cider. Better
yet, she did not have to listen to the prattle of women,
the booming voices of men, and the squeals of children
bored with being cooped up indoors.

Ermenilda loved this secret spot; it was her
sanctuary. Her father had told her the Romans built this
garden, and that it was a crumbling ruin when he had
first come to live in Cantwareburh. Since then, his wife
had poured her energy into restoring the secluded space.

As soon as she could walk, Ermenilda accompanied her mother to the garden, as did her younger sister. Even over the winter, the three women spent most afternoons out here—the garden was a passion they all shared.

At the far end of the garden, Ermenilda paused. There, she admired the snowy branches of her mother's prized quince tree. As she gazed upon it, a veil of melancholy settled over her.

Soon, I will have to leave this place.

Nervousness fluttered just under her ribs, replacing the sadness, before giving way to a lingering excitement.

Ermenilda had heard that Eastry Abbey also had a magnificent garden. Once settled there, she would no longer miss this one. She was hoping that her father would let her take her vows at Eastry in the spring. He had been noncommittal whenever she raised the idea, but she had time to convince him yet.

Dusk closed in, but still Ermenilda lingered. It was only when a shadowy figure emerged from the arbor, at the opposite end of the garden, that she realized she had been missed. Cloaked head to foot in fur, her younger sister hurried down the path toward her, her face rigid with purpose.

"I was beginning to think you had frozen to death out here! Come inside, Erme!"

Ermenilda sighed, irritated that her sister had shattered her solitude.

"I'll come in soon enough," she replied, waving Eorcengota away.

"You must come now," her sister insisted, her eyes shining. A mixture of cold and excitement had flushed Eorcengota's impish face. "We have guests this evening, and Fæder insists we join them for supper!"

"Guests?"

Ermenilda's irritation grew. She hated it when strangers arrived at her father's hall—especially if they were ealdormen, for she did not like how some of them leered at her.

"Yes, an exiled prince from Mercia," Eorcengota enthused, virtually hopping up and down on the spot with eagerness. "He and his men are stabling their horses as we speak. Fæder wants us indoors to greet him!"

A knot of apprehension formed in Ermenilda's belly. Unlike her silly goose of a sister, she did not like the sound of this visitor. Her father would be delighted of course; they rarely hosted royalty from Britannia's other kingdoms. The Kingdom of the Kentish often appeared of little importance in the wars, politics, and intrigue among the others who ruled.

Ermenilda reluctantly fell into step with Eorcengota, following her out of the garden and through the apple orchard. The trees were naked this time of the year, their bare, spidery branches dark against the swirling snow. Ahead, the outline of the Great Hall loomed. A high, timbered structure with a straw-thatched roof, it sat raised above the surrounding garden, orchard, and stables on great oak foundations. The hall cast a long shadow in the gathering dusk.

Shaking snow off her cloak, Ermenilda climbed the wooden steps to the platform before the doors. She nodded to the spearmen guarding the entrance and pushed the heavy oaken door open. Then she entered, with Eorcengota following close at her heels.

Just inside the door, she almost collided with a group of men who were in the process of removing their cloaks and weapons. Ermenilda realized with a jolt that these must be the Mercians. They were dressed for traveling in thick fur cloaks, leather jerkins, woolen tunics, and heavy boots. It appeared they had tended to their horses swiftly and entered the hall just ahead of the princesses.

Fæder will be cross.

Ermenilda feigned calm, shrugged off her fur cloak, and handed it to a waiting servant, aware that curious male gazes had settled upon her. She did not want to look their way but, against her own will, felt her gaze drawn to one of the men.

He stood near to her, little more than an arm's length away. The moment their eyes met, her breath rushed out of her—as if she had just tripped.

She had never seen a man so striking, so coldly beautiful. His eyes, ice blue, held her fast. His face was so finely drawn it appeared chiseled, and his long, white-blond hair fell over his broad shoulders. He was a big man, and she had to raise her chin to meet his gaze. The newcomer was dressed in leather armor and had just finished unbuckling a sword from around his waist, which he handed to a servant.

"Good eve, milady," he murmured.

The sound of his voice, low and strong, stirred something in the pit of Ermenilda's belly—a sensation she had never felt before—an odd kind of excitement mingled with fear.

"Wes þū hāl," she responded formally, trying to ignore the fact that her breathing had quickened. The man's gaze remained boldly upon her face, an arrogant smile curving his lips. Her father's booming voice saved her from having to converse with him further.

"Ermenilda!"

King Eorcenberht of Kent strode across the rush-strewn floor, sending servants scattering in his wake. He was a huge man, in both height and girth, a great fighting man in his youth. A thick beard, the color of hazelwood, covered his face—the same shade as the unruly mane, streaked through with gray, that flowed over his broad shoulders. Physically, his daughters—both slender and blonde like their mother—bore no resemblance to Eorcenberht.

"Apologies, Lord Wulfhere," Eorcenberht called as he approached. "My daughters were supposed to be here to greet you."

The blond man tore his gaze from Ermenilda and favored the Kentish king with a cool smile.

"And they are, Lord Eorcenberht. I have just been welcomed by one of them."

Something in the way the man spoke the words made Ermenilda feel flustered, as if she had done something wrong.

"Sorry, Fæder," she murmured before quickly sidestepping the Mercian lord. "I was in the garden and lost track of time."

"Join your mother," the king grumbled, "and help pour mead for our guests."

"Yes, Fæder."

Glad to be free of the Mercian's penetrating stare, Ermenilda cast her gaze downward and hurried away.

As always at this hour, the king's hall bustled with activity. A handful of servants were finishing preparations for the light evening meal—a supper of griddle bread, pickled onions, salted beef, and cheese—as the household ate their largest meal at noon. The servants had put out long tables where the king's thegns would take their meal, while the king and his kin dined upon the high seat.

Eorcengota caught up with her sister. They made their way toward a long worktable next to the nearest of the two fire pits.

"That must be Prince Wulfhere of Mercia," she whispered. "He's handsome, don't you think?"

"No," Ermenilda lied.

They joined their mother, Queen Seaxburh, upon the high table where she was pouring mead into cups.

"Fæder's guests are here," Ermenilda announced. She picked up another clay jug and began helping her mother.

"Yes, so I've seen."

There was no missing the acerbity in their mother's voice. Ermenilda saw her glance in the direction of the newcomers and glimpsed a flash of hostility in her mother's usually serene eyes.

"Mōder, what is it?"

"I have no wish to dine with Penda's whelp," the queen replied, her attention returning to her task. "Penda killed my father and brother. I would rather not break bread with his son."

Ermenilda glanced back at the blond man, who was now making his way across the floor. He appeared to be listening attentively while her father talked to him. She knew that her grandfather—King Annan of the East Angles—and her uncle, Jurmin, had both fallen three years earlier in battle against the Mercians. It had taken place in the marshes at Blythburgh, in the borderlands between Mercia and East Anglia. Her mother, who adored her father, had been inconsolable when she learned the news.

Seeing the look on her face now, Ermenilda saw that the grudge her mother bore Mercia ran deep. Not that Ermenilda blamed her. She cast a dark look at Prince Wulfhere and prayed her father send him quickly on his way.

Ermenilda had listened to many a tale about ruthless King Penda around the fire pit at night. The violent pagan, who would stop at nothing to expand his borders, had died in battle against Northumbria two years earlier, but that had not stopped the stories about him.

At least Fæder will not wed me to a pagan, Ermenilda assured herself as she finished filling the cups. Eorcenberht was a god-fearing man who, just a year earlier, had overseen the destruction of all the pagan idols in Cantwareburh. He also had insisted that the town observe Lent, the period of fasting after Ēostre.

Ermenilda sneaked a glance at the Mercian prince as he stepped up on the high seat. Frankly, despite his good looks and charisma, this man frightened her. He was different from her father, who was loud, bluff, and easy to read. The prince appeared to be a man who said little and thought much—she did not trust such men.

Taking a seat at the table upon the high seat, to the left of her mother, Ermenilda was disconcerted to see that their guest had sat down at her father's right—the spot usually reserved for his eldest son, Ecgberht. Prince Wulfhere was sitting directly opposite her, and she realized there would be no escaping his gaze during the meal.

Servants placed wooden boards, piled high with food, upon the table. Ermenilda watched Prince Wulfhere help himself to a generous serving of bread, cheese, and salted pork. The king watched him, smiling.

"I am glad you have come to dine at our table, Lord Wulfhere."

"And I am thankful for your hospitality," the Mercian replied. "You welcome an exiled prince into your hall on a cold night. For that, I am grateful."

Ermenilda stole a glance at her mother. The queen sat still and silent, hardly touching her food. The joviality on her husband's face was absent upon Seaxburh's.

"Not exiled for much longer, if I have anything to do with it," Eorcenberht replied, raising his cup high into the air.

The prince fixed him with a cool, level gaze.

"So you will help me regain the Mercian throne?"

"Aye, I have no wish to have Northumbrians preying upon my borders. Mercia has always been good to the Kentish people. I will not abandon you now."

The queen visibly paled at this, her grip on her bronze cup tightening. Ermenilda had never seen her mother so incensed. Yet, the king appeared oblivious to it. Heedless, he continued.

"I will gift you one hundred Kentish spears—my bravest warriors—to help you retake Tamworth."

The prince nodded and smiled.

"You are generous, Lord Eorcenberht."

Ermenilda watched their conversation with a growing sense of unease. She knew that the Northumbrian king, Oswiu, had held control over the Mercian stronghold of Tamworth for the past year. The Northumbrians had controlled southern Mercia ever since the murder of King Paeda, last Ēostre. It dismayed her to hear that her father was now involving himself in matters that did not concern him. If this exiled prince failed to retake the Mercian throne, there would be consequences for Kent.

Still, a woman's opinion mattered little when it came to politics, so she kept silent. Likewise, the queen held her tongue, although Ermenilda could see it cost her to do so.

The meal progressed, and the conversation shifted to other things. The king complained about the bitter winter that lay upon them and then asked the prince about his exile.

"How have you managed to escape capture?" he asked.

"I have been living in the woods of southern Mercia," Wulfhere replied, "and gathering men loyal to me. Local folk have been only too happy to hide me."

"My men tell me you arrived here with a white wolf?"

The prince smiled at this. It was the first truly warm smile that Ermenilda had seen him give.

"Her name is Mōna. I've left her in the stables while I'm here. She will trouble no one as long as she is left in peace."

"So the wolf travels with you?"

"She does. Mōna is my shadow."

Ermenilda suppressed a shudder; this man was most definitely a pagan. There was something wild—dangerous—about him. As if sensing her reaction, Prince

Wulfhere looked at her. Their gazes met for an instant, and Ermenilda saw his naked interest.

Heart pounding, she looked away and stared down at the remains of her supper.

"Your eldest daughter is quite lovely," Wulfhere commented. "Is she betrothed yet?"

"Not yet," the king replied. "She wishes to take the veil, but although I would like one of my daughters to serve god, I would prefer my eldest married well."

Ermenilda glanced up, shocked by her father's admission. She had been sure he would agree to let her join the nuns at Eastry. Of the two sisters, she was far more suited to such a life. Eorcengota was too spirited and silly to enjoy life as a nun, whereas Ermenilda craved quiet and solitude.

"Would you consider wedding her to me then?" Wulfhere asked.

Ermenilda watched her father's face and knew the offer had delighted him. However, he did not reply immediately. Instead, he leaned back in his chair and fingered the elaborately carved armrests while he mulled the request over. She glimpsed a shrewd glint in his eye and realized he was calculating something.

"It depends on two things, Lord Wulfhere," he replied eventually.

The Mercian put down his cup of mead and returned the Kentish king's gaze, his expression unreadable.

"And what are they?"

"The first is you must be baptized, renounce the old gods, and destroy all traces of them at Tamworth. I cannot wed my daughter to a pagan."

"And the second?"

"You must win back the Mercian throne before you and Ermenilda can be handfasted. Once you are the King of Mercia, she is yours."

Ermenilda slowly let out the breath she had been holding. Her father's conditions had made her relax slightly.

Wulfhere's father had flatly refused to be baptized, and she wagered that his son was cut from the same cloth. Plus, taking back Tamworth from the Northumbrians sounded like a difficult task at best. Perhaps a life at Eastry was not lost to her after all.

Unfortunately, Wulfhere's next words shattered her hopes. He glanced first at Ermenilda and smiled, although his eyes were hungry. Wulfhere's gaze met the king's once more.

"I agree to your conditions," he replied firmly. "I will accept your god and take Tamworth back for my people . . . and then . . ."

His gaze flicked back to Ermenilda, and she wilted under the heat of his stare.

"I will come to claim your daughter."

PART ONE

One year later . . .

Chapter One
Stalking Shadows

The Kingdom of Mercia, Britannia

Winter, 658 AD

The full moon sailed high in the sky. It drifted in and out of patches of wispy clouds, intermittently illuminating the world below in silver. The rain had cleared, as hoped, although the ground still squelched underfoot.

Wulfhere crept forward, alongside the eastern bank of the River Tame, his wolf at his heels. Mōna moved silently, alert and watchful, her white pelt glowed palely in the darkness, like the moon she was named after.

The pair were at the head of the group. None of the warriors carried torches, finding their way instead by the light of the moon. Although his men were trying to move as quietly as possible, the creaking of leather, the hiss of their breathing, and the whisper of their heavy treads seemed to echo through the stillness.

None of them wore helmets or carried shields—not even Wulfhere. For what lay ahead, they needed to be fast and deadly. Wulfhere had drawn his sword, Shield Breaker, ready for the fight.

Wulfhere's pulse started to accelerate as they approached the low gates.

After two years in exile he was about to take back his birthright. Yet caution tempered his impatience to enter Tamworth.

Is Aethelred loyal?

His success hinged on his brother's keeping his word. Aethelred had promised that when the moon had fully risen, men would open Tamworth's low gate. He had sent word to assure them that Oswiu's stewards were ignorant of their plans. Aethelred would be waiting for his brother in the Great Tower, with a group of men loyal to Wulfhere.

Wulfhere was wary. He trusted few men, and his brother was not among them. However, in truth, Aethelred had always been easier to like than Paeda, his elder brother.

Paeda had been a snake. He had betrayed their father on the eve of battle and given away true power over Mercia so that he could marry Oswiu of Bernicia's daughter, a young woman he had obsessed over.

Wyrd—fate—had turned against Paeda in the end. Rumor had it that Alchflaed, the flame-haired beauty Paeda had wed, had slain him while he slept, before fleeing into the wilderness.

Wulfhere pushed aside thoughts of his brothers and focused his attention entirely upon his destination. He could not afford to let himself be distracted now. He would discover soon enough if Aethelred coveted the throne for himself.

Ahead, he glimpsed a gap between the heavy oaken and iron gates. Wulfhere grinned, relief turning his mood from wary to jubilant. He need not have worried.

Inside, two spearmen awaited them. One of them stepped forward to greet Wulfhere.

"M'lord," he whispered urgently. "The high gate is also open. We must hurry before someone raises the alarm."

Wulfhere did not need warning twice. He nodded and motioned to the men behind him that it was safe to enter. Then, on winged feet, like Thunor himself, Wulfhere took off at a sprint up the main way that led to

Tamworth's inner palisade. Mōna ran at his side, as silent as a shadow.

Ahead, the Great Tower of Tamworth shone silver against the pitch black of the night sky. In daylight, the tower was a less prepossessing sight: dirty gray stone encrusted with lichen. A shiver went through Wulfhere as his gaze traveled down it. He was home.

No light shone from the tower's thin windows. Everyone inside slumbered. Wulfhere smiled once more and increased his speed, his soft-soled hunting boots barely making a sound on the roughly paved street.

As promised, the high gate was also open.

"Ready, milord?" one of his warriors asked, his voice a low rumble. The man's name was Elfhere. The tall, blond warrior had left Tamworth after the Northumbrians took control of it and had sought Wulfhere out in the wilderness. Elfhere limped slightly, from an old injury, but he was still one of Wulfhere's best. Wulfhere was glad to have him at his side.

"Aye," Wulfhere replied, flashing him a fierce grin. "Let's send these Northumbrians to meet Nithhogg!"

The thought of the great serpent, which resided in the underworld, feasting on the flesh of his enemies, caused a thrill to course through his veins. His bloodlust had awakened. No Northumbrian who came within reach of Shield Breaker tonight would be spared.

Once it was done, he would wed Ermenilda.

Even a year later, he could still picture her clearly. He had wanted Ermenilda from the moment he saw her. Young and slender, the Kentish princess radiated ethereal beauty, and it had ensnared him. Long, straight blonde hair, a few shades darker than his, flowed over her shoulders, framing a delicately featured face and soulful eyes the color of walnut.

The girl had a demure manner, yet she had held his gaze unflinchingly at the door to her father's hall. He had seen the way her face flushed when he stared at her, the way her breathing quickened. The image of how she had looked that evening remained with him. Ermenilda had been radiant as she entered, with rosy cheeks and snowflakes in her hair.

She was just one more reason he had to retake Tamworth.

Wulfhere reached up, his fist closing around the small iron spear he wore on a leather thong around his neck; it was the spear of Tiw, the god of war. He had not yet renounced the old gods, although the time was coming when he would have to do so. Wulfhere was not sure he would ever truly cast them aside, for the gods of his ancestors meant a great deal to him.

Tonight, Tiw would guide his sword and help him regain his birthright.

They stormed the tower in a fury, a tide of angry men surging into the Great Hall. One or two oil-filled clay cressets still burned around the perimeter of the hall, giving them enough light to discern friend from foe. Wulfhere had ordered his men to light the torches inside the doors as soon as he entered.

He wanted to see the look on his enemies' faces before he killed them.

Aethelred had sent descriptions of the two stewards. They were both powerfully built men, their arms glittering with arm rings. Wada was blond and Alfwald red haired. Wulfhere's brother had assured him they would be easy to spot—and Wada now slept high above the rest of the hall upon the King's Loft.

Wulfhere crossed the hall amid cries of the men, women, and children who had been sleeping upon the rushes. He saw Aethelred emerge from his alcove. His brother was fully dressed and gripped a seax.

Their gazes met and Aethelred grinned. Wulfhere knew that grin well—he had seen it often as a child, when he and his younger brother got up to mischief. He grinned back realizing that his fears for his brother's loyalty were unfounded. Aethelred would not betray him.

Wulfhere's men fanned across the hall. Three Mercian ealdormen had joined him: Immin, Eafa, and Eadbert. They were powerful, respected men, who had brought their own warriors with them. Wulfhere met Immin's eye as the hulking ealdorman with a mane of grizzled blond hair stepped up beside him.

Immin grinned. "Fire in your belly yet, milord?"

Wulfhere smiled, showing his teeth. In truth, he was more than ready. He longed to spill Northumbrian blood, to cut down those who had no right occupying his hall or commanding his people.

Some of his men had already engaged the Northumbrians. He spied Elfhere grappling with a warrior near one of the fire pits—but it was Werbode, the captain of Wulfhere's band, who led the charge. Tall and strong with a shock of black hair and a neatly trimmed beard, the warrior was a fearsome sight. Clad in boiled leather, Werbode howled his rage as he slashed his way across the rush-strewn floor.

Wulfhere turned his attention away from the melee and strode across the hall toward the ladder to the King's Loft. Men and women scrambled out of his way. It was not just Wulfhere they were frightened of but also the huge white wolf that stalked at his side.

Leaving Mōna to guard the foot of the ladder, Wulfhere sheathed his sword and drew his seax. Then, he clamped the blade between his teeth so that he could scale the ladder quickly.

Wada was scrambling out of the furs when Wulfhere reached the platform. He was naked. A young slave girl, the iron collar around her neck gleaming dully in the flickering torchlight, cowered behind him.

Rage twisted Wada's bearded face, whereas the slave had gone the color of milk.

"So the upstart pup has returned." Wada snarled, reaching for his sword that lay beside the furs. Even on the defensive, the Northumbrian ealdorman did not show a trace of fear. "Come home for a whipping have you?"

Chapter Two
The Taking of Tamworth

Wulfhere held Wada's gaze. He did not bother to reply to the insult—the steward was just trying to bait him. Instead, he inclined his head slightly and favored the Northumbrian with a cool smile.

Beneath them, the roar of battle shook the Great Tower of Tamworth to its foundations. The platform beneath Wulfhere's feet vibrated from the force of it. It was as if the gods were raging, and Wulfhere could taste the bloodlust in the air.

Wada lunged, but Wulfhere had anticipated him. Two steps took him up against the ealdorman, beyond the reach of his sword, where Wulfhere drove his seax blade up under Wada's ribs.

Wada inhaled sharply, his breath wheezing as if Wulfhere had punched him in the stomach. As the warrior struggled against him, Wulfhere withdrew the dagger and deftly slashed the Northumbrian's throat open.

The slave girl screamed, as the ealdorman slumped to the fur-covered floor, gurgling and thrashing.

Wulfhere let him fall. Ignoring the blood, which had splattered over him, he cast a glance at the cowering slave. Tears streaked her thin face.

"Please . . . ," she begged, her voice quaking. "Don't kill me . . ."

Wulfhere dismissed her; he was not interested in killing defenseless slave girls. There were others more worthy of death this night. He turned away and quickly descended the ladder to the main hall.

Mōna was savaging a Northumbrian warrior, who had tried to climb the ladder in an attempt to come to Wada's assistance. The man's screams echoed high into the rafters as the wolf pinned him to the ground, her huge jaws ripping at his flesh.

Wulfhere moved around them, leaving Mōna to her task, and stepped down onto the floor.

Men fought with seaxes, boning knives, or their fists. Although it was customary to leave your weapons at the door inside the Great Hall, many of the Northumbrians were armed. Surrounded by Mercians, they wisely carried their swords and seaxes everywhere.

Alfwald, the red-haired ealdorman, slashed at any Mercian who came within reach, the blade of his sword running dark. He strode now, toward Aethelred, who had just used his seax to kill one of the ealdorman's retainers. Alfwald's curses rang across the hall.

"Oath-breaking maggot!" he roared. "Come taste my blade!"

Aethelred spat on the floor and stepped forward to meet him.

Alfwald spied Wulfhere, and his face twisted with rage. He quickly forgot about the younger brother and turned to Wulfhere.

"Princeling," he growled. "So you show your face at last."

Wulfhere sheathed his seax and drew Shield Breaker.

"Aye," he replied with a chilling smile, "and this face will be the last thing you ever see."

***

A terrible hush hung over the Great Hall, broken only by the wet gasps of dying men.

Wulfhere lowered his sword and looked about him, taking in his surroundings for the first time since the attack had begun. Unarmed folk—men, women, and children—cringed against the sides of the hall or peered out at him from the alcoves. A carpet of bodies spread out around him, both Northumbrian and Mercian. The air stank of blood, offal, and fear.

It had been a bloody fight. The Northumbrian king had left his best men to rule Tamworth as his stewards, and Wulfhere's men had not expected to find them armed. Even so, the Mercians had prevailed.

Alfwald lay dead at his feet, while a few feet away, Aethelred wiped the blade of his seax on the cloak of the Northumbrian warrior he had just slain.

The brothers' gazes met and held.

Aethelred's mouth quirked into a half smile. "What took you so long?"

Wulfhere answered with a cool smile of his own. "Vengeance tastes best when it is savored. It did us all good to wait."

He retrieved a handful of rushes from the floor and cleaned Alfwald's blood off Shield Breaker. Then he sheathed the blade.

It's done.

Two years of waiting, planning, and anticipation were finally over. He stood inside the Great Tower of Tamworth, with the men who opposed him dead at his feet.

The fog of battle lust cleared from his vision, and he was aware that he had sustained a cut to his forearm—a blade had sliced right through his leather bracer. It was beginning to ache dully and, although not deep, would need attention.

Werbode approached him. The warrior was breathing heavily, still recovering from the fight, and bleeding from a shallow shoulder wound. Nevertheless, he was grinning.

"You did it, milord. Tamworth is yours."

Wulfhere returned his grin. "Aye, *we* did it."

The reality of matters was beginning to sink in. No longer would he have to hide in the woods like an outlaw. No longer would he live in tents and thatched hovels. He, the eldest surviving son of Penda of Mercia, now stood in his rightful place.

Elfhere also approached him. The warrior's face was splattered with blood, making his eyes look even bluer than usual. However, he appeared uninjured.

"What do you want done with the rest of the Northumbrians?" he asked, motioning to the men who stirred on the floor behind him.

Wulfhere's gaze shifted to the injured men. One of them was pulling himself across the rushes on his belly, in an attempt to reach a discarded seax. Wulfhere frowned; he could not afford to be merciful.

"Scour Tamworth for any Northumbrians who managed to escape the hall," he ordered, "and kill any of Wada and Alfwald's men who still breathe."

He turned to where a group of pale-faced slaves huddled against the far wall. "Clear the dead from the hall and tidy this place up," he commanded them. "By noon, I want no sign the Northumbrians were ever here."

Chapter Three
The Rightful King

Wulfhere sank deep into the hot water and let out a long sigh.

It was so long since he had taken a proper bath he had almost forgotten the sensual pleasure of it. The scent of lye soap—a smell that reminded him of his childhood—filled the alcove where he bathed. This small space had once been his mother's, and before that, his sisters had slept here. These days, it housed a huge cast-iron tub that took slaves many trips to fill.

The hot water soothed away the aches and pains of battle. He had rinsed the blood off his injured forearm, but no healer had yet looked at it. The wound ached, pulsing in time with his heartbeat.

Beyond the tapestry that shielded him from the rest of the hall, he could hear the sounds of industry: the clatter and thud of pots as the cooks began work on the noon meal and the sounds of sweeping and scrubbing as slaves washed the hall clean of blood.

Smiling, Wulfhere closed his eyes and relaxed into the hot water. Moments later, a tremulous female voice interrupted him.

"M'lord . . ."

Wulfhere's eyes snapped open, and he inclined his head to where a young woman had slipped into the chamber. He recognized her as the slave he had found with Wada. The girl was small and thin with a shock of golden hair. Unlike earlier this morning, she was now clothed, clad in a worn homespun tunic, girded at the waist.

"What do you want?" he asked.

"Your brother, Lord Aethelred, commanded me to attend you, m'lord," she murmured. "He told me you wanted your back scrubbed."

Wulfhere smiled. "Did he? That was generous of him."

The girl stared at him, her blue eyes glistening with unshed tears. He could see she was shaking.

"What's your name, girl?"

"Asha, m'lord."

"You're new to the Great Hall—I don't recognize you."

"I came here at Winterfylleth," she replied, her voice barely above a whisper. "My father killed one of Wada's warriors. They were drinking in the mead hall, and an argument got out of hand. I was part of the wergild he had to pay."

Wulfhere raised an eyebrow. Wergild—man payment—was the price a man had to pay after committing a crime, as compensation to his victim's family.

"So, your father killed a Northumbrian, did he?"

The girl nodded.

Wulfhere watched the slave a moment. She was young, barely out of childhood. Her pale skin bore bruises; Wada had clearly been rough with her.

Wulfhere sank back against the rim of the iron tub.

"Your father did us all a favor," he said finally. "I don't need my back scrubbed. Go to my brother and tell him that I release you from slavery. Then go to the smith and get that collar removed."

The girl gaped at him. "Really? Am I free, m'lord?"

Wulfhere waved her away. "You heard me, girl. Go and see my brother . . . and get him to fetch me Glaedwine. I need a healer."

Wulfhere crossed the floor toward the heah-setl—the high seat—where his brother and retainers awaited him.

This evening, the Great Hall of Tamworth bore no resemblance to dawn's scene of carnage. Fresh rushes crunched underfoot, and the aroma of roasting mutton and herbs replaced the stench of death, mingling with wood smoke from the hall's two enormous fire pits.

Long tables lined the floor, where men and women were taking their seats. He saw the smiles on their faces and shining eyes. They were pleased to have the rightful ruler of Mercia among them.

Aethelred was the first to greet him as he stepped upon the heah-setl.

"Good evening, brother."

Wulfhere nodded and took his place upon the carved wooden chair at the head of the table. This had been his father's chair, and it was the first time he had ever sat upon it.

Aethelred poured him a cup of wine and passed it to him.

"How does it feel?"

"What?"

"To sit in that chair."

Wulfhere smiled. "Better than you can imagine."

His gaze shifted to the other folk sharing his table. There were no other members of his kin here. His mother had taken the veil and gone to live in Bonehill, and both his sisters had left Tamworth to be handfasted, years earlier. Aethelred was all he had left. The others at the table were his retainers, Werbode and Elfhere among them.

The three ealdormen who had helped him take back Tamworth—Immin, Eafa, and Eadbert—were seated together at the far end of the table. Immin, big and blond, was flushed in the face from mead. Next to him was Eafa, a much smaller man with pale eyes and a bald head that gleamed in the light of the cressets that lined the nearby wall. The third ealdorman, Eadbert, was the youngest of the three. He was a tall, muscular man with a shock of black hair and a beard to match.

Eadbert caught his eye and raised his cup.

"To victory, Lord Wulfhere."

Wulfhere's smile widened into a grin. "Aye, I'll drink to that."

He raised his cup to his lips and took a sip of wine.

Werbode, seated at Wulfhere's right, also raised his cup. "And here's to your crowning, milord. Tomorrow?"

Wulfhere nodded. "At noon."

Slaves brought food to the table, interrupting their talk. Great slabs of roast mutton, fresh griddle bread, and pickled onions. Wulfhere's mouth watered at the sight of it; he had not forgotten how good the cooks were in his father's hall.

He helped himself to some mutton and broke off a piece of griddle bread, before his gaze shifted out across the hall to the sea of men and women who were now eating and drinking, their voices echoing up into the rafters.

I've completed the first of Eorcenberht's conditions, he thought. *Tamworth is mine, but there's just one thing I must do before I can return to Kent and claim Ermenilda as my own.*

Wulfhere turned back to Werbode. He fixed him in a penetrating stare until his thegn glanced up and met his eye.

"What is it, sire?"

"First thing tomorrow, I need you to do something for me."

Werbode nodded, his gaze curious.

"Go to the church and fetch me the monk, Seaxwulf. Before I can wear the crown, I must be baptized."

Chapter Four
Wulfhere's Prize

Cantwareburh, the Kingdom of the Kentish

One month later . . .

Ermenilda's breath steamed in the wintry air as she whispered the final words of her prayer.

It was a chill day, and with no hearth to warm the interior of the church, the cold seeped in through the princess's fur-lined boots and numbed her feet. Her hands, clasped before her as she knelt upon a pelt before the altar, were white with cold.

Constructed from oak and local stone, with a sea of slate pavers covering the floor, Cantwareburh's church was reputed to be one of Britannia's finest. Yet, it was no warmer than a burial chamber.

"The princess is praying . . . you cannot disturb her."

Behind her, Ermenilda heard the bishop, Frithuwine, chastise someone. Although Frithuwine's voice was barely above a whisper, it echoed in the silent church.

"I come from the king with an urgent message." Another man's voice echoed high in the rafters. "He wishes for Princess Ermenilda to return home immediately."

Frowning in annoyance that her peace had been shattered, Ermenilda unclasped her hands and rose to her feet. The candles burning upon the altar before her guttered as she turned to face the newcomer.

Her gaze fell upon the tall spearman with a thick fur cloak about his shoulders.

"What is it, Bercthun?"

The thegn, one of her father's favored retainers, dipped his head respectfully before replying.

"Apologies for interrupting you, milady. But, the king sends for you urgently."

Ermenilda watched him steadily but made no move to obey her father's instructions.

Bercthun shifted uncomfortably, his gaze flicking to where Bishop Frithuwine—a heavyset man of around thirty winters, wearing plush purple robes—also studied him.

"Cantwareburh has visitors, milady," Bercthun conceded, "from Mercia."

Ermenilda's feeling of inner calm, which her prayers always bestowed upon her, vanished.

"Who?" she demanded, her heart suddenly racing.

No, please don't let this be . . .

"King Wulfhere of Mercia, milady. He has retaken the Mercian throne and has come to speak with your father."

"The pagan prince who visited Cantwareburh a year ago?" the bishop asked, disapproval clear in his voice.

"Pagan no more, it seems," the thegn replied. "He has been baptized, and a priest is among his party."

A wave of nausea swept over Ermenilda, followed swiftly by dizziness.

Over a year had passed since Prince Wulfhere visited her father's hall, and she had begun to hope that her father would let her take the veil after all. There had been no word from the north, and she, like many, had assumed that Wulfhere had failed in his mission to take back the Mercian throne.

It was a shock to discover he had succeeded.

"Milady, are you well?"

Bercthun was frowning at her.

Not trusting herself to speak, Ermenilda nodded and drew her fur cloak close about her.

"Come then, we can delay no longer," her father's retainer urged her.

Reluctantly, she followed Bercthun across the floor, her boots whispering on the icy stone, and exited the church through wide oaken doors.

Outside, it was a bright morning but bone-numbingly cold. A freezing wind bit at Ermenilda's cheeks as she descended the stone steps before Cantwareburh's great church and fell in step beside Bercthun. They walked up a wide, cobbled way, in between the sturdy timbered halls of Cantwareburh's wealthiest inhabitants. They climbed a slight incline toward the wooden ramparts that ringed the Great Hall of Cantwareburh.

Eventually, the pair passed through the high gate and crossed a wide stable yard flanked by low buildings. The King's Hall rose up before Ermenilda—and for the first time ever, she was scared to set foot inside it.

Ermenilda crossed the floor toward the high seat, ahead of Bercthun, aware that all eyes within the hall appeared to be upon her.

One gaze in particular scorched her, as if she stood too close to the Yuletide fire.

King Wulfhere of Mercia stood upon the high seat, next to her father, and she tried her best not to look at him. However, the force of his stare was so strong that it drew her toward him, as if she were a pike dangling on the end of his hook. Unable to resist him any longer, she looked up and her gaze met his.

He was as she remembered—tall and powerfully built with a mane of white-blond hair—only he was dressed more elegantly this time. He wore a fine blue tunic, edged with golden silk. A plush ermine cloak hung from his shoulders, fastened by amber brooches. He was, frankly, the most handsome man she had ever seen.

His silver-blue eyes glittered as she approached, and Ermenilda's belly clenched. Her last, frail hope dissolved. His look made the situation clear. He had not changed his mind about wedding her.

"Lady Ermenilda," he murmured when she stepped upon the high seat next to him. "You are as lovely as I remember."

Ermenilda dipped her head, politely acknowledging the compliment.

"Thank you, Lord Wulfhere."

"Wulfhere is now King of Mercia, Ermenilda," her father spoke up. He stood to their left, with the queen beside him. Seaxburh was silent and pale, her gaze riveted upon the floor.

"Congratulations, milord," Ermenilda added, keeping her own gaze downcast.

"And he has foresworn the old ways and accepted the one true god," Eorcenberht continued, his voice booming with pleasure.

Ermenilda looked up and saw the small wooden crucifix that hung from around Wulfhere's neck. No reply came to her, so she remained silent. Her gaze shifted to where her sister stood a few feet behind their parents. Eorcengota's brown eyes were huge on her heart-shaped face. Like Ermenilda, she had not thought ever to see Wulfhere of Mercia again.

Ermenilda inhaled deeply and raised her gaze to meet Wulfhere's once more.

"So you have met my father's conditions, milord?"

"Aye, milady," Wulfhere rumbled, his pale gaze ensnaring her, "and now I come to claim my prize."

Ermenilda gritted her teeth. He made her sound like a trophy—like an enemy's sword he had claimed after victory to hang upon the wall of his hall. Wulfhere knew nothing about her, save what was visible to the eye. Judging from the look on his face, he did not care to know anything else. He was attracted to her, and he wanted her—that was all that mattered to him.

Her gaze left his and shifted to her father. The king was grinning like a fool, delighted with the match he had helped create.

Betrayal cut her deep, like a seax blade under the ribs. She had thought he had listened to her when she told him of her desire to become a nun at Eastry, but now she realized the truth. He had merely humored her.

"I shall arrange for the handfasting tomorrow," the king boomed, oblivious to his eldest daughter's despair. "The sooner the better, eh?" He winked at Wulfhere, who returned his gaze dispassionately.

"I've waited a year, Lord Eorcenberht," he replied. "I am a patient man."

Eorcenberht's dark eyebrows raised at this, but Wulfhere continued.

"I wish to be handfasted to Lady Ermenilda in my own hall. We shall depart from Cantwareburh at dawn tomorrow and return to Mercia."

Stunned silence met Wulfhere's words. Even Ermenilda was surprised by his response. The journey to Tamworth would take at least ten days—Wulfhere was a patient man indeed.

"My daughter should be handfasted here, and the ceremony blessed by Bishop Frithuwine." Queen Seaxburh broke the heavy silence, her voice sharp with anger. "Only then, should she be allowed to leave Cantwareburh. How do we know you will not dishonor her?"

Wulfhere regarded the queen a moment and inclined his head slightly.

"Do you not trust me with your daughter?"

"I trust no Mercian," the queen hissed.

"Seaxburh!" Eorcenberht roared. "Silence, woman!"

It appeared the queen would not hold her tongue. Seaxburh's face was chalk white, her blue eyes glittering with rage, when she turned on her husband.

"My father would turn in his barrow to see you like this—toadying and groveling to lesser men."

Eorcenberht stared at his wife, momentarily poleaxed by her outburst. Likewise, Ermenilda stared, stunned. Her mother, usually so meek and sweet, had never before shown such fire. For the first time, Ermenilda found herself in awe of the woman who had birthed her.

"Go to our quarters, wife," Eorcenberht rumbled, finally recovering his wits, "and not another word, or I will take my hand to you, right now."

The queen stared at him, her slender body shaking with fury.

"Go!" the king roared.

Finally, Seaxburh complied. Stiffly, she turned and stepped down off the high seat. Ermenilda watched her cross the hall, past staring men and women, before disappearing behind a heavy tapestry to the quarters she and the king shared.

Eorcenberht's face was the color of raw meat when he turned back to Wulfhere.

The Mercian king watched him, a faintly mocking smile curving his mouth. The Kentish queen had effectively shamed her husband this day, in front of men he wished to impress.

"Do you share your wife's views?" he asked mildly.

The Kentish king's mouth twisted. "A woman's opinion is not worth dog's piss. I will punish my wife for her insolence."

"So you don't harbor a secret grudge against Mercia?"

"Would I be giving my eldest daughter to you, if I did?"

Satisfied, Wulfhere nodded. His gaze shifted to Ermenilda, who had not spoken during the entire exchange.

"And what about you, Lady Ermenilda?" he asked, his voice iron cloaked in silk. "Do you agree with your mother?"

Ermenilda held his gaze and wished she possessed her mother's courage. She wished to tell him that the thought of being wedded to him turned her stomach—that baptized or not, king or not, she had no desire to have anything to do with him. His arrival had shattered her life, destroyed her dreams for a life of peace and seclusion. She hated him for it.

Yet, she did not say any of that. Instead, she merely shook her head and dropped her gaze to the floor.

Chapter Five
Leaving Home

Watery light filtered into Ermenilda's bower through a crack in the shutters, warning her that dawn was breaking.

Despite that she had not slept, the time had passed swiftly. She could still not believe this would be her last night in her father's hall. Her last night in Cantwareburh.

Events had spiraled out of control; she no longer felt as if her life belonged to her. This time yesterday, she had awoken serene and safe—and now a stranger was taking her away to a land she had never seen.

Ermenilda sat up and pulled the furs around her. Her eyes were puffy and sore, for she had cried all night, and her head felt as if it was filled with wool. Her gaze shifted to the leather trunks and packs stacked on the far side of her bower, and fresh tears welled.

No, it had not been a nightmare. She was indeed leaving.

"Erme . . ." Her sister's voice carried softly through the thick hanging. "Are you awake?"

"Yes," Ermenilda replied weakly. "Come in."

Eorcengota slipped into the bower, and Ermenilda saw that her sister's face was as miserable as she felt herself.

"Fæder says it's time," Eorcengota said softly. "I'm sorry."

Ermenilda nodded, not trusting herself to speak, and climbed out of the furs. She had worn a thin ankle-length tunic to bed, but the morning air had a bite to it. She shivered as she fumbled for the clothes she had lain aside for her journey: a long-sleeved undertunic and a thick woolen dress to go over the top.

Eorcengota watched her sister dress in silence for a few moments before she spoke once more.

"I can't believe you're leaving. It doesn't seem real."

Ermenilda turned from where she was buckling a belt around her waist and forced a brave smile. "It seems like a terrible dream to me."

Eorcengota's eyes filled with tears. "What will I do without you? I will miss you."

Ermenilda reached out and put her arms around her sister. "And I you," she murmured. "More than you will know."

When Ermenilda ended the hug, she saw that Eorcengota was scowling.

"Why is Fæder doing this?"

Ermenilda took a deep breath, choking back all the angry words she longed to unleash. Telling Eorcengota how she really felt would only upset her. Her younger sister was a fragile, gentle soul. Even at sixteen winters, she still wept over puppies and believed in fairies. Although she was only two years older, Ermenilda felt the need to protect her.

"He is doing this for our kingdom," she replied finally, "to strengthen our alliances with our neighbors. Mercia is powerful, and Fæder wishes to keep their favor."

"But will I ever see you again?"

Tears were running down Eorcengota's face now, and the sight made Ermenilda's breast ache with misery.

"I hope so," she replied, giving her sister a tremulous smile. "Perhaps, in the summer, I can visit."

Her sister wiped away her tears. "Really?"

Ermenilda nodded, not trusting herself to say anything else. She had just told her sister a white lie, to soften the blow of her departure.

In truth, she did not believe she would return to Cantwareburh soon—if ever.

Ermenilda emerged from her bower to find her father waiting for her. There was no sign of her mother, but a young woman Ermenilda did not recognize stood next to him.

Dressed in a plain woolen traveling tunic and cloak of the same material, the girl had curly auburn hair, forest-green eyes, and a pretty, if strong-featured, face. Something about her drew one's eye—an aura of warmth and vitality.

"Ermenilda," her father rumbled. "I have found a handmaid for you. Your mother is unhappy about you traveling unescorted, so Wynflaed will accompany you to Tamworth and see to your needs once you are there. She is the daughter of one of my thegns and will serve you well."

Ermenilda's gaze met Wynflaed's. The girl curtsied neatly and smiled.

"Milady."

Ermenilda nodded stiffly, too traumatized by the events of the past day to pay much attention to her new handmaid.

"Shall I help bring your things outside, milady?" Wynflaed asked brightly.

"Aye, thank you," Ermenilda replied, forcing a tremulous smile.

When the girl had disappeared behind the arras, Ermenilda turned back to her father.

"Where is Mōder?"

Eorcenberht frowned. "She is in our quarters but will come outside to see you off."

The pain in Ermenilda's breast, which had just started to subside after saying good-bye to her sister, returned. It felt as if a great fist were squeezing her heart.

"Please, Fæder, can I not say good-bye to her alone?"

Eorcenberht shook his head, his scowl deepening.

"You mother dishonored me in front of the King of Mercia, and she must pay for her insolence. She will not speak to you before your departure."

Ermenilda stared at her father, distraught. How could he be so cruel as to deny the queen a moment alone with her daughter?

"But, Fæder, I might never see her again," Ermenilda finally managed.

Her father's hard expression did not yield.

"She should have thought of that before she lost her temper yesterday," he replied, the tone of his voice making it clear that the subject was closed.

Frost crunched underfoot as Ermenilda crossed the stable yard to where Wulfhere and his men were making the final preparations for their departure. Wynflaed walked a few steps behind her, carrying a leather bag filled with her own possessions.

A clear sky stretched overhead, promising a bright and sunny, albeit cold, day ahead. It was the ideal weather to set out on a journey, yet Ermenilda felt nothing but despair at the thought of traveling this morning.

One of her father's men had saddled her palfrey for her, an elegant bay mare. Next to it waited Wynflaed's mount, a shaggy dun with a huge head.

It was not the horses that drew Ermenilda's gaze but the snow-white wolf that sat in the middle of the stable yard. The beast was huge with glowing yellow eyes—and the sight of it made Ermenilda's step falter.

The King of Mercia stood a few feet away from his wolf, his back to Ermenilda, as he tightened his stallion's girth. The wolf turned its attention to the approaching women, and it fixed Ermenilda in a chilling stare.

Breaking out in a sweat, Ermenilda halted, causing Wynflaed to run into the back of her.

"What is it, milady?" the young woman asked, stepping around Ermenilda. When the handmaid saw what her mistress was staring at, her next comment died on her lips.

Wulfhere turned at the sound of Wynflaed's voice, his crystalline gaze settling upon his betrothed.

"Good morning, Lady Ermenilda."

"Morning," she murmured in response, her gaze still riveted upon the wolf. The beast seemed to stare at her hungrily.

"Don't look so concerned," Wulfhere told her, humor in his voice. "Mōna will not hurt you. I told her of you; she is merely curious to finally meet the beautiful Princess Ermenilda."

Ermenilda dragged her gaze away from the white wolf and looked at Wulfhere.

"You talk to your wolf?"

"Aye, and unlike most folk, she's a good listener."

Ermenilda stared at him, not sure whether to think him mad or to laugh. She chose the former.

A tall warrior with long, thick black hair and a neatly trimmed beard stepped up next to Wulfhere. His dark gaze focused upon Ermenilda.

"You are terrifying the maid, milord," he told Wulfhere with a lopsided grin. "She looks as if she is about to take fright and run."

Wulfhere glanced over at the warrior and laughed softly.

"Not Lady Ermenilda. She may look like a lamb, but I'd wager she's tougher than she looks."

Ermenilda clenched her jaw. They were discussing her as if she was not there.

"I can see why you've waited for her, milord," the dark-haired warrior replied, running an appreciative eye over Ermenilda. "The princess is indeed a beauty."

Although he addressed the king respectfully, Ermenilda noted the tone of familiarity in the warrior's voice. It was clear that Wulfhere both liked and respected this man—although Ermenilda took an instant dislike to him. She did not like the leer in his gaze or the smirk on his face.

"Of course, Werbode," Wulfhere replied, his tone cooling slightly. "Do you doubt my taste in women?"

The warrior, Werbode, gave a soft laugh at that, before returning to saddle his horse. Meanwhile, Wulfhere crossed to Ermenilda and led her over to her palfrey, where he helped her mount.

Unspeaking, Ermenilda placed her booted foot in his cupped hands and sprang up lightly into the saddle. Beside her, a warrior helped Wynflaed up onto her dun gelding. The warrior was handsome, with twinkling blue eyes and shaggy golden hair. He favored the handmaid with a flirtatious smile before returning to his own horse. As he walked away, Ermenilda noted he had a slight limp.

Around them, the men readied themselves to move out, but Ermenilda focused on arranging her skirts— anything to keep herself occupied, to distract herself from the knowledge that she was about to leave the only home she had known.

Meanwhile, a group had gathered on the wooden terrace before the entrance to the King's Hall. Finally, Ermenilda looked their way and saw all her kin had gathered—her father, mother, sister, and two brothers. They were close enough for her to see the stricken expression upon the queen's face. Seaxburh's finely boned face was taut with grief, her eyes red rimmed.

Tears welled in Ermenilda's eyes as she met her mother's gaze. Her father's cruelty at not letting mother and daughter say their proper good-byes hurt her deeply. She hated to see her mother suffer so and felt a stab of resentment toward her father.

King Eorcenberht did not look as pleased with himself this morning, as he had the day before. His wife's behavior had soured the whole occasion, and her father wore a mutinous expression.

Eorcengota was openly weeping, and her younger brothers, Ecgberht and Hlothhere, were both struggling to hold back tears of their own.

Wulfhere rode up beside her, drawing Ermenilda's attention away from the distraught faces of her kin.

"Ready, milady?" he asked, his gaze meeting hers. There was an unspoken challenge in his eyes, almost as if he expected her to start sobbing and disgrace herself.

I will not let him see me weep.

"Aye," Ermenilda replied, barely able to speak, for her throat hurt with the effort she was making not to cry. "Let us go now."

Chapter Six
Silence

Cantwareburh had never looked as beautiful to Ermenilda as the day she left it.

The Mercian party rode north, along the western bank of the Great Stour, past clusters of timbered and wattle-and-daub dwellings. At her back, Ermenilda knew that the straw thatch of the Great Hall would be gleaming gold in the morning sun. However, she deliberately did not look over her shoulder.

She already struggled to hide her grief from her betrothed and knew that to gaze once more on the home she loved would break her. Wulfhere rode beside her, his stallion chafing at the bit, eager to move at a faster pace. The wolf, Mōna, trotted along at her master's side.

The wooden ramparts of Cantwareburh rose before them, and Ermenilda saw that the guards had opened the great oak and iron gates, so that Wulfhere and his escort could pass out of the city. Crowds gathered at the roadside, and folk craned their necks to catch a glimpse of Ermenilda's face.

Tired of being an object of spectacle, the princess pulled up her fur-lined hood. To the people of Cantwareburh, she was a highborn lady who enjoyed a life of privilege. No doubt, some of the young women in the crowd envied her. Wulfhere of Mercia was certainly a striking, virile man, who drew a woman's eye. The local women—daughters and wives of farmers, merchants, and artisans—probably imagined that she led a charmed life.

Nothing could have been further from the truth.

Eastry is lost to me.

The small silver cross that Ermenilda wore about her throat was the only thing she had left of her dream. She was not like other highborn women; her father's match would have delighted many, but she wanted a life away from the harsh world of men. She longed for a serene and simple life. Wulfhere had torn that from her.

They passed out of Cantwareburh and continued along the banks of the river to where a wooden bridge crossed the Great Stour. Marshes spread out to the northeast, glittering in the morning sun, but they were not headed in that direction.

Instead, the Mercians struck out northwest upon Watling Street, a wide, paved trackway built by the Romans. Ermenilda knew that this one, like all the great roads the Romans built, was long; it would lead them all the way into the heart of Mercia.

The Romans had departed these shores more than two hundred years earlier, but the road was still in a good state of repair. The horses clattered over the pavers, the sound echoing over the marshes to the east.

Ermenilda and Wulfhere rode close to the head of the column, where the lead riders carried Mercia's pennants high. The blue-and-gold banners flapped in the breeze. Around them was a sea of spears, bristling against the morning sky. Bitterness soured Ermenilda's mouth as she took note of how well protected they were. Wulfhere clearly wanted no harm to come to his Kentish princess.

The morning stretched out, and Ermenilda spoke to no one. Mercifully, Wulfhere did not attempt to engage her in conversation, and her thoughts turned inward. She paid no attention to the riders around her or to the rise and fall of men's voices as they chatted among themselves. Instead, her thoughts dwelled upon the two people she loved most—her sister and mother—and the look of anguish on their faces as they watched her leave.

Never had Ermenilda felt so alone.

**

They covered a lot of ground that first day. Wulfhere set a fast pace, clearly keen to reach Tamworth without delay.

By the time they stopped for the day, Ermenilda ached from head to foot. She enjoyed riding, but her outings from Cantwareburh were lazy treks that usually included flower picking and herb gathering with her sister. Wulfhere pushed his party, as if they were marching to war. When Ermenilda slid off her palfrey's back at day's end, she had to bite her lip to stop herself from crying out. Her thigh muscles were on fire.

They had made camp, around a furlong back from the road, in a wooded vale that was typical of the Kentish countryside. It was green and lush, with a brook trickling through the center of it. To the west, the sun was sliding behind the treetops in a blaze of pink and gold, promising good weather for the day to come.

Around her, Wulfhere's men got to work cutting branches and saplings in order to make tents, lighting fires, and gathering wood. Wynflaed proved herself to be an industrious young woman, as she helped the men carry her lady's belongings into the first of the tents.

Ermenilda noticed a few of the men glancing the girl's way. Wynflaed carried herself beautifully. She smiled and replied to the men's comments and questions, although she did not flirt. This pleased Ermenilda, for she did not want a handmaid who encouraged men's lechery, but a gentlewoman who took her duties to her lady seriously.

As she waited for Wynflaed to finish preparing her tent, Ermenilda saw a slight man—his brown hair shaved into a tonsure—making his way through the crowd toward her. The monk wore simple homespun robes and had a kindly, if careworn, face.

For the first time all day, Ermenilda's spirits lifted. In her misery, she had failed to note that a holy man rode among Wulfhere's band, although now she remembered Bercthun mentioning it when he had come to collect her from the church.

The monk stopped before her and dipped his head respectfully.

"Greetings, Lady Ermenilda. I am Seaxwulf."

Ermenilda smiled. "I am pleased to meet you, Brother Seaxwulf, and relieved that there is a man of god riding with us."

Her words evidently pleased the monk, for he smiled widely, the expression making him seem younger. "I baptized the king myself," he told her, "and Lord Wulfhere was adamant that I travel with him to Cantwareburh."

Ermenilda could not keep the bitterness from her voice when she replied.

"To convince my father that he is no longer a pagan?"

The monk's eyes widened, his smile fading. "Lord Wulfhere has shunned the old gods and destroyed all their idols in Tamworth," he told her firmly.

"Such acts are easy," Ermenilda replied. "It is what a man believes in his heart that really matters."

"The king is new to the word of Christ," Seaxwulf admitted. "However, with the gentle influence of a wife like yourself, he will surely come to believe as you do."

Ermenilda swallowed her next response. Angry, resentment-filled words were no use to her now, and the monk was starting to look genuinely alarmed by her comments.

"You speak wisely, Brother Seaxwulf," she replied eventually, forcing a smile. "Perhaps you are right, and Lord Wulfhere has indeed chosen another path."

Glancing right to where her betrothed was rubbing down his stallion, Ermenilda doubted it. Everything about Wulfhere of Mercia screamed pagan. He may as well have been wearing Thunor's hammer about his neck rather than a crucifix.

Ermenilda had retired to her tent and had just finished her supper of bread and cheese when Wulfhere visited her.

Wynflaed was busy laying out furs for her lady to sleep on, and Ermenilda was sitting next to the gently crackling fire. Wood smoke lay heavily in the air even though it filtered up, through a slit in the roof. Ermenilda was used to living in such an environment, for the fire pits in her father's hall burned day and night. Still, the fire took the chill off the cold evening air.

The moment that Wulfhere ducked low through the opening, the tent felt too small. He straightened up, his head nearly reaching the roof, and looked down at her. As always, his expression was cool, slightly aloof, although his gaze was searing in its intensity.

"Good eve, Lady Ermenilda," he greeted her. "I trust you are comfortable?"

Ermenilda nodded.

"My tent is next to yours, so if you require anything, please send your maid, and my men will see to it."

Ermenilda nodded once more, silently wishing he would go away and leave her in peace.

Silence stretched between them, and Wynflaed shifted uncomfortably. Ermenilda could feel her maid's gaze flicking from the king to his betrothed. The tension in the air was so heavy that Ermenilda struggled to breathe.

When it was clear that Ermenilda was not going to speak to him, Wulfhere hunkered down before her, so their gazes were level.

"It is rude not to respond when addressed," he said, his tone deceptively soft. "I was merely enquiring after your well-being."

Ermenilda felt her cheeks flame, suddenly feeling as if she were a child being chastised by her father.

"Thank you, Lord Wulfhere," she eventually murmured, her tone clipped. "I am well, as you can see."

He held her gaze for a moment longer. They were so close that she could see the flecks of darker blue in the silver blue of his irises. He smelled better than she wanted to admit—a virile smell of leather and horse, with the musky scent of maleness beneath.

"Good," he finally replied, rising to his feet. "Sleep well, milady. Tomorrow will be another long day. I want you well rested."

Ermenilda watched him leave, her heart hammering against her ribs. His presence unsettled her, filling her with confusion. She did not like the way he had demanded a response from her. If she did not feel inclined to speak this evening, after the trauma of leaving her kin behind, he should have understood.

Tears pricked her eyelids, and she glared down at the crackling fire.

"Milady," Wynflaed spoke up, her voice gentle and laced with concern. "Is something amiss?"

Ermenilda glanced up and met Wynflaed's gaze. Wordlessly she nodded and inhaled deeply to prevent the tears from escaping her burning eyes. When she replied, her voice was barely above a whisper.

"Everything."

Wynflaed's brow furrowed. "You do not wish to wed Lord Wulfhere, milady?"

Ermenilda shook her head vehemently. "I would rather wed an adder."

When Wynflaed looked shocked at that, Ermenilda continued.

"Do you know of his family, Wynflaed?"

"Only that his father was a great warlord," the girl replied cautiously.

"He was a ruthless pagan who killed my grandfather and uncle. Penda of Mercia's coldness and cruelty are legendary."

Wynflaed's frown deepened. "Wulfhere might be different from his father," she ventured.

Ermenilda gave her maid a scornful look. "Take one look at his son and tell me he is not cut from the same cloth!"

"He does appear quite cold," Wynflaed admitted, although she did not wilt under her lady's glare, "and his wolf scares me."

Ermenilda glanced down at the dancing flames in the fire pit before her.

"I wanted to become a nun," she murmured, "and my father was on the verge of allowing it when Wulfhere ruined everything."

"A nun?" Wynflaed replied, genuinely surprised by her mistress's admission. "Do you not want a husband and children?"

Ermenilda shook her head, vehement. "Not if it means being wed to Wulfhere of Mercia."

Chapter Seven
The Wolf and the Lamb

The Mercian party rode north, covering the furlongs swiftly, on the paved Watling Street. The weather remained good—cold with clear skies—although the outlines of skeletal trees reminded the travelers that spring was still some way off.

Four days out from Cantwareburh, they entered Lundenwic.

Ermenilda had heard much of this city from Bishop Frithuwine, but had not been looking forward to seeing Britannia's largest settlement. According to the bishop, Lundenwic represented everything that was wrong with the world of men. It was a ferment of corruption, debauchery, and greed.

Her first glance at the city did little to allay her fears.

They rode into Lundenwic, following the western bank of the mighty River Temese, a wide tidal river that flowed through the center of the city. The first thing Ermenilda noticed was how dirty the river was. It was littered with refuse, the corpses of dead animals, and floating excrement. The stench made her bile rise, and she covered her mouth with a piece of linen scented with rose water to prevent herself from becoming ill.

Farther upriver, they rode alongside wooden docks—pier after pier of moored longboats and cargo barges. The tide was rising, and it appeared some of the boats were preparing to leave. Men scurried to and fro, shouting to each other, tossing coils of rope, and carrying sacks and wooden crates onboard their vessels.

Overwhelmed by the sight, sound, and smell of so much humanity, Ermenilda glanced away, her gaze shifting to the east, where the ruined wall of the old Roman city glowed in the afternoon sun. Beneath it, a carpet of thatched roofs spread out and hugged the lazy bend of the river. Smoke from cooking fires and smiths' forges stained the sky.

Lundenwic represented everything Ermenilda had wished to shun. It was dirty, uncouth, and overwhelming—and it made her long for her garden sanctuary in Cantwareburh.

Riding next to her, atop her ugly roan, Wynflaed had the opposite reaction.

"I've never seen a city so large," she exclaimed, her wide-eyed gaze taking it all in. "There's life here—you can breathe it in."

"You certainly can. Lundenwic has something for all folk."

An appreciative male voice drew the women's attention to Wynflaed's left, where a blond warrior with startling blue eyes had ridden up beside them.

Ermenilda recognized him as the man who helped her handmaid mount in the mornings. His name was Elfhere, and he had clearly taken a shine to her comely servant.

"I wish we were staying here," Wynflaed admitted. "I would have liked to explore its streets."

"Perhaps, one day, you will have that chance," he replied.

Their gazes met for a few moments, before a slow smile crept across the warrior's face. Then, with a nod to them both, he urged his horse forward and moved off up the column, leaving the women alone once more.

Ermenilda pursed her lips. Although she instinctively liked Wynflaed, she found the girl's optimism and childlike wonder vaguely irritating. She also did not approve of Elfhere's interest in her maid; he was entirely too bold.

"Something for all folk? I smell nothing but dung and rotten fish," she commented.

To her chagrin, Wynflaed laughed.

"I know, isn't it wonderful?"

That was the last word Ermenilda would have used to describe this cesspit.

Around them, beggars had clustered at the roadside to watch the passing Mercians. Emaciated and filthy, they called out to the passersby, pleading for food or coins. Ermenilda wished that she had some bread to give to them, for the desperation in their gazes cut her to the quick. To distract herself from the pitiful sight, Ermenilda focused on her maid.

"You do not grieve for being parted from your family, Wynflaed. Why is that?"

Wynflaed tore her gaze from the crowd, where folk were chasing off a leper. Covered in filthy rags, the dirty, limping creature was a sorry sight.

"I am the youngest of five daughters," Wynflaed replied, her guileless gaze meeting Ermenilda's. "My father despaired of finding a husband for me, for three of my elder sisters are still unwed. To become the handmaid of a highborn lady is more than I could have hoped for. Truthfully, I was bored in Cantwareburh. My whole life, I have seen the same people and the same sights. It is a relief to be going to a new home."

"But your kin," Ermenilda pressed. "Do you not miss them?"

Wynflaed smiled. "Not as yet. They all wish me well, and I the same for them, but the time has come for us to take different paths."

Ermenilda listened to Wynflaed before lapsing into silence. Her maid's pragmatic approach to life stunned her. They were so different, and Wynflaed's boldness and fearlessness made Ermenilda feel like a frightened rabbit in comparison.

Ermenilda wanted nothing more than to flee from the world—but Wynflaed could not wait to embrace it.

"I can see you miss your family greatly, milady," Wynflaed observed.

Ermenilda nodded, her throat constricting. "My sister and mother are my best friends. I do not know how I will survive without them."

Wynflaed observed her for a moment, thinking upon Ermenilda's words, before replying. "I know it is not my place to say it, but I think you are stronger than you believe, milady."

Ermenilda frowned, her body tensing. "What do you mean?"

"Just that—you believe that away from your home and kin you are adrift and alone. Yet, I think that once you accept this change, it could well be the making of you."

Ermenilda stared at her handmaid. Her first reaction was outrage. How dare this thegn's daughter lecture her on the merits of change. She felt her face grow hot as she struggled to rein in her temper. When she did reply, her voice was ice-cold.

"I have just had all things I care about torn away from me. I do not wish to be any man's husband, least of all Wulfhere of Mercia's, and I do not wish to be queen. What I wanted was to be left in peace. Contrary to what you believe, this new life is likely to be the end of me."

Wynflaed's gaze widened at her mistress's sharp response, but this time she held her tongue. Stiff with indignation, Ermenilda turned her gaze back to her surroundings. She focused on the back of the warrior riding in front of her and ignored Wynflaed.

Yet, her handmaid's words lingered with her, needling her, long after their conversation ended.

They did not delay in Lundenwic. Wulfhere's men picked up some supplies, and then they resumed their journey. A vast wooden bridge spanned the River Temese, and the company clattered across it, before the Roman road continued northwest.

Wulfhere rode a few yards ahead of his betrothed. Ermenilda had proved not to be a chatty travel companion, and although he liked women who were not prone to prattle, Wulfhere soon wearied of her cold silence.

She will warm up soon enough, he reassured himself. *Once the Kingdom of the Kentish is far behind us.*

Wulfhere realized that Princess Ermenilda, for all her demure manners and speech, was surprisingly willful. After seeing her mother's display of anger, Wulfhere could see that there was more to his betrothed than met the eye. Queen Seaxburh looked as if a cross word had never parted from her lips, yet she had attacked him like a snarling wildcat. Her daughter clearly did not wish to be wed. He had heard from one of her father's thegns that the princess had planned to take the veil.

A terrible waste.

Wulfhere allowed himself a smile. He would enjoy teaching his lovely young wife the delights she was naïvely willing to give up. She may have not realized it, but there was a simmering sensuality within Ermenilda. He had sensed it the first time they locked eyes in her father's hall. He could see her own reaction to him flustered her. She may have been bent upon becoming a nun, but her body told another story.

"What are you smiling about?"

Werbode had ridden up next to him, although Wulfhere had been so deep in thought that he had not noticed him.

"Just thinking of my impending handfasting," he admitted, "and of my bride-to-be."

Werbode gave him a shrewd look. "She is indeed a lovely creature," he said, smiling. "However, she treats you coldly. She thinks herself better than you."

Wulfhere laughed at that, not remotely offended by his thegn's directness. Werbode did not bandy words, and Wulfhere liked that about him.

"Her coldness will pass," he assured his friend. "In time, the lamb will surrender to the wolf."

Chapter Eight
Upon the Bridge

The attack came on a gray, windy afternoon.

The Mercian company had left Lundenwic four days behind them to the southeast and had almost crossed the southern edge of the East Saxon kingdom. The borders of Mercia lay just a day's ride away.

Ermenilda rode in the midst of the company, as usual, with her handmaid traveling at her side, while the king had ridden up to the head of the column. They had spent the day riding across flat, largely nondescript countryside. Ermenilda had spied a few scattered East Saxon villages, but the Mercians had kept to the road and not stopped at any of them. Clearly, Wulfhere was keen to return home. He would not relax fully until he had crossed into his own kingdom.

Above, the sky was the color of weather-beaten slate from one horizon to the other, and the chill north wind had spots of rain in it. The princess was glad of her thick fur cloak, but even so, the biting wind numbed her face and hands.

Midafternoon, a wide, swiftly flowing river blocked their path. A huge bridge, made out of wood and stone, spanned it. The eastern bank from where they approached was grassy and led to wide meadows. Woodland crept down to the edge of the western bank, and the Roman way disappeared into the gloomy woods shortly after the river.

The first of the Mercians clattered onto the bridge, the sturdy structure vibrating under their weight.

Ermenilda urged her palfrey forward, following their lead.

Her horse had taken no more than a couple of strides onto the bridge when the unmistakable twang of a bowstring releasing cut through the air.

Moments later, men's shouts and the scream of an injured horse shattered the monotony of the cold, gray afternoon. The warriors in front of Ermenilda pulled up short, and she hurriedly did the same, causing her palfrey to toss her head and skitter sideways.

Wynflaed had brought her roan to an unsteady halt. The young woman was frowning as her gaze scanned the column ahead.

"What's happening, milady?"

"I don't know."

Suddenly, a man's voice, rough with anger, echoed across the bridge.

"We're under attack!"

Ermenilda's blood ran cold. She thought the Mercians and East Saxons were at peace these days. Surely, the East Saxon king would not be so bold as to attack his ally traveling across his land in peace. Neither could she imagine that outlaws would dare attack a king's party.

The fact remained that someone was attacking them. The sound of arrows, peppering the air like incensed hornets, caused her heart to pound erratically against her breastbone.

Of all the unpleasantness she was expecting to come from her new life as Wulfhere of Mercia's wife, being attacked on the way to Tamworth had not even featured in her fears.

Ahead, she caught a glimpse of her betrothed. Wulfhere was easy to spot, for his pale blond hair made him stand out, even on a dull day such as this.

"Protect the princess!" he shouted to the men behind him. "Form a shield wall around her!"

The Mercian warriors nearest to Ermenilda hurried to obey their king's order. They unslung their limewood shields from their backs and formed a tight circle around Ermenilda and her maid. The hollow thud of wood overlapping wood momentarily obscured the sounds of the fight up ahead. Sensing her rider's mounting panic, the palfrey danced nervously, snorting as the men formed a tight ring around them.

Murmuring soothing words, Ermenilda leaned forward and stroked the mare's quivering neck.

Now that Wulfhere's men surrounded them, she and Wynflaed could see nothing of the assault ahead. The noises told them that the fight was both violent and bloody—shouts, grunts, and screams, and the meaty thud of iron biting flesh. Arrows clattered against the perimeter of shields surrounding Ermenilda, and she bit back a scream when she saw one of the arrows find its mark.

The warrior directly in front of her gave a muffled cry. He toppled forward off his horse, an arrow in his belly.

Ermenilda caught a glimpse of the chaos beyond before the gap closed up. The men leading Wulfhere's company had dismounted their horses and were engaging the attackers on foot. The opposite end of the bridge was a writhing mass of bodies. In her brief glimpse, Ermenilda had seen men fall off the bridge into the swiftly flowing river below, while others were trampled underfoot.

Next to her, Wynflaed had gone as pale as milk. Tight-lipped, the handmaid clung on to the reins. To her credit, she did not start to weep or shriek in fear—and to her own surprise, neither did Ermenilda.

Wulfhere cursed under his breath and glanced over his shoulder, to where a barrier of shields protected Ermenilda from view. She was too close to the fighting, but there was no way he could help her now.

They were trapped. The bulk of his company had already crossed onto the bridge before the attack. They now formed a barrier so that those in front had nowhere to go but toward the enemy.

The moment the bowmen, hidden in the woodland on the western bank, ceased their onslaught, warriors clad in boiled leather and mail had erupted from the trees. Wielding axes, spears, swords, and seaxes, the attackers rushed onto the bridge howling like nihtgengan— goblins—released from the underworld.

Wulfhere's men had no choice but to meet them head on.

As soon as the first arrows sliced through the air, the king had swung down from the saddle and drawn Shield Breaker. Werbode and Elfhere fought at his side, their own blades slick with blood.

There were many attackers—but what had been their advantage quickly turned against them. The bridge was too narrow for the enemy to crowd onto all at once, and this diluted the strength of their assault.

Wulfhere slashed his way through the last group of attackers. His boots slid on the gore-covered surface, but he managed to keep his feet.

Howling his wrath, he ran at the few remaining men. One of the enemy warriors, suddenly realizing that he was almost alone on the bridge, lost his courage. One look at the face of the fair-haired warrior barreling toward him, sword raised, and the man leaped off the bridge.

As suddenly as it had begun, the attack was over.

An icy wind whistled across the bridge, mingling with the groans of the injured and the whimpers of the dying. Shortly after, the warriors surrounding the two women lowered their shields and moved away, giving Ermenilda a clear view of the carnage beyond.

At the foot of the bridge, she saw Wulfhere, splattered in blood, striding over to where his men had caught the attackers' leader alive.

The captive was tall and broadly built, with golden hair. Ermenilda could see that blood flowed down his left arm and that he had a deep gash on his right cheek. He snarled and struggled against his captors as he watched Wulfhere approach.

The Mercian King was an intimidating sight, clad from head to toe in leather armor and dripping with the blood of his enemies. He carried his sword, unsheathed, in his right hand, its broad blade coated crimson. His wolf, her snowy pelt streaked in blood, stalked behind him.

Wulfhere stood before his captive and looked down at him. When the king spoke, his voice, low and powerful, rang across the now-silent bridge.

"What is your name?"

The man's mouth curled in response and he spat at Wulfhere's feet.

A heartbeat passed before Wulfhere lashed out and hit the man hard across the face.

"Answer me, or I will make your death a slow and dishonorable one."

The warrior glared up at him, considering defiance once more before grudgingly giving a response.

"Sigric . . ."

"And where are you from, Sigric?"

The warrior's face twisted before he spat out his answer. "Ely."

Wulfhere went still, and a deathly hush fell. Watching the scene unfold, Ermenilda's throat tightened. Her betrothed was a terrible sight to behold when enraged. He was every inch the pagan warlord, a man who did not know mercy. His anger appeared cold and lethal, the quiet before a deadly storm.

"You are East Angles," Wulfhere said, finally.

"Aye." The captive gave Wulfhere a bloody grin.

"Did King Aethelwold send you?"

The warrior spat out a gob of blood, making his disdain for the East Angle ruler clear. "I follow Tondberct of Ely, not that pious coward."

"And what argument does Tondberct have with me?"

"His wife, Aethelthryth, is Queen Seaxburh of Kent's sister," the warrior replied.

At the sound of her mother's name, Ermenilda stopped breathing.

When Wulfhere did not reply, Sigric of Ely's bloody smile widened.

"The sisters seek reckoning for the death of their father and brother."

Listening, Ermenilda felt ill.

No, Mōder . . . surely you did not . . .

"And you were attempting to take it for them," Wulfhere said, finishing the man's sentence for him. He gave a cold smile of his own. "It is a pity then that you and your men fight like women."

"Mercian turd!" Sigric snarled. "Long have our people suffered under your yoke. We will have reckoning!"

"My father is dead," Wulfhere replied, his voice wintry. "You were a fool to rekindle an old blood feud, one that should have been let well alone. You have thrown away your men's lives for nothing—and for that you've earned a slow, painful end."

With that, Wulfhere lifted his sword and skewered the East Angle through the stomach.

The man's wails cut through the damp air like a newly sharpened scythe. Ermenilda covered her mouth with her hand, to prevent herself from screaming. She watched Sigric of Ely collapse, writhing, onto the bridge. The East Angle's screams went on and on. The stench of blood and gore made her bile rise.

Ermenilda watched, horrified, as her betrothed stepped away from the injured man. His cruelty sickened her. There was no reason to make the man suffer. Wulfhere's expression was dispassionate, while his pale eyes glittered. His gaze traveled over the bodies littering the bridge, many of whom were Mercian, and his face turned hard. Behind him, there were more bodies still, although most of these appeared to belong to the East Angle war band.

Wulfhere turned to face the rest of his company that awaited at the opposite end of the bridge. However, his gaze sought only one person: Ermenilda.

She lowered a shaky hand from her mouth and forced herself to meet his stare. Despite that they stood about twenty paces apart, Wulfhere's gaze bored into her, stripping her bare. This look was different from all the others he had given her till now. The other glances were of smoldering intensity, of unspoken desire or veiled amusement—but this one was chillingly cold.

Dread crawled across Ermenilda's skin, causing her to shiver with fear. She needed no words to understand the accusation behind the stare.

Wulfhere blamed her for the attack.

Chapter Nine
The Kiss

The Mercians made camp at a distance of about two furlongs northwest of the bridge where the East Angles had attacked them. It had taken Wulfhere's men a long while to pile up the dead into a pyre by the roadside and set fire to their corpses. Smoke stained the sky behind them when they finally continued on their way.

The wind had started to blow hard, bringing sheets of icy rain with it, when the men set to work. They erected their tents in the center of a wide clearing, not far from the road, and used saplings and tree branches as the frames. They stretched the rolls of hide they carried with them across the tops to create the tents.

Ermenilda was shaking with cold, her fingers numb as she attempted to unbuckle the girth to her saddle. Wulfhere had not spoken to her in the aftermath of the attack, but his rage terrified her nonetheless. Fortunately, with darkness swiftly approaching, other tasks appeared to absorb him, and he ignored her for the moment.

Elfhere relieved Ermenilda and Wynflaed of their horses, assuring the women that he would finish seeing to them. Wynflaed cast the warrior a brittle smile of thanks, her face still pale after the afternoon's trauma. Then, she turned to Ermenilda.

"Come, milady. Let's get you out of the cold."

Ermenilda did not need to be asked twice. Gratefully, she made her way across to her tent and ducked inside.

One of Wulfhere's men had just lit a fire, and Wynflaed hurried across to tend it while Ermenilda perched upon one of her leather packs and waited for the warmth to reach her chilled limbs.

Wynflaed finished feeding the fire with larger pieces of wood and straightened up, her gaze shifting to her mistress.

"You are very pale, milady," she observed. "Are you not well?"

Ermenilda forced a smile. "Well enough. I'm still a bit shaken, that is all."

"For the first time, I understand why men keep women away from war," Wynflaed replied, her voice subdued.

Ermenilda nodded, not trusting herself to speak. She would never forget the horror she had witnessed: Sigric of Ely's screams and sobs, and Wulfhere's chilling lack of emotion.

More than ever, she resented her father for tearing a peaceful life at Eastry Abbey from her. Instead, he had given her to a ruthless warlord, a man without mercy.

Gradually, it warmed within the tent. Outside, Ermenilda could hear men's voices as they finished making camp and seeing to their horses.

"I will make us a soup, milady," Wynflaed announced. She placed a small iron pot next to the fire and dug around in one of their packs for provisions. "That should calm our nerves."

"Thank you, Wynflaed," Ermenilda murmured. She appreciated her maid's practical attitude. Focusing upon other matters also made her feel better. She looked on as Wynflaed cut up carrots and onions and placed them in the pot with a few slices of salted pork. Wynflaed poured the contents of her water bladder into the pot and sat it among the glowing embers.

"It is simple fare," Wynflaed said, casting her mistress an apologetic smile, "but it will warm our bellies nonetheless.

"Wait." Ermenilda reached over to a satchel. "I have some dried herbs that should add some extra flavor."

She withdrew a linen pouch and plucked out a sprig of dried thyme. "This was from my garden."

The pungent, woody aroma of thyme gave her a pang of homesickness, reminding Ermenilda of the afternoons she had spent weeding, sowing, and harvesting with her mother and sister in their beloved garden. In the summer, the sun would release the herb's fragrance, and it would waft across the enclosure.

"Thank you, milady." Wynflaed took the sprig from her with a smile. "This should make the soup a little tastier."

Wynflaed had just added the thyme to the soup, and was stirring it with a wooden spoon, when the leather flap covering the entrance to the tent opened.

A tall man, his silver-blond hair mussed by the wind, entered. Ermenilda's fragile sense of peace shattered.

One look at Wulfhere's face and she knew she was in trouble. The king cast a glance at Wynflaed and jerked his chin toward the entrance.

"Leave us."

Wynflaed's eyes widened.

They both knew that she was supposed to chaperone her mistress. Ermenilda's mother had insisted upon it. Until they were handfasted, Seaxburh did not want her daughter and the newly crowned Mercian king left alone together.

"Milady . . . ," Wynflaed ventured, her expression pained. "I—"

"Leave us," Wulfhere repeated, his voice a low growl. "Now."

This time, the maid did not protest. Her face was taut with fear as she fled the tent.

Ermenilda rose to her feet, attempting to use outrage to cover the fear that caused her legs to tremble beneath her. "We cannot be alone together like this. Mōder insisted—"

"Nithhogg take your mother," Wulfhere snarled, advancing upon her. "Meddling bitch that she is."

He halted when they were barely a foot apart and grabbed her by the shoulders, holding her fast.

"Look at me, Ermenilda," he commanded.

She raised her chin and met his hard gaze. He was angrier than she had had realized; his skin was pulled tight across his cheekbones, his eyes narrow slits.

"I want the truth," he growled, his fingers digging into the soft flesh of her shoulders and upper arms.

"Th—the truth?" Ermenilda stuttered.

"Did you know of this attack?" he demanded. "Did you know what your mother had planned?"

Ermenilda's response was explosive and truthful.

"Of course not! I had no idea. That man was lying— my mother would never do anything so treacherous."

"I saw her hate for my father," Wulfhere countered, unmoved by her words. "She was bent upon reckoning. What did she promise Sigric of Ely? That when Penda of Mercia's whelp was dead, he could take you as his prize?"

Ermenilda was horrified. She brought up her hands and pushed against the hard wall of his chest in an attempt to free herself from him.

"No!" she cried. "You are a pig for suggesting such a thing!"

"I want the truth, Ermenilda." Wulfhere was relentless, his anger breaking over her in a great, cold wave. "Did you know?"

"I am telling the truth," she gasped, staring up at him, her vision blurring with tears. "I swear with god as my witness that I knew nothing of this attack."

He glared down at her, a muscle working in his jaw as he struggled to rein in his temper. Two heartbeats passed, and then, with a whispered curse, Wulfhere stepped even closer to her, so that their bodies were almost touching.

"I have no choice but to believe you," he murmured, leaning forward so that his breath feathered her cheek, "but I warn you—the one thing I cannot abide is a liar."

Ermenilda swallowed, her heart hammering against her ribs like a battle drum.

"I do not lie," she whispered, before dredging up her last shred of courage. "But, I also cannot abide senseless cruelty. Why did you have to stab that man in the belly? You gave him a slow, agonizing death, for no reason at all save to satisfy your own vindictiveness."

"That is good enough reason for me," he replied. "Sigric of Ely deserved it."

His lips brushed her cheek, and the sensation sent a jolt of liquid fire down Ermenilda's neck. She started to tremble, although this time it was not in fear. She did not like him standing so close. She did not like the way the touch of his lips on her skin addled her brain. Suddenly she could not think clearly—could not even form the words to protest his forward behavior.

"So beautiful," he whispered, "yet, so cold."

"I'm not . . . cold," she managed, the words nearly strangling her when his lips suddenly brushed hers.

"No?" His tone was gently mocking, and when his mouth brushed hers once more, Ermenilda let out a soft gasp. "Shall we see whether heat lies beneath the ice?"

Without waiting for her reply, for he clearly had no intention of listening to it, Wulfhere pulled her hard against him. His hands cupped the back of her head as his mouth claimed hers.

Despite the possessiveness of Wulfhere's touch, his kiss was surprisingly gentle. He brushed her lips repeatedly with his and then explored them with the tip of his tongue. He waited till her lips parted by their own accord before his tongue sought entrance. Even then, there was a melting gentleness to the kiss.

Ermenilda was boneless in his arms. If he had not been holding her, she would have crumpled to the ground. He overwhelmed her senses, and despite that her mind screamed in protest at the liberties this man was taking, her body utterly betrayed her.

She was caught in his web, and she could not break free. Her body no longer belonged to her; it ached to feel his hard, strong body against hers. It longed to feel his lips not just upon her mouth but everywhere.

When Wulfhere finally ended the kiss, her body pulsed with need.

Breathless, he stared down at her, surprise evident on his face.

"My mistake," he said, his voice oddly rough. "There is nothing cold about you, Ermenilda. To think you were about to give yourself as a bride of Christ—what a terrible waste."

His words had an immediate, dousing effect upon the passion that held Ermenilda in its thrall. Horrified, she twisted free of him and staggered back.

"How dare you!" she rasped. "Brute!"

To her fury, he merely gave a soft laugh, his eyes glittering.

"It's too late for that, princess. I now know that all that haughtiness is merely a ruse. Come our wedding night, you will enjoy being bedded as much as I will enjoy taking you."

Ermenilda gaped at him, her face burning, but Wulfhere had finished tormenting her. With a smoldering look, he turned and left the tent without another word.

Dusk had settled over the Mercian camp, and the wind tore through it, grappling at the stakes that formed the enclosure around the horses, and battering the tents.

Wynflaed ran a hand down her horse's neck and cast a nervous glance toward Princess Ermenilda's tent.

He should not be in there alone with her.

Guilt needled Wynflaed. She had made a solemn promise to the Kentish king and queen that she would ensure their daughter's virtue remained uncompromised until her wedding day. Both of them would be furious if they knew that she had left Wulfhere and Ermenilda alone together.

As if sensing her worry, Wynflaed's horse gently nuzzled her arm. The roan gelding had the biggest, ugliest head she had ever seen on a horse, but he had a sweet, steady nature, and Wynflaed had grown fond of him during the journey.

She stroked his furry forelock and inhaled slowly in an attempt to calm her nerves.

"I hope he is not bullying her," she murmured, speaking her thoughts aloud.

"Bullying who?"

A man's voice behind her made Wynflaed jump. She turned, squinting in the light from the nearby pitch torch, and recognized Elfhere. He stepped toward her, frowning.

"Is something amiss, Wynflaed?

The maid glanced once more at the tent, where she had left Wulfhere and Ermenilda. Wynflaed gave Elfhere a pained look.

"The king wanted to speak to Lady Ermenilda alone. He ordered me to leave."

Elfhere shrugged, seemingly unconcerned. "It is his right, as her betrothed."

Wynflaed stiffened. "I gave the queen my word that I would not let her daughter out of my sight."

Elfhere smiled. It was a lopsided, sensual smile, and Wynflaed wagered it had melted the heart of many a woman over the years. Despite walking with a slight limp, Elfhere was an attractive man with warmth and charm that made him easy to like.

"You cannot blame yourself, if the king ordered you to leave," he replied gently. "I doubt Lady Ermenilda will come to any harm. Do you not see the way he looks at her?"

"I do," Wynflaed answered tartly, "and that's precisely why I worry."

Elfhere chuckled at that, but his laughter faded when they spied Wulfhere duck out of Lady Ermenilda's tent and stalk off into the shadows.

Wynflaed cast a glance back at Elfhere, who was gazing at her intently.

"I must go to her," she muttered. "Good eve, Elfhere."

Not awaiting his response, she hurried across the windswept encampment and ducked into the tent. Inside, she found her mistress seated upon a leather pack near the fire. Nearby, the soup was bubbling furiously. The aroma of salted pork, thyme, and vegetables mixed with the smoky air inside the tent. However, the princess paid the soup no mind.

Ermenilda was weeping into her hands, her slender shoulders shaking from the force of her despair.

Chapter Ten
Anger and Arrogance

Winter had drained the world of any warmth. Under leaden skies and with a chill north wind in their faces, the company pressed on with the dawn.

The mood was somber this morning, for the attack had soured the previously convivial atmosphere among the Mercians. Until the attack, they had plenty to be happy about—a new king and an imminent handfasting. Now, many of their brothers would not be returning to Tamworth.

The news that Queen Seaxburh had betrayed them had altered many of their attitudes toward Ermenilda. This morning, she noted their cold glances and scowls. Despite her love for her mother, she felt a bitter stab of reproach toward her. Ermenilda's life in Mercia would be difficult enough as it was without folk turning against her. If the East Angle warrior had spoken true, her mother had committed a foolish act—something they would all pay for.

How could she be so reckless?

Ermenilda pulled up her fur-lined hood, in an effort to shield her face from the biting wind, and inwardly railed at her mother.

What did you hope to achieve?

"Good morning, milady."

The priest, Seaxwulf, appeared at her right, upon a stocky bay gelding. He had wrapped himself in a thick fur cloak, in an effort to ward off the chill, although his nose was red from cold.

"Good morning, Brother Seaxwulf," she responded dully. Usually, she welcomed the monk's cheerful, reassuring presence, but this morning she preferred to be left alone with her thoughts.

"Is anything amiss, milady?" Seaxwulf ventured, his quick gaze missing nothing.

Ermenilda shook her head. "No . . . I am just a little tired."

"Yesterday was enough to make me want to return to the life of a monk at Lindisfarena," Seaxwulf admitted quietly. "I never wish to experience such carnage, such brutality, ever again."

"Neither do I," Ermenilda agreed. "Although, I would rather not think of it at all today, if you don't mind, Brother."

Taking the hint, the priest nodded and reined his gelding back slightly, so that the princess rode alone once more. Grateful for the solitude, Ermenilda's gaze shifted up to the front of the column.

Ahead, she spied Wulfhere. He was riding alongside the dark-haired, bearded warrior, Werbode, who appeared to be one of his most trusted followers.

The men were conversing, although the roar of the wind made it impossible to overhear them. Wulfhere's fur cloak billowed behind him. As always, Mōna trotted along at his side, silent and watchful.

Ermenilda clenched her jaw as she observed Wulfhere. She stared daggers at his broad back.

She had called him a brute the evening before and meant it. He had no right to corner her, to accuse her, and to kiss her. He had humiliated her merely to prove a point. His comment about bedding her still lingered, filling her with terror. Yet, underneath her fear, there was an odd, churning excitement, which both confused and upset Ermenilda.

As the morning wore on, she ceased worrying about her mother and, instead, ruminated over Wulfhere's treatment of her. By the time they stopped for their noon meal, anger had twisted her belly in knots.

Last night, he had set a precedent. What was to stop him visiting her again tonight and taking greater liberties? She would not let him get away with humiliating her.

She would not let him have the upper hand.

The company had stopped by the roadside, at the top of a shallow valley. The wind blew Ermenilda's hood back off her face as she dismounted her palfrey, loosening strands of fine blonde hair from her braids.

Beside her, Wynflaed had just dismounted her gelding and was opening one of her saddlebags to fetch some bread and cheese.

"Shall we take a seat on those rocks over there?" she asked.

"Make a start without me, Wynflaed," Ermenilda told her handmaid firmly. "I must speak to the king."

"But, milady . . . is that wise?"

"Perhaps not, but it is necessary."

Ermenilda squared her shoulders and marched through the crowd of milling men and horses. She strode purposefully toward the front of the column. Aware of the men's stares as she walked among them, Ermenilda kept her gaze fixed upon her destination: the King of Mercia.

Wulfhere had just dismounted from his stallion and was saying something to Werbode. The dark-haired warrior spied Ermenilda first. He watched her for a moment, his gaze traveling the length of her in a way that made her boiling temper rise even further. Then, he lazily turned to Wulfhere.

"Milord, it appears your betrothed wants a word."

Wulfhere turned, his limpid gaze settling upon Ermenilda. The impact of their gazes meeting nearly caused her step to falter. Resisting the sudden impulse to turn and flee, she pressed on.

"Lady Ermenilda," he greeted her. "How can I be of service?"

"I would speak to you for a moment," she replied, stopping a few feet away from him. "Alone."

Wulfhere raised an eyebrow, while around them a few men sniggered.

Werbode gave a low whistle. "She's forward, this Kentish princess . . ."

Ermenilda threw him the coldest, most imperious look she could muster, but Werbode merely returned her gaze with a boldness that made her skin crawl. Suddenly, she felt like a lamb in a den of wolves. The anger that had propelled her off her palfrey and up to the head of the column was beginning to subside. She was starting to feel vulnerable.

"Come, milady."

Wulfhere cast Werbode a censorious look before he gently took hold of Ermenilda's arm and steered her away from his men. They reached the crest of the hill, a few yards away from the others, and halted. Behind them, to the north, Ermenilda could see the gentle folds of grassy downs stretching away to a cloudy horizon like a rumpled blanket.

Wulfhere turned and faced her. The look of thinly veiled amusement on his face made Ermenilda's ire rise once more.

"What is it?" he asked.

"I demand an apology," she replied, folding her arms across her chest as she faced him.

His amusement faded. "An apology . . . for what?"

"For your behavior."

Wulfhere stared at her, stunned. When he replied, his voice held a warning.

"I had every right to be angry, Ermenilda. I had just learned of your mother's treachery, and I believed you to be part of it. I am still yet to be convinced that you are entirely innocent."

"My word should be enough," she countered angrily. "Yet, that is not what I seek an apology for. You took advantage of a moment alone with me. You humiliated me."

His eyes widened. "A kiss is not humiliation. You are my betrothed—I have a right to kiss you. Even if I had taken you last night in your tent, it would have been my right."

Anger exploded within Ermenilda. She unfolded her arms and balled her fists at her sides.

Wulfhere observed her temper and raised an eyebrow.

"Definitely not the ice maiden I took you for. Do you wish to strike me?"

"If I were a man, I would," she replied between gritted teeth. "Do the promises you made my father mean nothing?"

Wulfhere gave a soft laugh. "And what promises are you referring to?"

"That you would follow god's word."

"I am baptized," he replied, "but I will not follow pointless rules when they do not serve me."

"Then you lied to my father," Ermenilda countered.

Wulfhere took a step toward her, his face hardening.

"I have not lied to anyone," he told her softly, "but if I wish to kiss you, I will. No priest, no father, and no god will stop me."

Ermenilda shrank back from him, her pulse pounding in her ears.

"When we are handfasted, I will do my duty, as a woman must," she snarled at him, "but until then, you will leave me alone."

She turned, with the intention of stalking back to where Wynflaed waited. However, Wulfhere grabbed her arm and hauled her back round to face him. He stood over her, his gaze hard with fury.

Then, he pulled her hard against him and kissed her.

This kiss was not like the night before—that embrace had been gentle, intimate, and overwhelmingly sensual. Instead, this kiss was possessive and brutal. He branded her as his, for all his men to see. Their hooting and catcalls rang in Ermenilda's ears when he finally released her. Her lips stung from the force of his kiss.

Without thinking, she lashed out and slapped him hard across the face. "Lutān!"

Wulfhere barely seemed to notice her blow. Instead, he stepped close to Ermenilda once more, his hard gaze pinning her to the spot.

"Perhaps I am a *lout*, as you say, princess," he told her softly, "but very soon I will be your husband, and you won't be able to deny me anything."

Ermenilda held her ground, even though his closeness was intimidating. Around them, Wulfhere's men were laughing and calling out to them, enjoying the display.

Ermenilda's cheeks flamed at the humiliation; this was even worse than the night before. Her temper had worsened an already tense relationship between them, and had given Wulfhere's men a spectacle to boot. However, she was still too incensed to care.

"You will be my husband," she told him, her voice trembling with the force of her anger. "But, you cannot force me to like you. I wish you dead. I loathe you, Wulfhere of Mercia. The devil take you!"

With that, she whirled away from him and pushed her way back through the crowd.

Chapter Eleven
Crossing the Line

Wulfhere stepped inside his tent and found Elfhere attempting to light a fire. Outside, night had fallen, and a vicious wind, even stronger than the night before, hammered against the tent. The hide snapped and billowed, causing the tender flames that Elfhere was trying to encourage to gutter and go out.

"Foul night," Elfhere observed, cupping his hands around the smoking pile of twigs. "The gods are raging."

Wulfhere grunted. He was not in a good mood this evening. The events of the last two days had soured his temper, and he had no desire for company. Instead of responding to his thegn, he sat down on the pile of furs in the far corner of the tent and began unlacing his boots. Elfhere took the hint and turned back to his task.

The warrior had just managed to coax the flames back to life, when the tent flap swung open and Werbode entered. He brought with him a gust of wind that put the fire out once more.

"Woden's balls!" Elfhere muttered. "Couldn't you have made a gentler entrance?"

Werbode gave the warrior a look of wry amusement before setting down the pack he was carrying.

"Looks like you're having trouble with that," he observed.

Elfhere threw him a dark look and turned back to the smoldering twigs.

Wulfhere observed the tension between them without comment. Although they were both unfailingly loyal to him, Elfhere and Werbode barely tolerated each other. Werbode saw himself as the king's most trusted thegn and often sought to discredit Elfhere. However, to Werbode's ire, Elfhere largely chose to ignore him.

"How about a cup of mead, milord?" Werbode asked.

Wulfhere nodded. Hopefully, a cup of the pungent fermented honey beverage would take the edge off his foul mood. "Pour yourself and Elfhere a cup while you're at it."

Werbode did as bade. He handed Wulfhere the first cup before wordlessly handing Elfhere his, once the warrior had succeeded in lighting the fire. Wood smoke filled the tent's interior before it found its way up through the slit in the roof.

The men sipped their mead in silence for a few moments, listening to the crack and pop of twigs as the flames took hold. Werbode spoke first.

"Will you have your reckoning against the East Angles, milord?"

"I will," Wulfhere replied without hesitation. "Although most of Queen Seaxburh's kin are now dead, her sister, Aethelthryth, and her ealdorman husband, Tondberct, reside at Ely."

"Shall we pay them a visit?"

Wulfhere nodded. "Once I am handfasted, I intend to do just that."

Werbode smiled, satisfied, his gaze meeting Wulfhere's.

"The Lady Ermenilda is feistier than she first appeared," he observed. "In her father's hall she appeared gentle and demure . . ."

"And now she has developed a forked tongue," Wulfhere said, finishing his friend's sentence for him. "The fact had not escaped me, Werbode."

"Her mother's behavior should have been warning enough," Werbode continued, "for a daughter often develops her mother's character with age."

Wulfhere frowned at Werbode and took a deep draft from his cup.

"She just needs time," he replied, although even to himself, the words sounded hollow. He knew that the Kentish princess did not want to wed him, but he had underestimated the depths of her aversion to him.

Still, she was a young woman full of contradictions. He had not imagined her reaction to his kiss the night before. Every time their gazes met, he felt her attraction to him. Try as she might to fight it, the pull between them grew stronger with each passing day. Surely, she could not deny it.

For his part, he was finding it increasingly difficult to resist her. Kissing Ermenilda had just stoked his hunger. Come their wedding night, he would be aching for her.

"Lady Ermenilda has lived a sheltered life till now," Elfhere said, breaking the weighty silence in the tent. "Her mother groomed her for a life as a nun, and she still hasn't accepted that it won't happen. But, I think you're right, milord. In time, she will soften toward you."

Werbode snorted into his mead, making his scorn for Elfhere's advice clear.

"You will need to take a firm hand with her, milord. The princess clearly has grown up among weak men. For all his bluster, the Kentish king is ruled by his shrewish wife. She cut off his balls years ago. Be careful her daughter does not do the same with you."

Wulfhere cast Werbode a quelling look. There were times when his friend pushed his frankness too far—and this evening was one of them.

"The day anyone—man or woman—rules me is the day I lie dead and cold in my grave," he replied icily.

Werbode, wisely, remained silent.

"Milady, you should eat something."

Ermenilda looked on her lap at the bowl of pottage she had hardly touched, and sighed. Her stomach had closed, and pottage was the last thing she wanted. Even so, she raised her wooden spoon to her lips and forced down a mouthful.

Wynflaed sat opposite her, on the other side of the crackling fire. The maid had finished her supper and was winding wool onto her distaff. The firelight softened Wynflaed's strong-featured face, darkened her eyes, and caught the strands of red in her curly auburn hair. Her expression was solemn as she regarded her mistress.

"Please, Wynflaed. Do not look so troubled," Ermenilda said finally. "I am not unwell."

"You are as white as milk, milady."

"I'm just tired."

Silence fell between them for a few moments, before Wynflaed ventured to speak again.

"I saw what happened this morning."

Ermenilda stiffened. "That's no surprise. The entire Mercian company viewed the spectacle."

"Yes, and most of them were entertained by it," the maid replied gently. "Yet, I am worried."

Ermenilda let out an irritated sigh. "I do not need another mother or a nursemaid."

"But you put yourself at risk today, milady," Wynflaed pressed on, ignoring her mistress's rebuke. "It's unwise to argue so openly with your betrothed. You risk humiliating him—and that could cause him to be cruel to you."

"He doesn't need a reason," Ermenilda countered sharply. "Cruelty comes naturally to Wulfhere of Mercia."

Wynflaed frowned, and Ermenilda could see the young woman pondering her words. Watching her, Ermenilda was struck how different her maid was to the two women she had grown up with: her mother and sister. Seaxburh was a sweet, if slightly aloof, woman, who hid her thoughts and feelings from others; whereas Eorcengota was impulsive, a little silly, and took the world at face value.

Wynflaed was not like that. She questioned everything, including her mistress, and it was beginning to wear upon Ermenilda. However, her handmaid had not finished.

"I think you misjudge him," she finally ventured. "It is true he is ruthless—kings have to be. Yet, I have seen how he looks at you. I don't think he would be cruel to you unless you forced him to it."

Ermenilda stared at Wynflaed, aghast. She put her bowl of pottage aside and drew herself up in outrage.

"Misjudge him? The man is arrogant and pitiless. You are softhearted, Wynflaed—and softheaded as well—if you think there is any goodness in him. He wishes to rule me, own me. I am like a new horse he wishes to add to his stable. One he intends to break."

Wynflaed held her gaze, although this time she did not respond. The young woman's cheeks had reddened at her mistress's insult.

Now incensed, Ermenilda continued.

"Wulfhere may claim my body, but he will never have my soul," she spat. "I would die first."

Chapter Twelve
The Storm

They crossed into Mercia under a heavy sky of brooding storm clouds. Rolling downs gave way to thick woodland of ash, beech, and oak. In the distance, Ermenilda heard the faint rumbling of thunder—odd for this time of year.

Although Ermenilda did not believe in portents, for those beliefs belonged to the ways of the old gods, there was something foreboding about the approaching storm. Both literally and figuratively, she could see nothing but darkness ahead. Tamworth, and her bleak future, lay just a few days to the northwest.

How can this be the will of god?

Ermenilda had struggled with the question since rising at dawn. She felt guilty at even contemplating the question, but still it niggled at her. Pagans believed that wyrd—fate—ruled your life. There was no reason, no plan behind events—fate merely took you where it willed, and you had no choice but to follow. Christians believed that god chose your path.

Is there something you must teach me?

Ermenilda's eyes filled with tears. She had been so content in her life, so sure that she would be able to devote her life to god. Perhaps, the lord was punishing her for her arrogance.

She rode alone this morning, deliberately so. Wulfhere sat astride his stallion a few horses ahead of her, while Seaxwulf and Wynflaed rode a couple of yards behind, leaving her to her solitude. The priest and handmaid were talking softly between themselves as another rolling peal of thunder drowned out their voices.

Ermenilda glanced up at the threatening sky and felt fat, cold raindrops fall upon her face. A bolt of lightning streaked across the woods in front of her, turning the gloomy day blindingly bright.

Her palfrey squealed in terror and reared, nearly unseating her. A nervy beast at the best of times, the mare tossed her head and bucked. Ermenilda reached down and stroked the mare's neck.

"Steady, girl."

Another lightning bolt struck. This one hit an old oak barely ten yards back from the road. The tree burst into flames, causing horses and men alike to shy away back from it.

The palfrey clamped the bit between her teeth and bolted.

Ermenilda heard shouts behind her, but all her attention was focused on stopping her horse. She pulled back on the reins with all her might, seating herself as deeply as possible in the saddle in an effort to slow her panicked palfrey. Blind terror had seized the mare. She tore through the ranks of Wulfhere's company and bolted into the forest.

Low branches clutched at Ermenilda, and wet foliage slapped her face as the palfrey galloped through the trees. Gasping with terror, she gave up trying to halt her horse and crouched low over the mare's neck in an effort not to be unseated by a low-hanging branch.

Fear froze her to the saddle. If the mare continued at this pace, fleeing without a thought to her or her rider's safety, she would soon fall and break a leg, or worse.

The end of a naked tree branch caught Ermenilda across the cheek, leaving a trail of fire in its wake. She gasped in pain and choked back a sob of panic. Once more, she tried to pull her mare up, but the horse still had her bit locked between her teeth, and showed no sign of slowing her pace.

The thud of horse's hooves to Ermenilda's left drew her attention. Out of the corner of her eye, she caught a flash of black. Someone had pursued her through the woods and had nearly caught up to her palfrey.

Wulfhere drew level with her, his black stallion easily keeping pace with the smaller mare. Reaching across he took hold of her reins in one hand and slowed his stallion with the other. Despite the terror that still pursued her like the devil, the palfrey had no choice but to respond. The horse squealed in protest, her neck arching upward—but she slowed her pace nonetheless.

The mare skidded to an unsteady halt. Her body trembled in the aftermath of her shock, and she was just waiting for another lightning bolt to set her off. Ermenilda swung down off her back, realizing as she did so that it was now pouring rain, and thunder was rumbling directly overhead.

Wulfhere dismounted from his stallion and ducked under the horse's neck before straightening to his full height before Ermenilda.

Her heart still racing from fear, Ermenilda pretended not to see him. Truthfully, it was taking all her concentration not to have her feet trod on, for her palfrey was now bucking and dancing on the spot, the whites of her eyes gleaming despite the sunless day.

"Give her to me," Wulfhere commanded.

Wordlessly, Ermenilda stepped back and let him take the reins. She looked on as the Mercian reached out and stroked the mare's quivering neck. The horse foamed at the mouth and looked as if she would bolt again, if given the chance.

Wulfhere remained calm. He murmured soothing, gentle words under his breath as he continued stroking the mare's neck. Gradually, the palfrey settled, her head inching lower until her nose rested against Wulfhere's chest.

Smiling, Wulfhere stroked the mare's head and forelock.

"That's it," he murmured. "It wasn't going to kill you after all, was it?"

Ermenilda watched, impressed, as the fear drained from her horse. She had never seen such a quick transformation.

"You are good with horses," she observed, albeit grudgingly.

Wulfhere turned his ice-blue gaze to her, and Ermenilda felt the same breathlessness that had assailed her in the tent two days earlier return. Only this time, she held it in check.

"Not with women, though?" he asked, his mouth quirking slightly.

Ermenilda refused to be baited.

"Thank you for helping me," she replied stiffly.

Wulfhere inclined his head slightly. "How could I not?"

He reached out and ran a fingertip down her cheek. "You're bleeding."

His touch made her stifle a gasp.

"It's just a scratch."

Thunder boomed overhead once more, and Ermenilda's palfrey gave a shrill whinny, her nervousness returning.

"We had better return to the others," Ermenilda said quickly. She pushed her wet hair, which had come loose out of its long braid down her back, from her face.

I must look a mess.

Angry with herself that she should even be worried about her appearance before this man, she reached back to pull up her sodden hood. However, Wulfhere reached out and stopped her.

"You are beautiful like this, all disheveled and wild," he said, his voice low and intimate.

Panic surged in Ermenilda's breast. He seemed to have forgotten their altercation the day before and the hate-filled words she had spat at him. It was as if they were already lovers. She had hoped her viciousness would have driven him away, but he was looking at her now as if he would devour her.

"Please, don't . . . ," she whispered.

"Please, don't what?"

"Say those things . . . I don't want to hear them."

His expression hardened, and his gaze narrowed.

"Most women like to be desired, to be complimented," he told her. "Why does it offend you so?"

"You know why."

She did not want to spell it out for him again. She did not want to tell him how she reviled him, for it made her feel cruel and small afterward. Wynflaed's chastisement the night before still rang in her ears, and despite that her feelings toward Wulfhere had not changed, she had no wish to wound him unnecessarily.

Wulfhere stepped close and placed a hand under her chin, tilting her head up so that their gazes met.

"This is not a battle you will win," he told her.

His hand left her chin and slid along her jawline. He tangled his fingers in her wet hair. Ermenilda's mouth went dry, and her pulse started to race. A strange torpor filled her limbs.

"So this is war?" she managed, her voice husky.

Wulfhere gave her a wolfish grin. "Aye."

"Please let me be," she pleaded weakly.

Wulfhere shook his head. He glanced back, from the way they had come. The sound of approaching horses, and the crunch of twigs underfoot, warned them that they had only a few more moments alone together in the woods.

It doesn't matter how much you deny it," he said softly. "Your body betrays you every time, lovely Ermenilda."

Blinking back tears of humiliation and rage, Ermenilda glared at him. She wanted to call him a liar, but the accusation would have been hollow.

Chapter Thirteen
The Great Tower

Tamworth appeared—a sprawling, dirty town, encircled by high palisades, with a huge gray tower looming over it like a grim watcher. The seat of the Mercian king sat at the intersection between two wide rivers: The Tame and the Anker. Thick woodland carpeted the land to the south and west, whereas wide meadows stretched east. To the north, there was a row of barrows; the grassy burial mounds of Mercian kings. The town's setting was idyllic, although to Ermenilda's anxious gaze, the settlement itself crouched menacingly at the heart of it.

Ermenilda rode into Tamworth at Wulfhere's side. He had insisted she did so, for his people would expect to see them arrive together. Even so, she made a point of not looking his way; an act of futility for even when she could not see him, she was keenly aware of his presence next to her.

They had barely spoken since he had rescued her in the woods a few days earlier. Since then, she had gone out of her way to avoid him and, mercifully, Wulfhere had not sought her out.

Now, with Tamworth before them, her reprieve had ended.

They clattered across the wooden bridge that crossed the lazy flow of the River Tame and rode up an incline to the low gate. It was a bright afternoon, unusually warm for the season. Folk had gathered at the roadside to welcome home their king and catch a glimpse of the Kentish princess he would wed.

Ermenilda saw the joy on their faces as she rode by. Children called out to her, and men and women cheered at the sight of their new queen. Mercia and the Kentish had always had an amicable relationship, although Ermenilda realized that she was more welcome here than she had anticipated.

Wulfhere reined his stallion in close to her, so that their legs were almost touching.

"The people of Tamworth are overjoyed to see you, Lady Ermenilda."

"I think it is their king they are pleased to welcome home," she replied, still avoiding his gaze.

"Ever since my father's passing, Mercia has lacked security," he answered. "My older brother, Paeda, was a puppet king, put in power by Oswiu of Northumbria. Paeda's wife—who was a Northumbrian princess—was never truly accepted here. You bring my people hope."

Ermenilda glanced at him, frowning.

Hope.

She had none for herself. How could she provide hope to anyone else?

They rode up the tangle of narrow, paved streets to the high gate and entered the inner palisade. A vast yard, flanked by low-slung buildings on either side, greeted them. Stone steps led up to the entrance to the Great Tower, where guards had opened the vast oaken doors to admit their king.

Ermenilda glanced around her as she slid to the ground and adjusted her clothing. Everything was on a much grander scale here than in Cantwareburh. However, her father's Great Hall was a much more welcoming structure, and a cursory glance around gave no sign of any garden, or even an orchard.

"Come, Lady Ermenilda." Wulfhere appeared at her elbow. His tone was reserved, polite. He was playing a role now, and he expected her to do the same. "My kin and retainers await."

"Brother! You did not exaggerate the Kentish princess's beauty, I see."

The man who had just spoken bore a startling resemblance to Wulfhere and stood upon the high seat awaiting them. As she and Wulfhere approached, Ermenilda noted the differences between the two men: Wulfhere was far more striking, with his mane of white-blond hair and regal bone structure. The man waiting on the high seat was sharper featured, his pale gaze shrewder. He wore his dark-blond hair cropped short against his scalp.

They had almost reached the high seat when the man stepped down to greet them. His face split into a grin, instantly making him devastatingly attractive.

Beside her, Wulfhere snorted. "Have you ever known me to exaggerate anything?"

Wulfhere turned to Ermenilda. "Lady Ermenilda, meet my brother, Prince Aethelred."

Unsmiling, Ermenilda nodded at the prince while he gave her an assessing, penetrating look in return. She shifted her gaze from Aethelred, noting that there was no one else standing upon the high seat behind the prince.

It was so different from her father's hall filled with her cousins, uncles, and aunts. A handful of men and women, all finely dressed, stood at the foot of the high seat. None of them bore any physical resemblance to the two brothers, so Ermenilda surmised that they were retainers rather than kin.

Where is the rest of his family?

She cast her gaze around the interior of the Great Tower of Tamworth. It was cold and damp and smelled faintly of mildew, despite the huge hearths burning at each end. Narrow, high windows appeared to let in very little light, while a number of clay cressets lined the circular walls, casting their warmth across the space. Above, Ermenilda noted that there appeared to be another floor, accessible via a ladder from the main hall.

"You will be weary." Aethelred clicked his fingers and motioned to a slave girl who was stoking one of the fire pits. "Bring the king some mead."

Wulfhere nodded. "It has been a long—and eventful—journey," he admitted.

Still keeping a gentle hold on Ermenilda's elbow, he led her up onto the high seat, where they sat down at a long table. Wulfhere and Ermenilda's chairs were beautifully crafted and carved from oak, with dragon's-head armrests.

Aethelred took a seat to his brother's right, his gaze bright with curiosity.

"So, when will you be handfasted?" he asked.

"This evening," Wulfhere replied without hesitation.

Ermenilda felt her belly contract at this news. She had known their wedding was looming but had hoped that he might have waited till tomorrow. Panic fluttered up into her breast. She was not ready for this; she would never be ready.

Aethelred smirked. "Impatient, eh?"

Wulfhere gave his brother a cool look. "Can you ask Immin's, Eafa's, and Eadbert's wives to make the arrangements?" he said, choosing not to reply to his brother's comment. "The ealdormen are still in Tamworth, are they not?"

Aethelred nodded. "They have eagerly awaited your return, Brother."

The slave girl appeared and poured each of them a cup of mead. Ermenilda took a sip from hers, before her gaze went to the iron collar about the girl's thin neck. Her father did not keep slaves; all those who served in his hall were free men and women. Frankly, she was not surprised that many slaves worked within Wulfhere's hall, although it did nothing to improve her opinion of him.

"Milord . . . " She spoke for the first time since entering the hall. "May I visit Tamworth's church now? Before the handfasting."

Wulfhere frowned. "The day grows late. You will need time to bathe and dress for the ceremony."

"It won't take long," she promised. "I will not linger."

"Very well," Wulfhere conceded. He rose from his seat and waved to the priest, who had just entered the hall. "Seaxwulf will take you there."

Ermenilda bowed her head. "Thank you, milord."

She rose to her feet, forcing herself to maintain the appearance of serenity. Wulfhere's brother was observing her. He had the kind of sharp gaze that missed nothing, and she wondered if he had noticed the tension between her and Wulfhere.

Without another word, she stepped down from the high seat and made her way toward Seaxwulf.

Wulfhere watched his betrothed cross the hall with the priest, Seaxwulf, at her side. He silently admired her proud posture; the long, slender curve of her back; and the way her golden hair spilled like honey over her shoulders.

The journey from Cantwareburh had been the longest of his life. He ached for Ermenilda. Over the past few days, he had been able to think of nothing else but his betrothed.

"She is indeed lovely."

Aethelred's voice drew his attention away from the Kentish princess, forcing his gaze back to his brother. He did not like the way Aethelred was smirking. As children, it had always been a sign that his younger brother was about to stir up trouble.

"She is," Wulfhere agreed guardedly, before taking a sip of his mead.

"Does she ever smile?"

Wulfhere sighed. Here was the barb he had known was coming.

"Not for me, she doesn't."

Aethelred favored him with a shrewd look.

"She dislikes you, doesn't she?"

Wulfhere glared at him. "Is it that obvious?"

"Only to the trained eye," Aethelred replied. "She is a highborn lady and hides it well enough. What did you do to offend her?"

Wulfhere sat back in his chair and raked a hand through his hair.

"The fact that I exist is offensive enough. Everything from having Penda of Mercia as my sire to the fact that I have prevented her from entering a nunnery offends Lady Ermenilda."

Aethelred raised an eyebrow. "And that doesn't worry you?"

Wulfhere shrugged, deliberately playing down how he really felt. He was not about to share his concerns with his brother. Aethelred was competitive enough to use any sign of weakness to his advantage.

"A wife doesn't have to like her husband," he reminded his brother, "and it won't prevent her from bearing my children."

Aethelred gave him a speculative look, clearly wanting to ask more. However, Wulfhere knew that his brother had noted the warning tone in his voice.

Wulfhere decided it was time to change the subject.

"Have you been to see Mōder?" he asked.

Aethelred nodded. "I visited her just after you left for Kent."

"How is she?"

"Well enough," Aethelred replied with a shrug. "Although, I'll never understand how life doesn't bore her death."

Wulfhere had not seen his mother, Cyneswide, since she had taken the veil two years earlier. The queen mother, once as proud a pagan as her husband, had chosen a life of seclusion in response to her eldest son taking the throne. She, like Wulfhere and Aethelred, blamed Paeda for her husband's death. Bonehill was a day's ride away from Tamworth, and Wulfhere knew he was overdue for a visit.

Wulfhere was about to ask his brother another question about their mother when Aethelred interrupted him.

"You said the journey home was 'eventful,'" he said mildly. "How so?"

Wulfhere took a deep draft of mead and exhaled before replying. He had hoped to wait before delivering this news, for thinking upon it soured his mood. It would not be long before Aethelred noticed some of the king's men were missing.

"We were attacked, upon a bridge on East Saxon lands, and lost a number of our men."

"Hwæt?" Aethelred slammed his cup down onto the table, sloshing mead over the brim. "Those bastards!"

"It wasn't the East Saxons," Wulfhere replied, forestalling him. "It appears that my betrothed's mother, Queen Seaxburh, and her sister, Aethelthryth of Ely, have been nursing a grudge against Mercia for a long while. They seek reckoning for the death of their father and brother."

"Annan and Jurmin? But that was nearly five years ago."

"Recent enough for their grief still to be raw," Wulfhere replied. "Long enough for their bitterness to fester."

"Are you going to let them get away with this?"

Wulfhere met his brother's gaze. "Attacking me was an act of war," he reminded him. "Never fear. Those responsible—Seaxburh, Aethelthryth, and that East Angle fool she wedded—will pay for it."

"Just one more street, milady."

Seaxwulf led the way up a narrow lane, to the right of where the inner palisade ended. "My church is close by."

Ermenilda favored him with a wan smile. She did not mind the walk at all; it gave her a moment of reprieve from the Great Hall and the wedding ceremony, which loomed ever closer. Wynflaed followed close at her mistress's heels, her gaze shifting around their surroundings with interest.

"The buildings are much bigger here," the maid observed.

Ermenilda had also noted the same—there were many more timbered dwellings in Tamworth, the homes of the king's wealthier thegns. It reminded her that her father's fyrd—his king's army—was considerably smaller than Mercia's.

Behind the two women and priest, four of the king's guard followed: Werbode, Elfhere, and two other men, whom Ermenilda did not recognize. Wulfhere obviously had no intention of letting his betrothed go about unescorted, especially this close to their handfasting.

Tamworth's church sat at the top of the rise. Although not nearly as striking as Cantwareburh's great church, it was a handsome structure of oak and local gray stone. Ermenilda picked up her skirts and followed the priest inside.

The moment she stepped within the silent, yawning space, her spirits lifted.

Wooden rafters formed the ceiling of the church, and high, narrow windows let in the watery late-afternoon light. Slate tiles covered the floor, and her boots whispered upon them as she followed Seaxwulf across to the altar.

Although Wynflaed and Wulfhere's men had entered, they stopped just inside the entrance, leaving her in peace. Grateful for the moment of silence and relative solitude, Ermenilda knelt on the fur rug.

"I would like to pray for a few moments," she told Seaxwulf. "If I may?"

"Of course, milady," the priest replied, giving a gentle smile. "You never have to ask permission. You are always welcome here."

His kindness made Ermenilda's throat constrict. She returned his smile and turned to the altar. Clasping her hands and closing her eyes, she began to pray.

Lord, please give me the strength to wed this warlord, she began. *I'm sorry but I feel so lost, so alone—please guide me.*

Nothing but silence echoed around her, making her feel even lonelier, even more lost. She squeezed her eyes tightly shut, for she could feel tears welling behind her eyelids.

I do not want to wed this ruthless, pitiless man, she continued, *but every time he looks my way, my pulse quickens.*

My body is weak.

Forgive me for it.

Chapter Fourteen
Man and Wife

Ermenilda sank with a sigh into the iron tub of steaming water. It had been difficult to keep clean during the journey to Tamworth, and no amount of cold washes with a bowl and cloth could compare to a soak in a bath.

She had never bathed in a tub this large before. She could soak right up to her armpits in it. The tub she used at home had been cramped and uncomfortable to sit in, whereas she could have luxuriated in this one all evening—or she could have, had she not felt sick with nerves.

The scent of lavender, from the oil her maid had added to the water, wafted through the space, a tiny bower hidden from the main hall by a heavy tapestry. The perfume went some way to calming her, although the rumble of men's voices behind the arras was a constant reminder of what was to come.

"Come, milady." Wynflaed had opened a pot of lye soap and was smearing some on a wet cloth. "We had better hurry, if you want me to wash your hair as well."

Ermenilda nodded before leaning forward and letting her maid wash her back. She closed her eyes, enjoying the heat of the water as Wynflaed poured it over her head and began to soap her hair.

"I have laid your dress out," Wynflaed told her. "It was the blue one?"

"Aye," Ermenilda murmured. "Thank you."

Once her hair was washed and Wynflaed had wrung it out so that it could start drying, Ermenilda took the cloth and washed the rest of her body. She glanced down at her pale, strawberry-tipped breasts, which bobbed like two small apples in the soapy water. Like her mother, she was slender and somewhat lacking in womanly curves.

What will he think when he sees me naked?

The rush of heat that followed this thought immediately made Ermenilda regret it.

Who cares what he thinks, she told herself, angrily scrubbing at her arms with the rough cloth. She only hoped that Wulfhere was the sort of man who preferred to couple in darkness.

It would make this whole ordeal much easier to bear.

"That's the last lace tied, milady," Wynflaed informed her, before stepping back to admire her handiwork. "You look radiant."

Ermenilda turned to face her handmaid, arranging her features into a calm mask. Inside, her innards were churning. She felt on the verge of tears, and panic was clawing its way up her throat. Yet, Wynflaed thought she looked radiant.

Indeed, the dress was lovely. It was low-cut, pushing Ermenilda's breasts together and, for once, creating a cleavage. The gown's cloth was a pale-blue heavy silk, a fabric that her mother had purchased from merchants who had brought exotic clothes and threads from the East. A gold chain girded her hips, and the dress had long bell sleeves hemmed with gold thread. On her feet, she wore slippers made of the same blue silk as her dress.

"Thank you," she replied, attempting to be gracious. Wynflaed was only trying to be kind.

"I think we should leave your hair unbound," Wynflaed continued. "It's prettier."

"It matters not," Ermenilda assured her with a brittle smile. "I'm sure that I'm presentable enough."

Wynflaed's brow creased at that, and she glanced down at her own dress—a sleeveless green tunic. Around her right bicep, the maid wore a bronze arm ring.

"I hope I am presentable," she muttered. "I feel shabby. I wish I had brought another dress with me."

Ermenilda smiled before shaking her head. Women were so critical of themselves. Wynflaed was even more striking than usual in that tunic, which showed off her enviable curves. Ermenilda was sure Elfhere would seek her out for a dance during the evening.

"You look lovely, Wynflaed," she assured her. "That tunic matches your eyes. You have no need to worry."

"Thank you, milady." Wynflaed flashed her a grateful smile. She picked up a vial of rosewater and unstoppered it. "Just one more touch, and you will be ready for your handfasting."

Ermenilda took a deep, steadying breath and prayed—once more—for the strength to see her through this evening, and the night to follow.

***

The ealdormen's wives had worked miracles in the short space of time Wulfhere had given them. They had spent the afternoon decking out the walls with ivy, sunny-yellow witch hazel flowers, and creamy-white winter honeysuckle.

A venison haunch was roasting over one of the fire pits, laboriously turned by a slave boy, while mutton roasted over the other. Other slaves were bringing in baskets of treats, baked in the ovens outside the hall: breads, pies, and honey seedcakes—the traditional handfasting sweet.

Two musicians, playing a sweet tune upon a lyre and a bone whistle, stood at the back of the high seat. A crowd of excited men and women—ealdormen, thegns, and their wives—almost drowned out the music with their chatter as they clustered around the high seat, where the handfasting was about to take place.

Eventually, both the music and the conversation stopped, and all gazes shifted to the man and woman about to be joined.

Wulfhere and Ermenilda knelt before Seaxwulf. The priest wrapped a ribbon around their clasped hands. He blessed them in the name of god and bid them both to pledge their loyalty to each other.

Ermenilda felt as if her throat was full of sand, but she did her best to speak clearly. Apart from the first glimpse of her betrothed, she had not looked Wulfhere's way since kneeling next to him. That first look had done nothing to still her pitching stomach. Wulfhere was breathtakingly handsome this evening, dressed in black leather breeches and a black quilted vest studded with amber and embroidered with gold. On his naked arms, he wore béagas—arm rings—of gold, silver, and bronze. His hair was loose, its silvery hue contrasting with the darkness of his clothing.

Kneeling next to him, Ermenilda caught the faint scent of lye soap. He had obviously also bathed in preparation for his wedding night.

Once they had completed their vows, Seaxwulf smiled down at the man and woman kneeling before him.

"May you be made one."

The priest gently unwound the ribbon that joined them. Wulfhere and Ermenilda completed the ceremony by sharing a small cup of mead and a bite of seedcake, as tradition dictated.

Wulfhere rose to his feet and, reaching down, pulled Ermenilda to hers. He leaned down and kissed her, and the Great Hall erupted in cheers and applause.

Once the kiss ended, Ermenilda stepped back from Wulfhere, grateful he had been gentle this time. He had barely brushed her lips with his, unlike that day in front of his men when his kiss had been possessive, demanding, and humiliating.

Wulfhere met her gaze. He smiled, his eyes glittering in the torchlight.

"Ermenilda, Queen of Mercia," he murmured, his voice low so that only she could hear. "My patience has been rewarded. Finally, you are mine."

The feasting and reveling went on late into the night.

Wulfhere and Ermenilda sat at the head of the table, upon the high seat, where slaves brought the dishes for them to try first. Wulfhere filled Ermenilda's trencher with the choicest cuts of meat and delicacies. He insisted on feeding her morsels from his own trencher—a sliver of aged cheese and a pickled quail's egg.

It took all Ermenilda's will to swallow the food he offered without complaint, for her stomach had closed. Between bites, she reached for her cup of sloe wine, draining it quickly. She held it up for a passing slave to refill, hoping that the wine would dull her senses.

Wulfhere offered her a piece of bread studded with fruits and nuts. She wordlessly took it, and he responded with a wry smile.

"The only pleasant memory I have of my brother's wedding was the handfasting feast," he admitted. "He spent the evening feeding his bride morsels and attending to her every need. It was the only occasion I saw Paeda pay Alchflaed any attention."

Surprised by his candor, Ermenilda gave Wulfhere her full attention.

"They were not happy together then?"

"Miserable," he replied, "although any woman wedded to Paeda would have been."

His words worried her. She wanted to ask more about his brother but was afraid that she would not like his answers. Instead, she looked down at her full trencher and forced herself to pick up a piece of venison.

Her second cup of wine emptied almost as fast as the first, and she held it out to be refilled. This time, Wulfhere put his hand over the brim, preventing the slave from obeying her.

"Bring my wife milk instead," he told the girl.

Ermenilda glanced over at Wulfhere, affronted, only to find him smiling. He leaned in close to her, so that no one else at the table could hear him. His breath tickled her neck, causing a shiver of heat to pass through her.

"I don't want your senses blunted tonight," he murmured. "I want you to remember every detail."

His words caused a wave of mortification, mixed with dizzying desire, to sweep over Ermenilda. Her breathing quickened, and she gripped the edge of the table to steady herself.

Without saying anything more, Wulfhere pulled away from her and resumed his meal. When Ermenilda had managed to master herself, she glanced at him. Her husband was now talking to his brother. He responded to something Aethelred had just said. Then, he laughed, and the expression transformed his face. The warmth of his laughter embraced her, as if she sat up to her neck in a heated bath.

God forgive her, she did not want to be this man's wife. Everything he stood for offended her. Yet, the sound of his voice and the feel of his gaze upon her skin melted her from the inside out.

And there was nothing she could do about it.

Chapter Fifteen
Another World

Wulfhere and Ermenilda were the first to dance once the feasting ended. The king led his wife out onto the floor, and they faced each other. He released her hand, stepped back, and bowed to her.

Ermenilda curtsied, bowing her head as she had been taught. She then picked up her skirts with her left hand and placed her right on top of his. They circled each other, shoulder to shoulder, their gazes holding.

Around them, Wulfhere's retainers cheered and clapped, caught up in the romance of the moment. Indeed, Ermenilda realized they made a striking couple—both blond and aloof.

It was just a dance, but the intensity of Wulfhere's gaze upon hers drew Ermenilda into another world, causing her to forget about their surroundings. For once, she did not care who watched her or that she was the center of attention. She had not consumed more than two cups of wine earlier in the evening, yet her senses reeled and she felt lightheaded.

Wulfhere never took his gaze from hers, and she drowned in the cool depths of his eyes.

The musicians played a gentle, lilting tune that forced the couple into a slow rhythm. The dance was formal, each movement precise. It was the dance of a lord and lady, with every step measured. The restraint of it only served to draw Ermenilda's attention to the heat that smoldered between her and Wulfhere. Her body's reaction to him both frightened and intrigued her.

When the dance finally ended, Ermenilda was almost sorry. Wulfhere led her back to the high seat, where they sat in silence. The musicians struck up a lively tune, and other couples took to the floor.

As she had predicted, Ermenilda saw Elfhere approach Wynflaed for a dance. Her handmaid sat at one of the long tables that ran on either side of the two fire pits. To Ermenilda's surprise, the young woman did not appear keen to dance.

Her face flushed pink, and she kept shaking her head. However, the handsome, blond warrior did not give up, and eventually Wynflaed allowed herself to be led out onto the floor. Ermenilda watched her maid curiously. Wynflaed was full of contradictions. During the journey here, she had appeared so confident and at ease with herself, yet she had clearly not wanted to dance.

As soon as the song ended, Ermenilda watched Wynflaed make a hurried excuse to Elfhere and hurry back to her place at the table.

The dancing went on for a while, and more mead and wine flowed. Still, Ermenilda and Wulfhere did not speak. She was aware of him seated next to her and the rumble of his voice as he conversed with Aethelred, but she deliberately did not look his way.

Eventually, the churning mixture of anxiety and excitement in the pit of her belly gave way to dread. It was now getting late, and the moment she had tried not to dwell upon approached.

When Wulfhere took her hand and rose to his feet, her mouth went dry.

"The queen and I will retire now," he announced to his retainers.

Cheers and ribald shouts of encouragement from drunken men met Wulfhere's words. Many of his warriors were now well into their cups, and some had drunk so much that they could barely stand.

Wulfhere ignored their shouts. Instead, he led Ermenilda off the high seat, and they crossed the floor together.

"Our quarters are in the 'King's Loft,'" he told her, motioning to the platform above. Ermenilda nodded dumbly, her heart thudding erratically against her ribs.

She climbed the wooden ladder, before Wulfhere, and was distraught to realize that her hands were slippery with sweat. By the time she reached the top of the ladder, she felt sick with nerves. Moments later, Wulfhere appeared, although the cheering and shouting from below continued.

"They'll tire soon enough," Wulfhere told her. "As soon as they open another barrel of mead, we shall be forgotten."

Ermenilda nodded, her gaze shifting around the platform in an effort to avoid looking at him. In her panicked state, she was having trouble taking note of her surroundings, although she could see the loft was warm and comfortable.

She stood upon a thick fur. Plush tapestries covered the damp stone walls around them. There also appeared to be a privy, protected from view by a hanging. Leather trunks lined the far wall, and Ermenilda recognized her own belongings among them.

However, the pile of furs in the center of the platform drew her attention. This was where she and Wulfhere would spend their nights. As if reading her thoughts, her husband stepped close to her.

"Finally . . . ," he murmured. "I thought I was a patient man, but this wait has tested me to my limits."

Ermenilda looked down at her slippered feet and pretended she had not heard him.

"So fair," he said, gently taking hold of her chin and tilting her face upward so that their gazes met, "yet not as cold nor as demure as you feign."

"I—I don't know what you mean," she stuttered, trying to ignore how close he was standing.

He smiled at her weak denial and, reaching out, stroked her face. "You fascinate me, Ermenilda of Kent," he said. "There are hidden depths to you that I look forward to discovering."

He was stroking her hair now, tangling its fine strands in his fingers. "I've wanted to do this since the first day we met," he told her. Ermenilda noticed his voice had roughened slightly, and she realized that she had stopped breathing.

Without another word, he leaned down and kissed her. It was gentle, his lips soft and warm upon hers. He pulled her into his arms and deepened the kiss. Ermenilda's lips parted, an involuntary gasp escaping her as his tongue sought entry. A heartbeat later, he was exploring her mouth, with such exquisite gentleness that her limbs dissolved. Their bodies were pressed against each other. His body felt hard and strong, in contrast to the softness of his kiss.

When Wulfhere ended the kiss, he was breathing hard, and his eyes had turned the color of a stormy sky.

"Turn around," he rasped, "so that I can unfasten your gown."

Ermenilda obeyed, although her limbs were barely able to hold her up. She had started to tremble and tried to stop it, but with no success. Her breathing stilled as she felt her husband undo the ties down the center of her back. While he did so, she was vaguely aware that the music had restarted in the hall below; laughter and drunken singing echoed up into the rafters.

When Wulfhere had finished undoing her gown, he pushed it off her shoulders. Ermenilda exhaled as the silken material slid to her feet, pooling around her ankles. She wore a filmy, sleeveless tunic beneath her gown, although she felt as vulnerable as if she stood before Wulfhere naked.

Wulfhere whispered something she did not quite catch and pushed aside her curtain of hair so that he could kiss the back of her neck. Ermenilda's gasp turned into a muffled groan.

Why does his touch do this to me?

His hands slid around her ribs to cup her breasts, and to her shame Ermenilda felt her nipples harden against his palms.

"Take off your tunic and turn to me," he whispered in her ear.

Her hands were shaking so much it was difficult to obey him. She eventually managed, wriggling out of the sheer tunic. The night air, warm from the fires below, caressed her naked skin. She turned around and stifled a gasp when she saw that Wulfhere was undressing. He did so swiftly—already naked to the waist by the time she swiveled to face him.

His gaze met hers before it slid down the length of her naked body.

"Even more beautiful than I imagined," he murmured.

Ermenilda watched him, transfixed as a moth circling too close to a naked flame. He was strong and broad shouldered, with a flat belly. Wulfhere was unlacing his breeches now, and he stripped them off to reveal a magnificent erection. His shaft lay swollen against his belly, and despite that she willed herself not to, Ermenilda could not take her gaze from it.

Seeing the direction of her gaze, Wulfhere smiled.

"No, certainly not as modest as I first thought."

He stepped toward Ermenilda and without warning scooped her up in his arms, carrying her over to the furs. There, he laid her down, before moving across her so that their bodies were pressed together. Ermenilda felt his shaft pressing into her belly, and excitement arched up within her like a wild thing. The feel of his naked skin on hers, the smell of him, and his overwhelming presence all drowned her senses. A hunger, unlike anything she had ever experienced, rose within her.

Wulfhere began to kiss her again—deep, sensual kisses that made her gasp. She could not stop herself from touching him; her hands wandered along the hard planes of his chest. Her mind screamed at her to stop, but her body was traitorous.

After Wulfhere had kissed her for so long that her head was spinning, her mouth bee-stung, he moved down to her breasts. He suckled each peak until she began to make soft, wordless cries.

"What is it?" he asked, breathless.

"I want . . . ," she gasped.

"What do you want?"

"I . . . I . . ."

Wulfhere gave a soft laugh before gently spreading her legs and stroking her between them.

"This?"

A shudder thrummed through her body, and an ache pulsed between her thighs.

What was he doing to her? She should have been mortified, yet all she could think about was the fact that he was now moving over her and had placed the head of his manhood at the entrance to her womb.

"I will try to be gentle," he murmured, "but this may hurt you."

Ermenilda had heard of the pain and blood that went along with a wedding night. Strangely, although those stories had frightened her in the past, she was not remotely afraid now.

All she wanted was to have him inside her. She felt as if she would die if he did not take her.

She whimpered as he slowly slid into her. She was tight, and had to stretch to accommodate him, but there was no pain—just an incredible fullness.

"Oh . . ."

"Aye," Wulfhere groaned as he seated himself fully inside her. "We were made to go together, you and me."

They stopped there for a moment, and Wulfhere stared down at her, his pupils dilated with pleasure. This time, Ermenilda held his gaze without shyness or embarrassment. The sensation of him inside her was exquisite. She could feel a slow pulse deep within her womb.

Wulfhere began to move inside her. The pleasure of his gentle movements tipped Ermenilda over the edge. She cried out—her fingernails digging into his back—hanging on as if she clung to a cliff's edge. Pleasure came in deep, aching waves that threatened to consume her, and she writhed beneath him.

Wulfhere answered by covering her mouth with his and kissing her deeply, his tongue mimicking the slide of his shaft within her.

The last vestiges of Ermenilda's self-restraint snapped, and she cried out. She arched her hips up against him and wrapped her legs around his hips. Wulfhere gave a strangled curse and began to move in slow, deep thrusts, as he too lost control.

By the time he spilled his seed within her, their cries echoing high in the rafters, both Ermenilda and Wulfhere were lost.

Chapter Sixteen
The Morning Gift

Ermenilda was the first to wake in the early dawn. She stirred among the furs, her body languorous. A sense of well-being, unlike anything she had ever experienced, filled her. For a few blissful moments, she was at peace—nothing existed but the softness and warmth of the furs and the soft breathing of the man beside her.

There's a man sleeping next to me.

Ermenilda's eyes snapped open.

Slowly, wishing she was dreaming, she turned her head to the left. Her gaze settled upon Wulfhere's face.

Asleep, he appeared a different man. The handsome yet austere lines of his face had softened in slumber, and he looked almost . . . vulnerable. Ermenilda inhaled slowly and reminded herself she was watching a sleeping predator. The moment those pale-blue eyes opened, there would not be anything remotely vulnerable about him.

Lord, forgive me.

Ermenilda rolled over onto her back and stared up at the smoke-blackened rafters.

I will be punished for such shamelessness.

To think just a few months ago she had been looking forward to taking her vows. Now, she was a wedded woman, and a bedded one too.

Ermenilda squeezed her eyes shut, mortification flooding through her.

She had planned to remain cold and detached with Wulfhere, to endure his touch and nothing more. Instead, she had gasped, whimpered, and groaned like a whore. She had not just suffered his lovemaking but encouraged every moment of it. Wulfhere had taken her twice more during the night, and she had eagerly accepted him each time.

I am a hypocrite, she railed at herself, and clenched her hands into fists so hard that her fingernails bit into her palms. She took slow, deep breaths, shame bathing her body in a hot tide, and eventually her panic and self-loathing subsided.

When she opened her eyes once more, Wulfhere was beginning to stir. Naked and virile, he stretched against the furs, his white-blond hair falling over his face.

Ermenilda's throat closed at the sight of him. She had never thought she would ever enjoy looking upon a naked man, but Wulfhere was beautiful to gaze upon.

Yawning, Wulfhere pushed his hair out of his eyes and rolled to face her.

"Good morning," he said, favoring her with a slow, sleepy smile. "Did you sleep well?"

Ermenilda nodded, not trusting herself to speak.

"Are you hungry?"

Truthfully, she was. She nodded once more.

"Good." Wulfhere climbed to his feet and strolled over to where his clothing lay discarded a few feet away. "I shall return shortly with something for us to break our fast together," he told her.

Ermenilda watched him dress in breeches and a quilted vest, before he disappeared down the ladder into the hall below. It was still quite early, and a hush hung over the Great Hall of Tamworth. Ermenilda imagined that after the previous evening's revelry, few folk—except for the slaves who worked hard from dawn till dusk—would be awake.

As soon as Wulfhere disappeared, Ermenilda jumped off the furs and pulled on her undertunic. She dug around in one of the leather trunks she had brought and pulled out the plainest, most demure woolen overtunic she could find. By the time Wulfhere reappeared, she had dressed and braided her hair down her back.

"Not one to lie abed, I see," her husband observed, raising an eyebrow. He did not seem to notice Ermenilda's prim posture as she sat rigidly upon the edge of the furs.

Her husband had somehow managed to climb the ladder one-handed, while in the other he balanced a platter of bread, cheese, fruit, and a jug of milk, with two wooden cups. He carried the food over to the furs and sat down next to Ermenilda, placing the platter between them.

Wordlessly, he poured her a cup of milk before helping himself to some bread and cheese. Then he gave her a slow smile.

"A night like that gives a man the hunger of a wolf."

Ermenilda felt her face grow hot, and she looked away. She took a piece of bread, studded with walnuts, and studiously ignored him. However, she knew she could not chastise Wulfhere for his comments, not after her behavior the night before.

They finished their meal in silence, and Ermenilda was brushing crumbs off her dress, wishing there was a deep well she could throw herself down, when Wulfhere spoke once more.

"Since you are dressed, there is somewhere I wish to take you."

Ermenilda glanced up, surprised. For the first time since awaking, she found her voice.

"Really, this early?"

"It is your morning gift," he told her with a secretive smile, "so this would be the best time of day to give it to you."

It was a chill, frosty morning in Tamworth. The sun had barely risen, sending shafts of golden light over the tops of the trees to the east and blinding Ermenilda as she followed Wulfhere across the yard toward the high gate.

Despite her discomfort, Wulfhere's cryptic words intrigued Ermenilda. The morgen-gifu—morning gift. She had forgotten about the tradition of the new husband bestowing a gift upon his wife on the morning after their handfasting. Her father had given her mother a fine palfrey for a morning gift, whereas her aunt, Aethelthryth, had actually received an island from her new husband.

They had almost reached the high gate, with Ermenilda walking a few paces behind Wulfhere, when he turned left and made his way down a lane between the stables and the storehouse. Ermenilda hurried to keep up with his long strides, nearly running into his back when he abruptly stopped.

Ermenilda peered around her husband and saw they were standing at the entrance to a small enclosure. Around twenty yards long and ten wide, the rectangular area was nothing more than a stretch of pitted earth, still frozen hard with frost. A tall brush fence encircled the area.

Confused, Ermenilda turned to Wulfhere.

"Where are we?"

"This area used to house fowl, but I have had them shifted to another spot," Wulfhere replied. "Welcome to your new garden . . . or it will be once you do something with it."

Ermenilda stifled a gasp of surprise.

"How did you know I like gardening?"

A slow smile crept over Wulfhere's face. "Your father told me of your love for the garden behind his hall. He said you would pine for it."

Ermenilda was at a loss for words.

"I know it does not look like much now," Wulfhere continued, "but the soil is good, and if you have the skill your father boasts of, you will soon transform it."

"It is a thoughtful gift," Ermenilda finally murmured, finding her manners. Truthfully, the gift humbled her, although she was still taken aback. "Thank you, milord."

"Ermenilda, look at me," he commanded.

She looked up, her gaze fusing with his.

"My name is Wulfhere," he told her, his tone brooking no argument. "We are now man and wife. Enough with the cold formality."

He reached into the pocket of the quilted vest he wore and withdrew a small object.

"A patch of bare earth is not my only gift." He held out a necklace, a golden nugget of amber encircled by gold, which hung on a gold chain. "This is also for you."

"It is beautiful," she replied, before turning so that he could fasten it about her neck. "Thank you . . . Wulfhere."

Truthfully, despite its beauty, the necklace was a mere bauble compared to the plot of land for her garden. Suddenly, she did not feel so trapped at Tamworth. She had feared she would spend endless days cooped up inside the oppressive stone tower, spinning and weaving. Now, she had a means of escape, a means of self-expression.

She had her husband, the man she had openly reviled on the journey here, to thank for it.

Ermenilda turned back to Wulfhere, her gaze meeting his once more. His expression was shuttered, although his eyes were keen. He may have not wanted to show it, but she sensed her reaction to his gifts mattered to him.

"These are generous gifts," she began timidly, "and I am grateful."

He reached out and gently stroked her cheek. Her skin thrilled at his touch, and her breathing stilled.

"Do you no longer loathe me then?"

"I . . . do not," she managed.

His hand slid to the nape of her neck, where he stroked the sensitive skin there.

"So you could come to tolerate me?"

Ermenilda swallowed and tried to ignore the dizzying lust that melted her limbs like butter set too close to the fire.

"I . . . could."

"I know you wished for another life," he continued, "but I promise that you will want for nothing here. Gold, jewels, and finery—whatever you wish for, you will have."

Ermenilda did not reply. His words had brought her swiftly to her senses. Desire drained from her, leaving her feeling slightly sick. Wulfhere had unwittingly ruined what had been a tender moment between them.

Gold, jewels, and finery. So, you think you can buy my affection?

Ermenilda stepped back from him, forcing Wulfhere to withdraw his hand.

"I have no need of riches," she told him firmly. "The life you took from me was one of solitude, peace, and worship. Those things cannot be bought."

She thought her response would anger him, but Wulfhere merely watched her, his gaze narrowing slightly.

"One thing my father taught me," he told her quietly, "is that everyone has their price. From the highest to the lowest, we will all bargain. It's just a matter of finding what yours is."

PART TWO

Two months later . . .

Chapter Seventeen
Gardening

Wynflaed straightened up, brushing aside a lock of auburn hair that had come free of its braid. "It's starting to rain, milady. We should go inside."

Ermenilda sighed and glanced up at the threatening sky. Drops of cool rain splashed onto her upturned face, and thunder rumbled in the distance. Her afternoon's work was about to be cut short. She had lingered in church after the noon meal, and now the weather was turning. It was proving to be a wet spring. At this rate, they would never prepare the beds for planting.

Brushing dirt off her hands, Ermenilda climbed to her feet and looked about her. She stood at the heart of the garden, enveloped by the scent of damp earth. Her surroundings bore no resemblance to the bare plot Wulfhere had gifted her two months earlier. It was still far from the garden she had left behind in Cantwareburh, but now she could visualize how it would eventually look.

Even so, she wished her mother and sister could have seen how much work she and Wynflaed had put into this garden. At the thought of Seaxburh and Eorcengota, a blade of homesickness twisted under her ribs. There were days she missed them so much that it felt as if her soul ached.

Blinking back tears, Ermenilda surveyed the area. They had laid down gravel paths—one down the center with smaller paths running out to the perimeter—and planted roses around the edges. The bushes were bare and scrawny now, but as soon as the weather warmed, they would flourish with deep-red blooms.

In the largest bed, she and Wynflaed had sown early-spring greens, and the seedlings were just beginning to poke through the dark earth. If all of Ermenilda's planting went to plan, kale, cabbages, onions, turnips, and carrots would fill the other beds by midsummer.

Ermenilda picked up her wicker basket of wooden gardening implements. Wordlessly, she led the way toward the gate, her boots crunching on the gravel underfoot. Just before leaving her garden, she glanced back at it, as was her habit every afternoon once she had finished work. Despite the melancholy that always settled upon her when she thought of her family, the sight of the work she and Wynflaed had done never failed to fill her with a sense of achievement.

The rain started to fall heavily, turning the earth muddy beneath the women's feet as they hurried back to the Great Tower. By the time Ermenilda reached the oaken doors, the deluge had soaked her woolen cloak through. Likewise, Wynflaed was completely drenched, her hair plastered against her scalp.

They stepped through the doorway, into a passage that led up to the main hall, with store rooms off to the right and left. They were peeling off their wet cloaks when Ermenilda saw Elfhere emerge from the hall and make his way toward the main doors.

"Good afternoon, Lady Ermenilda . . . Wynflaed." He greeted them both with a smile, although—as always—his gaze lingered upon Wynflaed.

"It is not so good," Ermenilda replied with a grimace, shaking water out of her hair. "I would not venture outdoors, if I were you."

Elfhere nodded, his gaze remaining upon Wynflaed.

"I have not spoken to you in a while, Wynflaed," he said, his smile fading. "Is all well?"

The maid nodded, favoring him with a polite smile in return. "Aye, all is well—thank you. We have been busy preparing the garden."

She turned away from him, signaling their conversation was over.

Ermenilda watched Elfhere step back, his expression shuttered. He nodded to Ermenilda and moved past them, disappearing outside into the rain.

Ermenilda watched him go, frowning, before turning to Wynflaed.

"Has that man done something to offend you?"

Her maid turned to her, surprised.

"No, milady. Why do you ask?"

Ermenilda shrugged. "You rebuff him every time he tries to speak to you. I thought you were friends with Elfhere?"

Wynflaed's cheeks reddened slightly, revealing that Ermenilda had indeed hit a nerve.

"We are not friends," she replied quietly. "Before I left Cantwareburh, your father made it clear that I was not to encourage any men in Tamworth. He told me that I was to dedicate myself entirely to serving you, and that should I form an attachment with a man, I would be dismissed."

Ermenilda's eyes widened. This was the first she had heard of it.

"My father never said anything of this to me," she replied. Oddly, had they had this conversation two months earlier, she would have been inclined to agree with her father. Her family had strong views when it came to the behavior and chastity of female servants. Her mother in particular would not tolerate "immoral" behavior from them. However, the past two months had changed Ermenilda's view of the world and blurred the lines between what was and was not acceptable.

Her union with Wulfhere challenged everything she had been brought up to believe and had made it difficult for her to maintain the rigid views her parents had instilled in her from birth.

"I understand my father's concern," Ermenilda told her maid as they made their way across the entrance hall, "but I do not want you to be miserable on my account. If you wish to talk to Elfhere, to form a friendship with him, I will not punish you for it."

Wynflaed smiled at that, her usual sunny countenance reappearing.

"I'm certainly not miserable, milady," she assured her. "And Elfhere won't die of a broken heart. There are plenty of other maids for him to flirt with here in Tamworth. I am happy in my service to you."

Ermenilda shook her head, smiling at her maid's ever-practical approach to life.

They entered the hall, which was busy this afternoon, as everyone had escaped indoors to avoid the rain. Ermenilda could hear the hiss of the rain lashing against the tower. She spied two leaks coming in from the roof, under which slaves had placed wooden pails to collect the water. The air smelled of smoke, wet wool, and dogs.

Upon the high seat, next to his brother and Werbode, Ermenilda saw her husband.

As always, the sight of Wulfhere made her feel as if there was not enough air inside the hall. Even after two months, she felt a dizzying excitement whenever he was near.

Wulfhere saw Ermenilda and waved her over.

She went to him, forcing her expression to remain neutral, even though her stomach fluttered with anticipation. From the beginning, she had fought her reaction to him, for she had been determined to hate Wulfhere of Mercia. After their explosive wedding night, she had tried to keep him at arm's length, but once the first day of their union had passed, she realized it was impossible. Wulfhere had cast a spell upon her, one that grew stronger with the passing of time.

"You are wet through, wife." Wulfhere greeted her with a smile. "Don't tell me you were gardening in the rain?"

Ermenilda shook her head and took a seat next to him. "The storm caught us by surprise," she admitted, taking the cup of warmed mead he passed her.

"How is your garden coming along, Lady Ermenilda?" Aethelred spoke. His voice was polite enough, although she could see the faint mockery in his eyes. Next to him, Werbode was smirking. She knew they all thought Wulfhere indulged her, that gardening was the work of the cottars who tilled the fields outside Tamworth—not the task of a highborn lady.

"Very well, thank you, Aethelred," she replied, glancing down at her hands. To her dismay, she saw they were filthy, with dirt encrusted under the nails. Embarrassed, she put down her cup of mead and hid her hands discreetly under the rim of the table. "The beds are almost ready for the summer vegetables, and the first of the spring greens are coming up."

"Will it soon rival your garden in Cantwareburh?" Werbode asked, still sneering. As usual, his gaze upon her was disturbingly intense, and Ermenilda wondered if Wulfhere ever noticed the way his thegn looked at her. Nonetheless, his mockery vexed her.

"I did not know that gardening interested you, Werbode," she replied, her tone sharpening. "You are more than welcome to join Wynflaed and me in our afternoon work. I'm sure I can find plenty of tasks worthy of you."

Laughter erupted at the table. Aethelred let out a loud guffaw, and even Wulfhere grinned. Werbode pursed his lips as their mirth bubbled around him, his eyes narrowing to angry slits.

Ermenilda held the thegn's gaze unflinchingly. She was tired of his lecherous, derisive looks. She would likely pay for that comment, but it was worth it to put Werbode in his place this once.

Chapter Eighteen
A Shadow Falls

Wulfhere watched his wife dress.

Her slender body glowed palely in the light from the flickering cressets and the faint dawn that filtered in from a narrow window high above. Not looking his way, even though she knew he watched her, Ermenilda retrieved a long, sleeveless tunic and pulled it on over her head. The movement thrust out her chest and gave him an unobstructed view of her milky, pert breasts, before the linen rippled down over her lithe form.

It was their morning ritual, one that he would never tire of. Once they awoke, she would rise first while he waited in the furs. Initially, his keen observance of her embarrassed Ermenilda—but these days she pretended not to notice.

On top of her undertunic, she pulled on a form-fitting woolen overdress, which she girded around her narrow waist with a leather belt. She braided her long blonde hair and pinned it in a bun at the nape of her neck. Since their handfasting, she no longer wore her hair loose, as only unwed maids did so. It made the sight of her flowing hair even more attractive to Wulfhere, for he was the only one who now saw it.

Ermenilda turned to him, which was a deviation from her morning routine. Usually, she would leave the platform after dressing without uttering a word. Their gazes met, and Wulfhere saw that her dark-brown eyes were serious.

"It is Ēostre," she began quietly. "Will you come with me to church this morning?"

Wulfhere hesitated. He was tempted to refuse her, for he had no interest in wasting his morning in church, listening to Seaxwulf drone on about the resurrection of Christ. But, the look upon her face was so earnest that he checked himself. In truth, Christianity and its dull god bored him witless. He had only agreed to be baptized in order to win Ermenilda's hand, and since then it had been difficult not to reveal his underlying contempt for her religion.

He was in a good mood this morning, relaxed after a particularly passionate night in the furs with his wife. Although Ermenilda never took the initiative with him, there was nothing passive about her responses. The depth of her hunger for him often surprised Wulfhere, as it had last night.

Eventually, she would learn that his faith was in name only, but it would not be today.

"Aye," he answered his wife with a lazy smile. "I will."

Despite that winter now lay behind them, the air still held a distinct bite this morning. Ermenilda was glad of the fur cloak about her shoulders as she descended the steps before the Great Tower and followed her husband across the stable yard. An entourage followed them—Aethelred and a group of the king's most favored retainers, Werbode and Elfhere among them.

Ermenilda glanced up at the high clouds streaking across the sky. It was a typical spring day, reminding her that Cantwareburh, farther south than Tamworth, would have fully embraced the new season by now. A riot of spring flowers would cover the meadows outside the town.

The thought made her long for her mother and sister. She wondered how Eorcengota was faring on her own. Had their father found a husband for her, or would he give her to the church? Perhaps Ermenilda could visit them next year, once she and Wulfhere had settled properly into life together.

Next to her, Wulfhere glanced toward Ermenilda and smiled. This morning, he wore a black leather tunic and doeskin breeches, which contrasted against the ermine cloak rippling from his shoulders. As always, his smile made heat radiate out from the pit of Ermenilda's belly.

Images from the night before returned to her, and heat rose up her neck. Wulfhere had pulled her astride him on his lap and guided her so that she slid down the hard length of his shaft. Then, he had showed her how to ride him, while he stroked her body.

Breathing hard, Ermenilda looked away.

Stop it, she chastised herself. *That's the last thing you should be thinking about this morning.*

Ignorant of her heated thoughts, Wulfhere reached out and drew her arm through his, so that that they walked together through the high gate into the town beyond. It was a tender gesture, and Ermenilda did not resist him.

They had not walked far when Ermenilda spied the remains of a bonfire. The embers were still smoking. Frowning, she glanced up at her husband, but Wulfhere was looking straight-ahead.

Lighting bonfires at Ēostre was a pagan ritual. Wulfhere had promised her father that all the old traditions would cease at Tamworth, but evidently, that had not happened.

They rounded the corner, taking the street that led up to the church, and passed a group of girls clad in flowing white. Resembling a flock of white doves, the young women ran past, barefoot despite the chill morning. Some of the men behind the king and queen called out to the maids, asking for their blessing. Light, feminine laughter echoed across the street behind them as the girls answered.

Ermenilda clenched her jaw. The girls had dressed to resemble the pagan goddess of spring and rebirth, Ēostre herself. Once again, Ermenilda glanced toward her husband, but Wulfhere ignored her.

He knows that he has ignored his promise, she thought angrily, *but he does not care.*

Wulfhere listened to Seaxwulf's hypnotic voice and stifled a yawn.

When is that priest going to finish?

It was cold inside the church, for the space had a stone floor and a lofty ceiling, and Wulfhere was glad he had not removed his cloak. Seaxwulf's voice reverberated, and he lifted his arms high. It was the only movement in the stillness, save the guttering tallow candles on the altar behind the priest.

Wulfhere shifted his weight from his right foot to his left and glanced at his wife. He had sensed Ermenilda's disapproval upon seeing the bonfire and the white-clad maids on the way up here but had deliberately chosen to ignore it. Surely, the fact he had agreed to come here and endure Seaxwulf's unending preaching would be enough. If the folk of Tamworth still chose to worship Ēostre according to the old traditions, he did not see the harm of it.

Ermenilda did not notice him glance her way, for she was watching Seaxwulf, her gaze luminous.

A blade of jealousy knifed Wulfhere through the chest.

She never looks at me like that.

It was not entirely true. She did when they were in the furs together—but that was a physical rather than emotional response. If Seaxwulf had been a virile young man rather than a scrawny monk of middling years, Wulfhere would have suspected his wife of being in love with him. Such was the look of rapture on her face.

As it was, Wulfhere still did not like it, for it was a stinging reminder that while he may have possessed his wife physically, he did not hold her heart. She was still aloof with him, an enigma that he could not solve.

Finally, Seaxwulf's interminable droning ended. Wulfhere let out a long sigh in relief and turned to usher Ermenilda toward the door.

"Wait," she breathed, her gaze still gleaming. "I wish to speak to Brother Seaxwulf a moment."

Without even asking her husband's permission, she stepped around him and crossed to the altar. Stifling irritation, Wulfhere followed her.

"I just wanted to thank you, Seaxwulf." Ermenilda took the priest's hand and squeezed it gently. "That was a wonderful sermon."

Seaxwulf beamed at her before his gaze shifted to where Wulfhere had stopped a couple of paces behind her.

"I am glad you enjoyed it, milady," he replied. "We all need reminding of the sacrifice Jesus Christ made for us and the miracle of his resurrection."

Wulfhere ground his teeth. There was no mistaking that the priest's words were meant for him.

"My Lord Wulfhere." Seaxwulf addressed him direct now. "I am glad to see you here. You have set a good example for your retainers."

Wulfhere nodded, barely masking his irritation.

"It has come to my attention that many in Tamworth have reverted to their old traditions this Éostre," the priest continued, his voice rising. "They have put up shrines to the heathen goddess throughout the town and have placed offerings of food for her."

Wulfhere shrugged, feigning indifference, although his ire was rising at the priest's meddling.

"There will be many in Britannia who still worship the old gods," he replied. "You cannot change centuries of tradition overnight, priest."

Seaxwulf drew himself up, although he was not a physically imposing man and was nearly half a foot shorter than his king.

"They must be punished," the priest insisted, the slight tremor in his voice betraying his nervousness. "It is the only way folk learn. Bread and water only for forty days, for those who have transgressed."

Wulfhere heard sniggering behind him and realized that some of his men had gathered to hear what Seaxwulf had to say. Wulfhere folded his arms across his chest.

"And how do you suggest I enforce such a punishment?"

"Have your men scour Tamworth. Find all those who still worship the heathen goddess and punish them."

"And if folk still transgress?"

Seaxwulf's mouth thinned. He was a gentleman and clearly did not like to speak of such things, but he had gone too far down this road to turn back now.

"Another forty days of bread and water."

Wulfhere laughed. A moment later, his men joined him, their mirth booming through the church.

"You would make the folk of Tamworth cheap to feed."

"But you cannot let this go unpunished," Seaxwulf insisted. He had now gone red in the face. "They must learn that—"

"Enough." Wulfhere raised a hand, making it clear that Seaxwulf would continue at his own peril. "There will be no punishment. If you want the folk of Tamworth to worship at your altar, you will have to find other ways of convincing them."

They were outside, making their way back down the incline away from the church, when Ermenilda finally dredged up the courage to speak to her husband.

"You were very rude to Seaxwulf," she said quietly. "He did not deserve it."

Wulfhere gave her a quick look, an eyebrow rising. "He overstepped the mark."

"But he was right," Ermenilda persevered. Outrage had emboldened her. "How will people change their ways if their king does nothing?"

Wulfhere frowned, his face hardening, and Ermenilda realized that she too had overstepped the mark. Like the priest, she had gone too far to turn back now.

"You made a promise to my father. Does that mean nothing to you?"

A chill silence hung between them for a few moments before Wulfhere finally replied.

"I did what I needed to, in order to get what I wanted."

Finally, he admits it.

Wulfhere had just confirmed the suspicions that she'd had about him, right from the beginning—only it brought Ermenilda little pleasure in being proved right.

"So you lied," she choked out the words. "You still worship the old gods."

Wulfhere stopped in his tracks and swung round to face her. His gaze had narrowed. Ermenilda tried to step back from him, but he reached out and placed his hands on her shoulders, pinning her to the spot.

"I did what was necessary. I was baptized. A priest sanctified our marriage. That is enough."

"No," Ermenilda whispered, horrified at his ignorance. "None of that means anything if you do not believe—"

"Lord Wulfhere!"

A young female voice interrupted them.

Ermenilda tore her gaze away from her husband's angry face to see a young woman standing before them. She was small and pretty with a mane of golden hair, and she was staring at Wulfhere with adoration.

White-hot jealousy lanced through Ermenilda.

Who is this girl? A lover?

The strength of her reaction unbalanced her. One moment she loathed the man in front of her, the next she was enraged by the thought of him touching another woman.

"Do I know you?" Wulfhere growled, irritated at the interruption.

"My name is Asha," the girl replied, favoring him with a timid smile. "I do not expect you to remember me."

"Asha . . ." Wulfhere gave her a hard look, his anger fading. "I do recall you . . . from over a year ago."

The young woman nodded. "I have not forgotten your kindness, m'lord."

Perhaps seeing Ermenilda's perplexed look, the girl smiled at her.

"I was a slave in the king's hall," she explained. "When Lord Wulfhere reclaimed the Great Tower of Tamworth, he slew my captor and gave me my freedom."

Ermenilda watched the girl's eyes fill with tears and felt a sting of remorse for her earlier jealousy. Her anger toward her husband ebbed slightly. Perhaps, despite everything, there was good in him. This young woman obviously thought so.

"You saved my life," Asha told Wulfhere earnestly. "I'm eternally grateful."

Chapter Nineteen
Reckoning

The conversation started like many others.

Upon the high seat, Wulfhere and his brother bantered, as usual, teasing each other about their hunting trip. Spring was slowly easing into summer, and they had returned to Tamworth with many boar and deer carcasses slung over the backs of their horses. Aethelred had just recounted how he single-handedly brought down the biggest stag in the forest.

Ermenilda, who sat silently at Wulfhere's side, noted that the prince's story appeared to be highly entertaining the warriors seated around him.

"Those antlers shall grace this hall," Aethelred boasted, before grinning across at his brother, "as a constant reminder of who is the best hunter among us."

Wulfhere snorted into his cup of mead.

"Just like Paeda, you suffer from an overinflated sense of your own worth, little brother."

This comment drew a roar of laughter from around the table.

Ermenilda, who was observing them all, noted that one of them did not join in the mirth and good cheer. Werbode sat among them, scowling into his cup.

"Enough of hunting and boasting." The thegn spoke up once the laughter had died down. "We have waited long enough. When will we have our reckoning?"

The warrior's comment brought forth a hum of excited whispering and murmurs around the hall. Ermenilda frowned, her gaze shifting to where Wulfhere sat beside her. She appeared to be the only one present who did not know of what Werbode spoke.

"What reckoning?" she whispered to Wulfhere.

Her husband either did not hear her or pretended not to. His cool gaze had settled upon Werbode, and his face wore a pensive expression.

"I have not forgotten," he answered, finally, when the chatter around them had ceased. "There are some things a man never forgets."

Werbode leaned forward, his dark eyes gleaming. Unlike many of the warriors who grew their beards long, the thegn trimmed his close to his chin, with a pointed end.

"When then?"

"We are on the eve of Thrimilce," said the king. "If we begin our preparations now, we will be ready to leave midmonth."

"It is a good month for travel." Aethelred spoke up, his gaze shining. "The East Angle marshes will be easy to cross this time of year."

Ermenilda went still, while the conversation continued around her.

"How many spears will we need?" Werbode asked. "I will begin gathering your fyrd tomorrow."

"At least two hundred," Wulfhere replied. "Speak with Immin, Eafa, and Eadbert and request they and their men join us."

Werbode nodded, his mouth thinning. "They will," he assured Wulfhere. "There is not one warrior in your hall who would deny you. We all thirst for vengeance for the death of our brothers on that bridge."

Panicked, Ermenilda turned to Wulfhere.

"No! You cannot attack my kin!"

Wulfhere looked at her, his gaze hooded.

"Excuse me?"

"You're planning an attack on my aunt in Ely, aren't you?"

"War is not a woman's business." Wulfhere's voice held a warning. "You should keep out of this, wife."

Ermenilda stared at him, anger rising in her breast.

"If you speak of attacking my uncle and aunt, then it is my business," she replied. Although she kept her voice low, it was difficult not to spit the words out at him.

"Tondberct of Ely will rue the day he did his wife's bidding and sent men to kill us," Aethelred interrupted. His face was hard as he glared at Ermenilda. "You are fortunate indeed that my brother does not blame you—as he does your aunt and mother."

"Aethelthryth of Ely tried to kill me," Wulfhere continued, casting a quelling look in his brother's direction. "I cannot let that go unpunished."

"The men who attacked you are all dead," Ermenilda countered. "Surely, that is punishment enough?"

She was suddenly aware that most of the men at the table were now staring at her with hard, accusing eyes. She knew she should hold her tongue, for she was sailing into dangerous waters. Yet, the cruelty of what Wulfhere was planning had caused her to cast aside her usual reticence.

"It's not enough," Wulfhere replied. His voice was deceptively soft, a tone that Ermenilda knew meant his anger was quickening. "And you would do well not to pursue this further, wife."

Ermenilda heeded his warning and looked down at her half-eaten trencher of pottage. Outrage pulsed within her. She bit down on her tongue to prevent herself from screaming accusations at him.

You cannot be surprised, a cruel voice within mocked her. *You knew who you were wedding. You have let lust cloud your judgment. Wulfhere of Mercia is a merciless and cruel warlord, just like the men before him.*

"Milord." Ermenilda broke the weighty silence that had descended over the high table. "May I be excused? I wish to go to church."

Wulfhere nodded curtly. He glanced up the table to where Elfhere sat. "Elfhere—take three men and escort my wife."

"Aye, milord."

Ermenilda rose from the table and, not casting a glance at any of the men seated around her, stepped down from the high seat. Then, stiff-backed with fury, she walked out of the Great Hall, with Elfhere following close behind.

Wulfhere watched Ermenilda leave the hall before turning his attention to Werbode.

"You would have done better not to have brought that up in the queen's presence."

Werbode's mouth twisted, and Wulfhere saw something move in the depths of his eyes. The thegn looked as if he wished to say something but wisely decided against it. Instead, he raised his cup to his lips and took a deep draft of mead. However, Aethelred, less prudent than Werbode, spoke his mind.

"She would have found out soon enough, Brother. What's wrong? Are you afraid of your wife's wrath?"

This comment brought a few choked laughs and smirks from those present, although the mirth rapidly faded when Wulfhere drew his seax.

Aethelred had been resting his left elbow on the table, his right hand spread upon the pitted oak surface. Quick as a barn owl diving for its prey, Wulfhere launched himself at his brother, sinking the blade deep into the wood between the prince's splayed fingers.

Aethelred cursed and yanked his hand back, catching the edge of the blade with his forefinger. He cursed again as blood trickled down his hand.

"Mad bastard!" he roared. "You nearly cut my hand off!"

Wulfhere yanked his seax out of the table and slid it back into its scabbard at his waist.

"Insult me again and you'll lose more than a hand."

Wulfhere's gentle tone belied the anger that was coiling in the pit of his belly. The prince had gone red in the face, and his pale eyes glittered with anger, but he held his tongue. Likewise, the other men at the table refrained from voicing their thoughts.

Truthfully, Wulfhere was as angry with himself as with his mouthy brother. Most of the time, his wife epitomized the ideal highborn lady: demure, polite, and soft-spoken. However, he had seen flashes of a different woman—a strident, opinionated harpy, who would not hold her tongue if angered.

Wulfhere sat back down upon his carved chair and poured himself another cup of mead from the clay jug before him.

Fæder never had this problem with Mōder, he thought darkly.

All the years they were together, Wulfhere had never once seen Cyneswide openly contradict Penda. Perhaps when they were alone she had done so, but never in front of others. Wulfhere knew that his father would never have tolerated it. He thought of his elder brother, Paeda, and the brutal way he had responded to his Northumbrian wife when she dared challenge him. Wulfhere could not bring himself to treat his own wife in that manner, even if he could see that many of his men thought less of him for not doing so.

I don't want Ermenilda to fear me.

Yet, he could not let her question him again in front of his men like she had today. Something would have to be done.

Ermenilda strode across the yard in front of the Great Tower of Tamworth, her vision blurring with tears.

It was a windy evening, and the sun was setting in a blaze of gold behind the racing clouds to the west. The wind tugged at her hair, pulling tendrils of it free from her braid. It was cool outdoors, and she had no cloak. Such was the force of Ermenilda's anger that she did not care.

Ignoring the curious glances from the guards at the high gate, and Elfhere who silently followed her, she strode through it and turned left. The streets of Tamworth were largely deserted at this hour, and she saw few folk as she strode up to the church. On the way there, she feverishly went over what she had just heard inside the Great Hall.

Aethelthryth and Tondberct were in danger—she had to warn them.

Seaxwulf was the only one in Tamworth with the power to help her.

Reaching the church, Ermenilda left Elfhere outside. She ran up the steps and burst inside through the heavy oaken doors. Seaxwulf was there, as she had expected. He was sweeping the paved floor with a broom. Ermenilda entered the church so quickly that he looked up in alarm, the tallow candles guttering around him.

"Lady Ermenilda! What is it?"

His concern caused something inside Ermenilda to snap, and she choked back a sob.

"My husband is a monster," she gasped. "I married a foul warmonger who plans to attack my kin!"

Seaxwulf's eyes widened at this news, and he cast his broom aside, taking a few hesitant steps toward her.

"Please, milady. Tell me what happened . . . and start from the beginning, for your words make no sense to me."

Ermenilda took in a deep, shuddering breath to prevent another sob and brushed at the tears streaming down her face. She managed to tell him the tale, as best she could, gasping the words while she struggled to contain her tears. When she had finished, the priest's face was solemn. Ermenilda did not like the look of resignation in his dark eyes.

"I am sorry to hear this," he admitted quietly, before he looked down at the stone pavers beneath his sandaled feet. "I had suspected that the king would not let that attack go unpunished."

"They are my family," Ermenilda replied, her voice rising. "We must warn them. I am not able to write, but you can. Please write a note for my aunt and see that it is delivered to her. She must learn of this before my husband marches upon Ely."

Seaxwulf's head snapped up.

"Lady Ermenilda," he gasped. "What you ask of me is treason."

"What I ask of you will save lives," she countered.

Seaxwulf shook his head, his expression turning stubborn.

"I do not wish to see your kin in Ely harmed, but I cannot do what you ask."

Panic surged within Ermenilda. The priest was her only hope of getting word to Aethelthryth. She had been so sure he would help her.

"I thought you were a good man, a Christian man," she said bitterly, "but now I see you are like all the rest. Interested only in saving your own hide."

The priest held up his hand, as if to ward off her venom.

"Lady Ermenilda," he replied sternly, not remotely cowed by her accusation. "What you ask would cost me my own life. Is that what you want?"

Ermenilda had not considered that.

"Wulfhere would never know," she replied weakly.

Seaxwulf shook his head. "He would learn of it eventually, and he would cut off my head. You must not get in the way between a king and his reckoning, milady."

Chapter Twenty
A Stormy Farewell

Dread dogged Ermenilda's steps during her walk back from visiting Seaxwulf. It was nearly dark outside when she slipped into the Great Tower. Inside, slaves were tidying and cleaning up after the evening meal, and a group of women—thegns' wives—were working at their distaffs as they chatted around one of the fire pits.

Ermenilda crossed the rush-strewn floor, making straight for the wooden ladder on the far side of the hall. Wulfhere and his men were drinking and talking upon the high seat, and she felt some of their gazes shift to her. However, she ignored them all.

She climbed up to the King's Loft, exhaling in relief when she was finally away from the gazes of the hall below. This platform, in the times when she retired for the night before Wulfhere, was her sanctuary. Slaves had been up here already and lit the oil-filled clay cressets lining the walls. They had placed a jug of watered-down wine for the king and queen upon a low table near the furs.

Ermenilda poured herself a tall cup, wishing that the wine was not diluted. She dreaded the moment when Wulfhere would join her this eve. It was not just his anger she feared but her own. After learning of the reckoning he and his men planned, she could not bear to look upon him.

The wine, weak though it was, calmed her jangled nerves, and she took a seat on the edge of the furs. She did not feel like sleeping yet, for she was too nervous, so she reached for her distaff instead and began winding wool onto the wooden spindle. Owing to the amount of time she passed in her garden, she had been lax in this chore of late. She had a mountain of wool to wind.

The repetitive action calmed her somewhat, and she listened to the rumble of voices from below the platform as she worked. Still, when Wulfhere finally appeared at the top of the ladder, it took all her effort not to gasp in fright.

As she had expected, his face was thunderous.

"Not waiting for me naked this eve?" he queried.

Ermenilda looked away from him, staring down at her distaff, and shook her head.

She heard the rustle of his clothing as he began to undress. A lump lodged in her throat. The last thing she wanted was for him to touch her.

"Put your distaff aside," he commanded quietly, "and look at me, Ermenilda."

She clenched her jaw, bristling at the order, before she obeyed him. Wulfhere had just stripped off his tunic and was unlacing his breeches. Usually, his gaze was heated when he did this, dark with longing. This eve, his face was as hard as she had ever seen it, and his gaze was glacial.

"You angered me today," he told her. "You know that, don't you?"

Ermenilda swallowed her rising ire and forced herself not to glower at him.

"Aye," she replied softly.

Wulfhere crouched before her so their gazes were level.

"There are husbands who would beat a wife for publically contradicting him."

Ermenilda's breathing hitched, fear shimmering through her.

"Fortunately for you, I am not one of them," Wulfhere continued.

Their gazes held.

"Ermenilda, if you wish to argue with me, wait until we are alone."

"You are planning an attack on my kin," she replied, her voice husky with the effort she was making not to show her fear. He had not yet laid a hand on her during the marriage, but she did not like the implied threat in his words. "I had to say something."

"No you didn't," he countered, his voice hardening. "You could have waited till we were alone. In future, you will."

She stared at him, her vision blurring with tears. It was like talking to a boulder, as inflexible and hard as granite. Here she was, upset because he and his army were about to march on her East Angle kin, and all he cared about was the fact she had embarrassed him in front of his men.

"Is there not a shred of mercy in you?" she asked. "Does the fact that I abhor what you are about to do not matter?"

He stared at her a moment, before his gaze narrowed.

"You don't understand what it means to rule. Reckoning is like fate—it cannot be avoided."

"In the old world, it was so," she replied, vehement, "but not now. The old gods demanded reckoning, and fate treated us like pawns—but no more. The one true god does not demand you spill blood on his behalf. It is he, not wyrd, who determines your future."

Wulfhere's lip curled at that. He rose to his feet and stripped off his breeches, his movements angry.

"Everything comes back to your religion, doesn't it?" he snarled. "Every argument, every plea. Do you actually hold an opinion that wasn't fed to you by a priest?"

Ermenilda gasped and leaped to her feet, facing him.

"You can't be surprised," she choked out, anger almost rendering her speechless. "I never wanted to wed you. I wanted a life as a nun, and you took it from me. If you wedded a woman with a strong faith, you have only yourself to blame."

"Careful, Ermenilda." Wulfhere stalked over to her, even more intimidating than usual in his nakedness. "There are times when you have a forked tongue."

He was standing close, too close. Ermenilda breathed in the spicy male scent of him and felt her senses reel. Even when she was angry with him, this man affected her.

"I wouldn't," she managed, trembling as he reached out and stroked her cheek. The gentleness of his touch was at odds with the anger in his voice. "If you did not offend me so deeply."

"Those are harsh words," he replied, before leaning down and kissing her neck. The feel of his lips on her skin made Ermenilda's limbs go weak. Without meaning to, she leaned toward him, stifling a groan as his arms went around her.

"They are my only weapons," she murmured, trying in vain to keep track of her thoughts. "You are a harsh man . . ."

Wulfhere gave a soft laugh and unpinned her hair, letting it tumble down her back.

"I thought women liked cruel men?"

"I don't . . . I . . ."

Wulfhere claimed her mouth, kissing away her protests, her anger. He undressed Ermenilda with practiced ease before stripping away her clothing so that he could run his hands over her naked body. She gasped, trembling under his touch.

He scooped her into his arms and stepped over to the furs. By the time he laid her down upon them, Ermenilda could think of nothing else but Wulfhere.

He was her world, her past, her future—her penance.

***

The days leading up to Wulfhere's departure flew past with frightening swiftness.

Ermenilda grew increasingly anxious. Even the afternoons spent in her garden, working alongside Wynflaed, could not calm her. Tamworth was a hive of activity. Men flooded in from nearby villages, warriors willing to wield a spear, axe, or sword for their lord. The clang of iron, as smiths forged weaponry, shattered the peace of each dawn and twilight.

Ermenilda increasingly saw less of Wulfhere as the day he and his fyrd would march drew near. He spent his days overseeing preparations or practicing with his sword and seax alongside his men.

Although she was grateful not to see him, her husband's absence did little to settle Ermenilda's nerves. She retired in the evenings, long before he did, and would often pretend to be asleep when he crawled into the furs next to her. After their argument on the day Ermenilda had learned of his plans, they did not speak of it again.

Their differences still lay heavy between them, unspoken. Tension filled Ermenilda whenever she sat down next to her husband upon the high seat. In the past, Wulfhere had attempted to converse with her at mealtimes. Now he let her eat in silence while he discussed tactics with his men.

On the morning of Wulfhere's departure, Ermenilda was withdrawn as Wynflaed helped her dress. They stood in the small alcove that housed the iron bathtub. Seeing one's husband off on a military campaign was a great occasion, and folk expected to see the queen in all her finery.

Wynflaed laced Ermenilda up in a dove-gray gown with bell sleeves and fastened the delicate amber necklace the king had gifted his wife around her mistress's neck.

"Are you unwell, milady," Wynflaed asked with a frown.

Ermenilda shook her head. "I've spent the morning praying. I'm weary both in body and soul."

"I wish there was something I could do," Wynflaed said, her green eyes clouding in sadness. "I do not like to see you so melancholy."

Ermenilda sighed and favored her maid with a wan smile.

"I dared to hope my husband was not the brute I initially believed," she replied quietly. "There is little joy in being proved right."

Wynflaed shook her head.

"He is taking a dark road. Your father will be angry when he hears of the attack."

Ermenilda shook her head, bitterness stinging the back of her throat.

"My father will say nothing. He, like other rulers of lesser kingdoms, would never risk angering the King of Mercia."

A crowd had gathered in front of the Great Tower, when Ermenilda emerged to bid her husband farewell.

To her surprise, Werbode—clad head to foot in leather—was waiting for her at the door. He insisted on escorting her down the steps to where Wulfhere had almost finished saddling his stallion.

"You look ravishing, milady," Werbode said, leaning in close and breathing in the rose scent she wore, "and you smell good enough to eat."

Ermenilda drew back from him in shock. Usually, the thegn kept his distance from her, his admiration consisting of hungry looks. His departure had made him bold.

Too bold.

Ermenilda cast him a look of cold disapproval, but that only caused Werbode to smile.

"Aye, and too haughty by half," he murmured.

At the base of the steps, Werbode stepped away from her and bowed. Ermenilda saw the mockery in his face and wished she could have a quiet moment alone with Wulfhere, to tell him of his thegn's disrespect.

Of course, Werbode had known she would not have the chance to tell the king—that was why he had done it. Ermenilda was only grateful that the warrior was marching to war with Wulfhere, and would not be left behind to protect her.

Wulfhere finished tightening his horse's girth and turned, his gaze settling upon her.

"You are late in coming to see me off," he told her. His voice was gruff, although his gaze was softer than usual.

"Wynflaed took an age with my hair," Ermenilda replied, motioning to the elaborate pile of curls and braids atop her head. "She wanted me to look my best today."

"Aye," Wulfhere stepped close to her, "and you do."

He looked down at her, and the heat of his gaze made Ermenilda feel as if she were standing in the noon sun, even though there was a cool breeze this morning.

"I know you do not give this battle your blessing," he said quietly, "but surely you wish me to come home unharmed."

Ermenilda stared at him, conflicted. Part of her wanted never to see him again—that way she could take the veil and live out the rest of her days in peace. Still, another—traitorous—part of her twisted at the thought of this man coming to any harm. She had not even thought of the possibility that this campaign might claim his life.

She hated what he was setting off to do, and she despised him for ignoring her pleas to abandon his quest for vengeance. It was this anger that she clung to now, as she faced him.

"I wish you a safe return, milord," she told him, "but only if you do not harm a soul during this campaign."

"There is no battle without death," he replied, faintly mocking.

Ermenilda held his gaze, resisting the urge to lash out and slap him. His arrogance galled her. Inhaling deeply, she took a step back from him, creating a gulf between them, before answering.

"Then, I will pray to god that it ends in yours."

Chapter Twenty-one
In the Marshes

The sky was immense here. The earth a mere strip of dirt, swamp, and reeds against its vastness. Wulfhere did not like it. He preferred the soft green of Mercia, with its cool forests and rolling hills. The Kingdom of the East Angles looked like a land fit for frogs, and little else.

He swatted at the cloud of midges whining around his head and glanced at where Werbode rode silently beside him.

"How can folk live here?"

Werbode grunted, his dark gaze sweeping over the waterlogged fens.

"Forsaken by the gods," he agreed. "There is a reason why folk named our destination *Eilig*—Isle of Eels."

"What manner of morning gift is an island in the midst of stinking swamp?" Wulfhere muttered.

To his left, Elfhere gave a humorless chuckle. "I heard that Lady Aethelthryth was so delighted with Tondberct of Ely's gift that she immediately insisted they move there."

"The woman must be mad, as well as conniving," Werbode commented sourly.

Wulfhere was inclined to agree with him.

They were drawing close to Ely now. After days of traveling through fenland, Wulfhere knew the island was near. They rode upon a narrow causeway. The road was in need of repair—boggy and crumbling in places. The

Romans had built this dike, and it had not been touched since.

It was a hot day, and the humidity in the fens made Wulfhere's skin itch. Under his leather armor, he was sweating heavily. His mood, like every day since departing from Tamworth, was dark.

Ermenilda's last words to him still rang in his ears, as did the dislike on her face. For a moment, he had truly believed she never wished to see him again, that she hated him. Then, he remembered how she welcomed him in the furs, and the passion they shared every night, and told himself her anger would pass.

By the time he returned to Tamworth, she would have missed him.

Fæder always insisted that women would never understand warfare or a man's need to do battle with his enemies.

Queen Cyneswide had never challenged the king on his decisions to go to battle. In truth, she had never shown the slightest interest in her husband's campaigns—but Ermenilda was different. Although he tried to deny it, Wulfhere knew his conflict with his bride would not end here.

"Brooding again, milord?"

Wulfhere glanced right, to see Werbode observing him.

"Aye, what of it?" he replied moodily.

The thegn gave him a shrewd look.

"A wife should not trouble a man so."

"Leave it, Werbode," Wulfhere growled. "My marriage is my own business."

Werbode shrugged, as if he could not care less, although his parting comment had a sting.

"A wife should know her place. If you do not teach Ermenilda hers, you will have no end of trouble."

Wulfhere turned on him, and was about to respond harshly, when Elfhere interrupted.

"Milord! Ely is before us."

With Werbode's impertinence cast aside, Wulfhere's gaze shifted to the northeastern horizon, where the tip of straw-thatched roofs thrust skyward, and smoke rose lazily, dirtying the pale-blue sky.

An island of clay and gravel sat among glittering fenland, joined to firmer ground by a narrow causeway. As they approached, Wulfhere spied the wooden ramparts encircling the settlement, with guard towers at each corner. The East Angle flag—a red cross upon a field of white with a blue shield and three golden crowns in the foreground—hung limply from one corner, for there was no trace of breeze this morning.

The tallest roof within the ramparts did not appear to belong to ealdorman Tondberct's hall but to a great church. It perched upon the island's highest ground, dominating the surrounding landscape for furlongs.

Wulfhere reined in his stallion and took in every detail of the scene before him.

"What now, milord?" Werbode asked. "Shall we attack?"

"Not before I hear what the ealdorman has to say," Wulfhere replied. "I shall have his guilt confirmed before I deal with him."

"Does it matter? You know he did it."

"Aye, but I'm curious to see what he will do, now that the consequences of his actions have come calling."

Wulfhere turned his full attention upon Werbode. The warrior had worn upon his nerves for days, and he decided it was time Werbode learned to mind his tongue. They had fought shoulder to shoulder many times, and he trusted the warrior with his life. However, of late, Werbode seemed to forget who the lord was, and who the servant.

"Ride into Ely on my behalf," he ordered. "Tell Tondberct that if he offers himself and his wife up to me, I will spare the lives of those in Ely."

Werbode glowered at him, and Wulfhere could see he chafed under the order. With the eyes of many—including his rival Elfhere's upon him, he swallowed his resentment and nodded curtly.

Wulfhere watched the dark-haired warrior kick his horse into a trot and ride up the column toward the town. He saw Werbode approach the gates and hesitate there for a moment, before they opened to admit him.

"What now, milord?" Elfhere asked beside him.

"The fox is now among the fowls," Wulfhere replied, smiling grimly. "Now, we must wait."

***

"Tondberct, there is an army outside our walls!"

Aethelthryth of Ely swept into the hall, her skirts billowing behind her. Her pretty face, framed by a white headrail, was pinched. Her eyes were huge.

"Hwæt?"

Tondberct looked up from where he had been playing hnefatafl with his brother. Between them lay a wooden board, marked out into twenty-six squares. He put down the carved figurine of his king and stared at his wife.

Aethelthryth had stopped before him. She was a small woman, with delicate features. Beneath her headrail, her hair was dark as a raven's wing—like her mother's—although her eyes were dark blue as her father's had been. Despite her tiny frame, she was a force of nature. She placed her hands on her hips and regarded Tondberct, her eyes turning hard.

"What will you do about it?"

Tondberct rose to his feet. Although he towered above his diminutive wife, she did not appear the least intimidated.

"Who is it?"

"I know not," she replied, "but they have sent a man to us. I just saw him pass through the gates."

Tondberct muttered a curse under his breath and glanced across at his brother, Cedric.

"Satan's spawn," he spat.

Cedric's sea-blue eyes widened. "Wulfhere?"

"Aye, who else?"

The ealdorman turned to Aethelthryth and met her eye. "Did I not warn you'd bring doom upon us?"

She did not reply, although the hardness of her gaze told him she was not remotely sorry.

Tondberct strode out of the hall, his wife and brother at his heels. Aethelthryth had to run to keep up, but the ealdorman did not slow his pace for her. He would have preferred her to stay behind; yet, it was futile to try to impose his will upon her.

They had just emerged from the hall when a man rode into the market square before them. He was a big warrior, with a thick mane of dark hair and a neatly trimmed black beard. His gaze was hard as it settled upon him.

"Ealdorman Tondberct of Ely?"

Tondberct nodded. "And who are you?"

"My name is Werbode. I am thegn and chief counsellor to King Wulfhere, son of Penda."

The newcomer's hard gaze shifted to Tondberct's left, where Aethelthryth stood.

"And is this your wife?"

"What does it matter to you?" Tondberct asked, his temper rising.

"It matters, for what I have to say is for both of you to hear."

"Go ahead," Aethelthryth spoke up, her voice cold and clipped. "Speak your missive."

The warrior raised a dark eyebrow, his gaze lingering upon Aethelthryth a moment longer, before he replied.

"King Wulfhere would have you confirm that you ordered the attack upon us three months ago."

When neither Tondberct nor his wife replied, Werbode continued.

"Sigric of Ely and his band attacked us upon a bridge on East Saxon lands. He claimed that you sent him. Do you deny this?"

Indeed, Tondberct was tempted to deny it. He had argued with his wife for nearly a year over her insistence that he avenge her father's and brother's deaths. He had warned her that attacking the King of Mercia would bring trouble upon him, but she had not listened.

He had sacrificed his men to please her. Sigric had known that attacking Wulfhere of Mercia would likely result in his death, but he had departed without a word of bitterness. Tondberct had sometimes wondered if his most trusted retainer had been secretly in love with his wife. He did not blame him—Aethelthryth had a way of making men do her bidding.

I've never been able to deny her anything, the ealdorman thought. *I should have known she would one day bring doom upon me.*

In the years they had been married, Aethelthryth had always gotten what she wanted. Even if he initially resisted her, she always persuaded him in the end. She had even convinced him on their wedding night that she should remain forever chaste, in preparation for one day serving god as a nun. Initially, he had been furious, although she had finally convinced him to leave her a virgin.

Over the years, he had shared the furs with many women—none of them his wife.

"It is true," Aethelthryth answered for him, filling the weighty silence.

Tondberct wheeled toward her, furious. "Aethelthryth!"

"I will not lie and cower before these men," she told him, raising her chin imperiously. "Sigric was loyal to us, and I will not pretend I did not know him."

Werbode was watching them keenly.

"Now that your wife admits it, I have a choice for you both," he continued. "Wulfhere will not let your crime go unpunished. Either come with me now, as prisoners of the King of Mercia, or we will lay waste to Ely and every soul residing within it."

"Monsters!" Aethelthryth cried. "Seeking reckoning for my father's and brother's deaths was no crime. Why should we, or the folk of Ely, be punished for it?"

Werbode grinned, and his gaze met Tondberct's.

"Does Lady Aethelthryth rule here? It appears you have lost your tongue."

"I rule Ely," Tondberct ground out. Anger had rendered him temporarily mute, "but I agree with my wife. You have no right to come here, into another kingdom, and issue threats. Be gone!"

"If you refuse to come with me, we will raze this pile of twigs to the ground." Werbode gestured to the surrounding hall, church, and low-slung thatched dwellings surrounding them. "Choose wisely, ealdorman."

Folk had now gathered to listen to the argument. Tondberct could see the fear on their faces, and he felt impotent rage swell within him. This was his town, his people, and he had sworn to protect them.

"I will go with you," he said finally, "but my wife remains here."

Werbode shook his head. "Both of you must come with me—or we attack Ely."

Tondberct glanced at Aethelthryth. Her delicate face had gone hard, and her eyes glittered with fury as she glared at Wulfhere of Mercia's emissary. Not for the first time, Tondberct marveled at her strength, her courage. Aethelthryth should have been born a man; she was too strong-willed to make a good wife. Nevertheless, he loved her and would do anything to protect her.

His gaze met hers, and he saw her iron resolve. She would not bend to Wulfhere's demands, and neither would he. Tondberct turned back to Werbode, who was watching them both keenly.

"Tell Wulfhere that if he wants us, he will have to take us by force."

Werbode's lip curled at his answer.

"Leave us now." Tondberct took a menacing step toward him, unsheathing the sword at his waist. "Scurry back to your master, or I'll send your head back to him and feed the rest of you to my dogs."

Chapter Twenty-two
A Woman's Lot

"More bread, Lady Ermenilda?"

"No, thank you, Aethelred."

Ermenilda took a sip of watered-down wine and regarded her brother by marriage over the rim of her cup. The prince had been exceedingly polite to her ever since Wulfhere's departure. However, the frosty edge to his voice did not escape her.

They sat alone upon the high seat this noon, as they had since the king and his warriors had departed. The other residents of the Great Hall ate their meal at the two tables running along either side of the fire pits. The rumble of voices, punctuated by laughter and good cheer, surrounded Ermenilda and Aethelred's table, only serving to highlight their forced civility. Aethelred eventually broke the weighty silence between them.

"It is ten days since Wulfhere left. I wonder how he has fared."

Ermenilda could think of no polite response to that, so she made a noncommittal murmur and took a mouthful of mutton, onion, and turnip stew. Another awkward silence stretched between them before she finally ventured a question.

"Did you not want to go with him?"

Aethelred snorted and took a deep draft from his cup.

"And leave Tamworth undefended against our enemies?"

"But surely one of his ealdormen can protect the hall while you're away?"

"After having our hall occupied by Northumbrians for two years, he does not want to leave us vulnerable," Aethelred told her with a frown, "and I don't blame him."

Ermenilda studied him a moment. Prince Aethelred was somewhat of an enigma; she could not decide if he was a worse or better man than Wulfhere. There were times—when his smirks and calculating looks wore upon her—when she imagined being wedded to Aethelred would be far worse than to his brother. At other times, like now, he wore an introspective expression, and his gaze was troubled.

Watching him, Ermenilda wondered if his arrogance and apparent ambition were merely a shield for the insecure youth beneath.

"What is it?" Aethelred had noticed her penetrating look. "You stare at me as if I were an ugly earthworm you have dug up in your garden."

Ermenilda laughed. Her reaction was unexpected and caused others in the hall to turn to look. Covering her mouth with her hand, Ermenilda realized that it was the first time she had laughed in a long while. Life had become so serious of late that it felt odd to find something humorous.

"I am glad I amuse you," Aethelred said, although his disgruntled expression told her that the opposite was true.

"I was just trying to gain your measure," she admitted. "Before leaving Cantwareburh, I thought I was a good judge of character but these days I no longer trust my own assessment."

The prince raised an eyebrow.

"That change is probably for the better. People are rarely what they first appear—good, bad, or otherwise. It never pays to make quick judgments about a man's character."

Ermenilda took a sip from her cup and mulled over his words. She knew there was some truth to what he said, but she preferred a world she could understand. She liked to know what was good and what was bad—there was comfort in it.

Everything had become so confusing of late. She had wedded a man she both detested and desired. On the one hand, Wulfhere's absence had been a blessed relief, and on the other, she found herself unexpectedly missing him—especially at night. Worse than that, she found herself missing the low timbre of his voice and the sight of him prowling into the hall, his white wolf stalking at his heels. She missed the flutters of excitement in her belly every time his gaze met hers.

Now it was Aethelred's turn to observe. She had been so deep in thought that she had not realized the prince was watching her closely.

"You are not like other women," he said, finally, "although neither was the princess Paeda wed."

"That does not sound like a compliment," Ermenilda replied, stiffening.

Aethelred's mouth curved into a mocking smile. "It was not meant as one."

"And how am I so different?"

"You think too much, question too much. It appears a recipe for unhappiness, if you ask me."

Ermenilda stared at him, stunned. "You believe other women don't think?"

"Well, if they do, they have the wits to hide it from their menfolk."

Although she chafed at his comments, Ermenilda knew Aethelred had spoken true. She had eyes—she knew most highborn women saw much but said little. The bitter truth was that husbands preferred their wives that way.

Her mother had brought Ermenilda and her sister up to be modest ladies, but some of Seaxburh's fire burned in her firstborn daughter's veins. Fortunately, Seaxburh had married a god-fearing man who ruled a peaceful kingdom. Until the day before Ermenilda's departure, she had never really seen her parents argue. Unluckily, for Ermenilda, her father had given her to a warlord.

Wulfhere brought out a side of her she had not known existed—a side she did not like.

"There you go, thinking again," Aethelred teased. "I don't need to be a seer to read your face, Lady Ermenilda."

"So I think too much, do I?" Ermenilda muttered, stabbing her small wooden trowel into the damp soil. "So men prefer women to be witless fools?"

Nearby, Wynflaed looked up from where she had been planting seedlings.

"What's that, milady?"

"Lord Aethelred shared his opinion about my character with me at nón-mete," Ermenilda replied, not bothering to hide the scorn in her voice. She was used to being frank with her handmaid, something Wynflaed appeared to appreciate. "Apparently, I have too much to say for myself. A cleverer woman would keep her eyes open and her mouth shut."

To Ermenilda's chagrin, Wynflaed laughed. The sound—light and musical—echoed across the garden, where rows of cabbages, turnips, carrots, and onions now grew. The scent of roses from the first blooms edging the garden mingled with the woody aroma of thyme and rosemary that they had planted near the paths. Ermenilda sat back on her heels and glared at Wynflaed.

"My mother always told me that was so," the maid admitted, still smiling. "She said that it's a rare man who wants a woman to be his equal. Most men believe our brains are smaller, that we are incapable of understanding anything beyond the realm of the home and children."

"And you find that funny?"

Wynflaed shook her head, not remotely perturbed by Ermenilda's glare. "I find it ridiculous," she replied, "and any man who thinks so deserves to be cuckolded."

"Wynflaed!" Ermenilda scolded her, although she was now fighting a smile.

The handmaid shrugged and reached for another seedling.

"I said the same to my mother, and she pretended to be outraged as well. Yet, she knew the truth as well as me—the cleverer a woman is, the more careful she must be to hide it from her menfolk."

"In such a world, it's better for a woman to remain unwed," Ermenilda replied, viciously pulling out a weed and tossing it into her basket.

Wynflaed looked up from her work, a frown marring her smooth brow.

"But, we need men to protect us, to provide for us. Why else do you think womenfolk put up with it?"

"Nuns don't have to," Ermenilda reminded her.

"They still have rules to live by. We all do."

A male voice interrupted their conversation.

Both women started slightly and turned to see the priest, Seaxwulf, standing in the gateway to the garden.

"Apologies, if I startled you." The priest gave an embarrassed smile. "I didn't mean to eavesdrop."

"Good afternoon, Brother Seaxwulf," Ermenilda greeted him coolly. Ever since he had refused to aid her, she had avoided him, preferring to pray by her bedside than visit his church.

The priest nodded and took another step forward, his gaze surveying his surroundings.

"You have worked miracles with this plot," he said. "I've never seen anything so beautiful."

Despite her disappointment in Seaxwulf, Ermenilda smiled at his compliment. It felt nice to have someone admire her and Wynflaed's hard work.

"Thank you," she replied.

It was then that she noticed the priest was dressed for traveling, in a dark woolen cloak, with a leather satchel slung across his front.

"Where are you off to?"

Seaxwulf glanced down at his attire and smiled. The cloak was too warm for the afternoon's humidity, and his brow glistened with sweat.

"I am traveling to Bonehill. I usually visit the abbey twice a year, to make sure the nuns have everything they need. I bring them grain and salted meat and cheeses to replenish their stores."

Ermenilda stood up and brushed soil off her hands. "Bonehill? I too would like to visit. How far is it from Tamworth?"

"Just under a day's ride, southwest of here. Once the king returns, I will ask him if you can accompany me on my next visit, if you wish it, milady."

Ermenilda smiled. His offer pleased her. "Yes, I would like that very much, thank you."

Seaxwulf moved back toward the gateway. "I must leave you now. I just wanted to stop by and say good-bye. I meant to depart this morning, but I've been delayed. At this rate, I will not reach Bonehill till tomorrow morning."

"Well then, I bid you a good journey."

Ermenilda watched Seaxwulf depart. She knelt down once more and retrieved her trowel. Wynflaed was observing her, a thoughtful look upon her face.

"What is it?"

"Would you really have preferred a life as a nun, milady?"

"Aye," Ermenilda replied without hesitation. "I know their life can be hard, and austere, but I would prefer it to being wed to Wulfhere of Mercia."

Ermenilda paused there, her stomach clenching. "I shudder to think what he will do to my kin in Ely. If he returns with their blood on his hands, I will never forgive him."

Chapter Twenty-three
Ely Burns

"Murderers! Devils!"

Aethelthryth of Ely faced the men who strode into her hall, their blades slick with fresh blood. She stood alone in front of the fire pit. All her servants had fled, and the men had gone outside to fight. She trembled as the warriors approached but held her ground.

Wulfhere respected her for that.

He crossed the floor, taking in the cleanliness and order of the empty ealdorman's hall as he went. The servants had thrown down their brooms and left their preparations for supper scattered across the workbenches, yet he could see that every surface gleamed. The air, though smoky, carried the scent of lavender and rosemary. Clearly, Lady Aethelthryth was an industrious woman and ran her husband's hall well.

"So you come at last," she hissed at him when he came to a halt five feet from her. "To finish the job your father started."

Wulfhere inclined his head before motioning to Mōna, who had stepped up next to him and was growling low in her throat. The wolf, her jaws dripping with blood from the fight outside, was ready to savage this woman.

"Quiet, Mōna."

"And you have brought your hellhound with you," Aethelthryth observed, although her voice shook with fear. Her gaze flicked to the white wolf, now sitting by Wulfhere's side.

"I have no quarrel with your family," Wulfhere said finally. "However, you made a mistake in not letting the past lie. Did you not think that attacking me in a time of peace would bring my wrath upon you?"

Aethelthryth's lip curled, and he could see her hatred for him burned deep.

"I could not abide you wedding my niece." She bit out the words. "A girl of pure body and spirit, destined to serve Christ. You have ruined her."

Behind him, Wulfhere heard Werbode snigger.

"I told you the woman had a mouth on her," the warrior said.

Wulfhere did not respond to Werbode's comment. Instead, he continued to watch Aethelthryth of Ely. She was younger and prettier than he had expected. Eventually, she broke the weighty silence between them.

"What have you done with my husband?"

"He is dead, as are all his warriors."

Aethelthryth went the color of milk at this news and swayed slightly on her feet.

"You are a monster," she whispered.

Wulfhere inhaled slowly, quelling his mounting irritation. "I warned you both what would happen if I attacked Ely," he told her. "You had the chance to come away willingly, but you refused. All this death is your doing."

"Kill me too then," she spat at him; her face, framed by a white linen headrail, was gaunt with fury. "Finish it!"

Wulfhere shook his head. "And make you a martyr, Lady Aethelthryth? I think not. You are coming back with me, to Tamworth, as my hostage. That way, your sister in Cantwareburh will think twice before continuing her blood feud."

"No!"

Aethelthryth's hard-won self-control snapped. She lunged for the nearest worktable, where a knife lay next to a pile of carrots. Her fingers had just fastened around the bone hilt when Wulfhere reached her. He grabbed hold of her wrist and squeezed until she dropped the weapon to the rushes.

"What were you going to do with that?" he asked, kicking away the knife. "Stab me?"

Aethelthryth did not answer. Instead, she struggled against him, kicking and clawing like a cat. For a small woman, she was remarkably strong.

"I'd say she was going to slay herself," Elfhere commented. The blond warrior stepped up and deftly bound the woman's wrists behind her back while Wulfhere held her still. Aethelthryth was weeping now, her shoulders shaking with soundless sobs.

Elfhere was frowning as he watched her. "Is she hurt?"

Wulfhere shook his head. "Nor is she as helpless as she appears. Keep an eye on her."

They left the ealdorman's hall behind and led their captive out into the ruined town. Smoke filled the afternoon sky, and around them thatched dwellings burned. Above it all, Ely's great church had gone up like a great funeral pyre, flames licking high into the eggshell sky.

Aethelthryth gave a choked cry when she saw it. She dropped to her knees and began whispering a fevered prayer.

"The woman grates upon my nerves," Werbode grumbled. "Can we not gag her?"

Wulfhere shook his head. "She will quieten soon enough."

Smoke hung heavily in the air, causing Wulfhere's eyes to water. The roar and crackle of the flames devouring the timber church behind them drowned out the groans of the dying men he stepped over. He could feel the heat of the inferno on his back.

The bodies of Tondberct's men lay thick around the perimeter of Ely, and their blood had stained the earth dark at the gates, where the fighting had been most intense. Wulfhere had lost a few men in the attack, but once they breached the gates, the fight had ended quickly.

Outside the gates, they passed two heads atop pikes.

Aethelthryth let out a long wail when she saw them. Tondberct and his brother, Cedric, stared back at her. They both wore their final moments upon their faces. Tondberct's eyes were wide, his mouth gaping, whereas his brother's face had twisted in a rictus of agony.

"They both fought bravely," Elfhere told her quietly. "They died with swords in their hands."

Aethelthryth ignored the warrior and began to sob— loudly this time—before sinking to the ground. Her wails echoed across the fenland, louder even than the roar of the burning church.

Wulfhere watched her grief and felt an odd sensation fill him, one he could not define.

He had never liked watching a woman weep.

He had thought that his reckoning would feel better than this: that exacting revenge against Seaxburh and Aethelthryth would fill him with a sense of vindication. Instead, he just felt strangely hollow.

Smothering the sensation, Wulfhere turned to Elfhere.

"If she will not walk, carry her to the horses. We're leaving."

"So soon?" Werbode stepped up, frowning. "We have not yet plundered the town. There will be plenty of riches to be had in Tondberct's hall."

Wulfhere shook his head. Suddenly, the need to be away from Ely was the only thing that mattered.

"Leave them," he ordered. "The folk of Ely will need gold to rebuild their town when they return."

"Hwæt?" Werbode's face turned thunderous. "Do you deny us the spoils of battle?"

Wulfhere lashed out, his fist connecting with Werbode's left eye. The warrior grunted, before dropping to the ground like a sack of barley.

Massaging his bruised knuckles, Wulfhere cast a gimlet-eyed glare at his men, who had gathered around him. White-hot rage pulsed through him. He would kill the next warrior who crossed him.

"Does anyone else have anything to add?"

Only silence answered him.

"Good. Ready your horses—we ride for Mercia."

Chapter Twenty-four
A Cold Welcome

Ermenilda was at her loom, working on a tapestry that would one day grace the wall above the high seat, when she heard that Wulfhere had returned.

"The king's fyrd has entered the low gate, milady." Wynflaed had just stepped up onto the high seat, her cheeks flushed from running. "Shall I help you change into another dress?"

Ermenilda's stomach contracted at the news. She looked down at the plain green sleeveless tunic she wore, girded at the waist with a simple cord. Her state of dress was the least of her worries.

"There is no time," she replied.

Ermenilda rose to her feet and tucked away a lock of hair that had come free of its long braid. She had known that Wulfhere was due to return any day, but the realization that he would shortly enter the Great Tower caused her heart to quicken with a strange mix of dread and excitement.

"Come," she said to Wynflaed, her tone brisk to mask her nervousness. "We should go out to meet them."

Outside the Great Tower of Tamworth, the sun shone bright and warm on what was the warmest day of the year, so far. Heat bathed Ermenilda's face when she stepped out of the tower's entrance and halted at the wide ledge before the steps.

Beyond the high gate, she could hear the thunder of approaching horses. Her heart began to hammer against her ribs, and she placed her hand on her breast, in an attempt to calm her pulse.

Moments later, men poured into the wide space before the Great Tower. The late morning's peace shattered, as warriors and their horses filled the yard. The jangling of bridles, the creak of leather, the clunk of limewood shields, the rumble of men's voices, and the snorting of horses greeted her. The noise washed over Ermenilda in a roaring tide.

She spotted her husband easily. He rode into the yard, with Mōna loping at his side. He was helmetless, his pale hair spilling over his shoulders. Her breathing stilled at the sight of him. Try as she might to deny it, Wulfhere entranced her; his presence dominated any space he entered.

She watched Wulfhere glance toward the tower, seeking her out, and their gazes met. The intensity in his pale eyes caused her to inhale sharply. She might have gone on staring at him forever had a woman's voice not echoed across the yard.

"Ermenilda?"

I know that voice.

Tearing her gaze from Wulfhere's, Ermenilda looked behind him at where Elfhere was helping a woman dismount. The female was small and dressed in a gray-blue tunic that matched her eyes. Her white headrail was disheveled and stained.

Ermenilda picked up her skirts and hurried down the steps toward the swirling crowd.

"Aethelthryth . . . is that you?"

Her aunt was as beautiful as Ermenilda remembered. She was Seaxburh's older sister, but she seemed younger than the queen of the Kentish. Perhaps it was because Seaxburh had given birth to four children, whereas her sister had remained childless. Her face was as smooth and unlined as Ermenilda's.

Aethelthryth rushed across the yard toward her. As her aunt approached, the bravery on her face seemed to dissolve and her eyes filled with tears. She threw herself into Ermenilda's arms, nearly knocking her over. Ermenilda put her arms around her aunt and felt her body quaking.

What have they done to her?

Ermenilda glared over Aethelthryth's shoulder at where Wulfhere was now unsaddling his horse, but he had his back to her.

Her aunt was now sobbing against her shoulder, inconsolable, and Ermenilda found herself at a loss for words. It was just as well, though, for Aethelthryth was in no state for talking.

Werbode sauntered past. Ermenilda noticed he was sporting a black eye. His gaze raked over the women before he smiled at Ermenilda. It was not a pleasant expression, more of a leer. The nape of Ermenilda's neck prickled—concern flowering into alarm.

"Come, Aunty." She gently pried Aethelthryth off her shoulder and placed an arm around the woman's trembling form. "I will prepare you a hot bath and fetch you something to eat."

She felt Wulfhere's gaze shift to her. He had turned from unsaddling his horse. She could sense that he wanted her to look his way.

Ermenilda ignored him.

Seeing Aethelthryth so distraught boded ill and filled her with fear. She would not speak with her husband until she had spoken to her aunt in private.

Wynflaed watched her mistress lead the sobbing woman away. She glanced to the right and saw that the king was also observing his wife walk back toward the Great Tower.

Wulfhere's gaze had narrowed, and his expression turned stony. Wynflaed watched him, alarm fluttering up from her belly.

She should have come forward to greet him properly.

Wynflaed liked the woman she served. Ermenilda was lively, clever, and sensitive. Despite that their opinions sometimes clashed, she treated her handmaid well, and over the months they had been at Tamworth, a strong friendship had grown between them. However, there were times when Wynflaed wanted to shake her. Did she not realize the trouble she was making for herself?

Wynflaed was about to move off, to follow the queen back inside the hall, when a man spoke behind her.

"Were you going to greet me?"

Wynflaed swiveled to find Elfhere waiting there, smiling.

"Did you miss me, fair Wynflaed?"

Wynflaed gave an unladylike snort in an attempt to mask the heat flowering in her cheeks. "As much as I'd miss one of my father's hounds."

Elfhere laughed at that, and Wynflaed noted—not for the first time—how handsome he was.

Yes, and I'm sure he knows that too.

"How did the campaign go?" she asked him, in an attempt to steer the conversation back to safer waters.

The laughter drained from Elfhere's face.

"Well enough," he replied, glancing askance at his king. Wulfhere was not paying him any attention, for he was barking orders at his men.

"What does that mean?" Wynflaed pressed, frowning. "Did the king have his reckoning or not?"

"Oh, he had his reckoning. Ely is nothing but a smoldering, pyre and the ealdorman and his brother are slain."

Wynflaed went cold at this news. She could see from Elfhere's expression that he was not pleased to be the bearer of such tidings. Wynflaed glanced toward the hall where Ermenilda and the weeping woman had just disappeared.

"And his lady?"

"Lady Aethelthryth is now King Wulfhere's hostage," Elfhere replied, his gaze shuttered, and all trace of his earlier good humor gone, "to do with as he sees fit."

Ermenilda showed Aethelthryth over to a stool and helped her sit. They had taken refuge in the tiny space that held the iron bathtub. A heavy tapestry screened them from the rest of the hall, giving the women a moment alone.

Ermenilda knelt before her aunt, her gaze riveted upon Aethelthryth's flushed face. Tears still streamed down her cheeks, although she had managed to rein back her sobbing.

"Aunty," she said finally. "You must tell me what happened—"

At that moment, the tapestry shifted as Wynflaed poked her head inside the chamber.

"Milady . . . can I help you?"

"I've asked the slaves to prepare water for a bath," Ermenilda replied. "Please bring my aunt something to eat and drink."

Wynflaed nodded before disappearing back into the hall.

Ermenilda turned back to her aunt. She reached forward and took Aethelthryth's hands—they were ice cold.

"Please," she whispered, dread rising within her, for her aunt's silence was damning. "Talk to me . . ."

Aethelthryth looked up, her eyes glittering.

"They killed Tondberct and Cedric," she gasped, her voice breaking. "Put their heads upon pikes outside the gates."

Ermenilda stared at her aunt, horror stealing through her. But Aethelthryth had not finished.

"They burned Ely," she continued, choking out each word as if she was struggling to breathe. "They destroyed my church."

Aethelthryth leaned forward, her face twisting with the force of her anguish.

"Your father was a fool," she spat. "Wulfhere is no Christian. He is an unrepentant heathen, and his soul will burn for what he has done."

Ermenilda continued to stare at her aunt, unable to respond. Aethelthryth's news sickened her to the core.

"Did they spare anyone?" she finally managed, bile creeping up her throat.

"Only those who did not fight them," Aethelthryth replied. "Any who tried to stop them from entering Ely, they cut down."

"I am so sorry," Ermenilda whispered. Tears now escaped her burning eyes and scalded her cheeks. "I tried to stop him from marching on Ely, but he would not listen."

Aethelthryth did not appear to be listening to her. Such was her rage against the man who had killed her husband and taken her hostage that she almost appeared to be in a trance.

"And now I'm his prisoner," she choked out. "To be kept here as a trophy."

"Did he or any of his men hurt you?"

Ermenilda asked the question that she had been dreading to ask since she had seen her aunt. Despite everything, she could not imagine Wulfhere as a rapist—but, at that moment, she was ready to think the worst of him.

Aethelthryth's lip curled and her stormy gaze hardened at that question. Eventually, she shook her head.

"It appears that even wolves have some scruples," she admitted grudgingly. "He told one of his men to watch over me and warned the others not to touch his hostage."

Relief, giddying in its intensity, flooded over Ermenilda. It was short-lived, for a deep anger now burned within her.

Night fell over Tamworth in a hazy twilight of mauve and pink, bringing a hot early summer's day to a close. The aroma of roasting mutton greeted Wulfhere as he climbed the steps up to his hall. He was exhausted. His eyes felt gritty with fatigue, and his limbs ached from days in the saddle.

Inside, his gaze sought out his wife. He found her, sitting with her aunt in a far corner. Ermenilda was winding wool onto her distaff while Aethelthryth sat, eyes downcast, her hands folded onto her lap. His hostage was dressed in a clean light-brown tunic, with a fresh veil obscuring her hair from view.

Both women ignored him as he entered.

Wulfhere clenched his jaw—his wife's coldness stung. Taking a deep breath, he looked away from Ermenilda and continued across the hall, calling for a hot bath to be drawn. There would be time for them to talk later.

Across the hall, Aethelred waved to him. The prince was grinning.

"How about a horn of mead to celebrate victory?"

"After I wash the smell of horse off me," Wulfhere called back, his mood lifting slightly. At least his brother was happy to see him.

Chapter Twenty-five
Rage

Mead flowed on the evening of Wulfhere's victorious return to the Great Hall of Tamworth.

There was a feast of roast venison and platters of roast vegetables, served with wheels of aged cheese and slabs of freshly baked griddle bread. Slaves circuited the hall, filling feasters' cups to the brim with frothy mead, while dogs positioned themselves under tables, eagerly awaiting morsels of food that would drop onto the rushes.

A scop stood at the far end of the high seat. The youth strummed a lyre as he sung a poem about a wronged king and his glorious reckoning.

Ermenilda sat in silence next to her husband and listened.

> *Wise sir, do not grieve.*
> *It is always better to avenge dear ones*
> *than to indulge in mourning.*
> *For every one of us, living in this world*
> *means waiting for our end.*
> *Let whoever can win glory before death.*
> *When a warrior is gone,*
> *that will be his best and only bulwark.*

The young man had a hauntingly beautiful voice, and thunderous applause echoed up into the rafters after each verse.

Ermenilda grew increasingly upset as the song progressed.

The scop sung of the old ways, of a warrior's life dedicated to glory in battle—as if nothing else mattered. Ermenilda looked about the table and saw how the scop's words affected Wulfhere's men. Werbode's eyes glittered as he listened. Elfhere stared down at his cup of mead, an intense expression upon his face. Some of the other men silently wept. Only two people at the table did not appear moved by the poem: Seaxwulf and Aethelthryth.

The priest sat at the far end, next to Ermenilda's aunt. Seaxwulf's expression was cool, although Ermenilda could see the disapproval in his eyes. Aethelthryth sat, head bowed, her face deathly pale.

It is always better to avenge dear ones than to indulge in mourning.

Was that why Aethelthryth and Seaxburh had plotted to kill Wulfhere?

They were both deeply religious women, but in the end, the lust for vengeance had triumphed over their beliefs.

Watching her aunt's stricken face, Ermenilda felt a wave of pity consume her. Revenge was a never-ending cycle, like a serpent consuming its own tail. Once you awoke the beast, it would not die till it had consumed itself.

Finally, the scop finished his poem, his voice echoing in the silence before the feasters climbed to their feet and applauded him.

Ermenilda remained seated when Wulfhere joined them. Her husband held his drinking horn high in the air as his men cheered.

"To victory!"

Ermenilda stared at her trencher piled high with venison, roast onions, and carrots and knew she was too angry to eat a mouthful of it. She tried to quell the outrage building within her, but the impulse was too strong.

When Wulfhere sat back down beside her, she turned to him.

"What manner of victory is it to attack a town with barely the means to defend itself?" she asked.

Although she kept her voice low, it seemed to ring across the table.

"What glory is there in burning down the homes of folk who have never done you wrong?"

Her gaze met Wulfhere's, and she saw the warning in the pale depths of his eyes. Around her, the hall went ominously silent, but Ermenilda did not heed it. She wanted Aethelthryth to see this; she wanted her aunt to know that she did not condone her husband's behavior.

"You were baptized, and yet you burned Ely's church to the ground. Why?"

"As a reminder, a warning," Wulfhere replied, his voice quiet and devoid of emotion, "to all those who trespass against the King of Mercia."

"But you swore an oath!"

"I serve no master. My choices are my own to make."

"You're a beast!" Ermenilda shot back, aware that her voice had turned shrill. "You made a promise you had no intention of fulfilling. You are a liar!"

A hiss of outrage reverberated around the hall, and Ermenilda emerged from the red haze that had made her blind to all else till this moment. She glanced about her and saw anger on their faces. Only Aethelthryth appeared pleased—her face flushed with pride at her niece's outburst—and her eyes gleamed. Ermenilda looked back at her husband, and her stomach twisted with dread.

Wulfhere had gone pale—his handsome face all taut angles. His eyes were two glittering slits as he rose to his feet.

"Enough," he growled.

He took her by the upper arm, his fingers biting into her skin, and propelled her toward the ladder that led up to the King's Loft.

"Go upstairs," he told her, his voice rough with barely contained anger. "I will deal with you later."

Ermenilda, truly afraid of her husband for the first time since meeting him, did as he ordered. Her shaking limbs were as much from fury as from fear, as was her thundering pulse. She climbed the ladder, aware of the gazes of all burning into her, and staggered across to the furs.

There, she shakily sat down and tried to calm the rage that still pulsed in her breast.

Wulfhere returned to his seat and took a deep draft of mead from his drinking horn. Unfortunately, the honeyed mead, which had previously tasted so sweet, now left a bitter tang in his mouth.

Damn her. She has gone too far this time.

Next to him, Aethelred shifted uncomfortably. His brother was frowning, his gaze fixed upon Wulfhere.

"Save it," Wulfhere growled at him. "I'm in no mood to listen."

To make himself clearer still, Wulfhere stabbed the knife he had been using to cut meat into the table next to his trencher. His brother, perhaps remembering what had happened last time he had voiced his opinion on Wulfhere's relations with his queen, held his tongue.

Around Wulfhere, conversation eventually resumed, although it was without the earlier joviality and sense of celebration. Ermenilda had achieved what she intended—to humiliate him in front of his kin and retainers.

Wulfhere's gaze traveled to the far end of the table, where Seaxwulf was gloomily staring down at his half-eaten meal. Aethelthryth of Ely sat next to him, but she was not downcast and defeated, as she had been earlier.

Instead, his hostage was staring at him, her eyes as hard as iron. She met his gaze unflinchingly and held it, in wordless challenge.

The women in this family. They're all shrews with tongues like seax blades.

As if reading his thoughts, Aethelthryth favored Wulfhere with a hard smile, full of spite. Wulfhere tore his gaze away from her and glanced up at the loft he shared with Ermenilda. Perhaps his brother, and Werbode, had spoken true. He had been too soft, too permissive, with his bold-tongued wife and was now reaping what he had sown.

Ermenilda was still sitting upon the edge of the furs, her hands clasped together in front of her in a silent prayer, when she heard the scrape of Wulfhere's boots on the rungs of the wooden ladder.

Mother Mary, save me. He is coming.

Heart hammering, Ermenilda rose to her feet and wiped her damp palms on her skirts. It was best to face him standing; he would not see her cowering in the corner, pleading for forgiveness.

Even so, she nearly quailed at the sight of Wulfhere climbing onto the platform. It had been almost a moon's cycle since he had stood inside their private chamber beside her, and like before his departure, Wulfhere's presence dominated the space. She felt tiny in comparison.

He stalked across the platform toward her, but Ermenilda held her ground.

Will he hit me?

He had not yet raised a hand to her, but Ermenilda braced herself for the blow. Against his warnings, she had once again humiliated him in front of his kin and retainers. Her husband would not let that go unpunished.

His punishment, when it came, was not what she expected.

Wulfhere roughly pulled Ermenilda into his arms and kissed her.

She gasped in shock, and his tongue thrust into her mouth, silencing any protest. The kiss was punishing. With one hand, he held her pinned against him, while with the other, he unbraided her hair so that it tumbled down her back.

He reached down between them and grasping the bodice of her tunic ripped it down the front. The sound of rending material filled their chamber.

Ermenilda gasped again. The sound slid into a cry of shock when he ripped the thin undertunic from her as well, so she stood naked before him.

Wulfhere stared down at her, his gaze glittering under hooded lids, before it raked over her body. Her nipples hardened, her breasts straining traitorously toward him. Ermenilda realized her breathing was coming in short gasps.

Wulfhere pushed her toward the furs.

"On your hands and knees," he ordered.

When she did not comply, he pushed her down. Ermenilda's limbs began to tremble, although not just from fear, but also desire. She knew he was doing this to dominate her, to prove she had to do his bidding in all things, but suddenly she did not care. After long days without his touch, her traitorous body ached for him.

She heard Wulfhere move behind her, his breathing harsh. A moment later, he entered her in one hard thrust. It was so sudden, so powerful, that Ermenilda cried out. This was nothing like the man who had made love to her so gently on their wedding night or in the months after. This man was claiming what was his without any tenderness at all.

Wulfhere thrust into her again, so hard that she had to clutch onto the furs to prevent herself from flying forward off them. Ermenilda whimpered, heat exploding in her loins as he filled her. He took her savagely, his fingers digging into her hips as he thrust deep.

To her shame, Ermenilda loved every moment of it.

She was incapable of any coherent thought. Her body pulsed in exquisite pleasure, excitement making every nerve ending shiver. Ermenilda began to shudder uncontrollably, her cries echoing around her. He thrust deeper still, bringing her to the edge between pleasure and pain.

Wulfhere finally climaxed—his own cry hoarse. He collapsed on top of her, and Ermenilda could feel his heart racing like a galloping horse, against her back. The sensation of his weight on her felt like the most natural thing in the world.

Wulfhere did not remain there, prone, for longer than a few moments. He withdrew from her and got to his feet. Ermenilda, still struggling to recover her breath, rolled over to face him.

Watching him, she shivered. The temporary madness caused by passion drained from her.

The look on Wulfhere's face told her everything she needed to know. The cold disdain in his eyes and the twist of his mouth caused her throat to close in dread.

"So that is what you prefer?" he told her, his voice chilling. "To be used like a whore?"

Ermenilda stared at him in dismay, horror choking her throat, making it impossible to reply.

"You are my queen, and I wanted to treat you like one," he snarled, lacing up his breeches. "But, you would prefer to shame me in front of my hall and have me rut you like a goat afterward."

Wulfhere finished lacing his breeches and moved toward the ladder. Before he stepped onto it, he turned back to Ermenilda, his cold gaze raking over her.

"You accused me of being a liar, Ermenilda, but you are no better. You say one thing and do another. From now on, I will treat you like the deceitful bitch you are."

Without another word, Wulfhere descended the ladder.

Chapter Twenty-six
Foraging in the Rain

E rmenilda watched Wulfhere disappear.

The pain in the center of her chest felt as if he had reached inside her chest and ripped out her beating heart. She felt sick, cold, and horrified—both at his cruelty toward her and at her own behavior.

Naked, she sunk back onto the furs and curled up into a ball. It hurt to breathe, to think, to exist. Pain engulfed her.

It was wrong, all of it. They were locked into a battle till death.

I wound him and he wounds me. If this continues, we shall destroy each other.

The tears came, burning her cheeks as she wept silently. She felt the furs under her cheek become soaked, but she did not move. Wulfhere's words had cut her deeply, yet the truth of his accusation echoed in her mind like a tolling church bell.

Deceitful bitch.

She should have tried to continue her argument with him when he had climbed up into their loft, not fallen into his arms like a slut. He was right—one moment she treated him like the devil himself, the other she could not wait to open her legs for him.

At that moment, Ermenilda loathed herself. She could not imagine continuing life in this way or remaining wedded to such a heartless man.

I cannot continue. I will not, she finally decided, struggling to form coherent thoughts through the haze of pain.

This has to end.

***

It rained the next day. The clouds rolled in long before dawn, and by the time light stole across the land, the two buckets sitting under leaks in the Great Hall were full.

Ermenilda was quiet as she broke her fast upon the high seat next to her husband. She did not look his way and ate no more than a mouthful of bread before sipping at a cup of hot broth. Likewise, Wulfhere ignored her.

Aethelred attempted to draw his brother out of his morose mood, but Wulfhere merely gave one-word responses. Eventually, he too fell silent. Ermenilda paid no one at the table any mind. Her thoughts had turned inward, and they were as heavy as the rain clouds that hung over Tamworth that morning. She felt as if she were wading through deep water.

At the far end of the table sat Aethelthryth. Her aunt ate sparingly, her gaze resting frequently upon Ermenilda, willing her to meet her eye. Ermenilda found she could not do so. Such was the depths of her shame, her self-loathing, that she could not bear to meet her aunt's gaze.

Finishing her broth, Ermenilda left the high seat and went to find Wynflaed. Her handmaid was sitting next to one of the fire pits, chatting to another servant as she mended one of the queen's undertunics—the one that Wulfhere had torn off Ermenilda the night before.

"Wynflaed," Ermenilda greeted her handmaid briskly, deliberately averting her gaze from the item of clothing the girl was mending. "I wish to gather herbs this morning. Will you join me?"

Wynflaed frowned. "This morning? But, it is pouring with rain outside, milady."

"The rain does not bother me," Ermenilda replied briskly, "and besides, I have need of some fresh air this morning, rain or shine."

Wynflaed nodded, although she was still frowning. Ermenilda saw the concern in her maid's eyes and knew that Wynflaed—like everyone else—had witnessed her argument with Wulfhere the previous night.

"I will fetch my cloak and basket," Wynflaed replied, putting aside her sewing.

Ermenilda nodded. "I will meet you at the door shortly."

She fetched her own fur mantle, which would provide ample protection from the rain, and a basket of her own. The hall was busy this morning, after the previous night's revelry. Slaves scrubbed down work surfaces and made pies from leftover venison.

Wulfhere had remained upon the high seat, and was watching Aethelred and Werbode play knucklebones. He sat, never once looking her way, his gaze hooded.

Ermenilda was grateful Wulfhere had decided to ignore her this morning. It merely affirmed the decision that she had come to the night before was the right one. She had lain awake, curled up on the furs, all night. Mercifully, Wulfhere did not return to their loft, leaving her alone. She had listened to the muffled sounds of those in the hall below, and when the rain started, she had found the rhythmic drumming against the walls of the tower calming.

By the time the first watery light of dawn filtered in through one of the high windows, Ermenilda had made up her mind.

Wynflaed was waiting for her by the doors, and together the two women made their way outside into the rain. Her basket tucked under an arm, Ermenilda strode purposefully across the muddy stable yard, taking little care for her boots, while Wynflaed did her best to skirt the largest puddles.

"Milady," Wynflaed hurried to catch up to her. "Shouldn't we tell the king that we are leaving the town? His men usually accompany us."

"Not this morning," Ermenilda replied firmly. "Just once, I wish to be free of the company of men. We need no escort to gather herbs."

They left Tamworth via the low gate. As Ermenilda had anticipated, the guards there frowned when they saw the queen and her maid leaving unescorted.

"We will not be long," Ermenilda told them, her tone brooking no argument. "There are a few herbs I wish to pick, which grow alongside the Tame. We shall return shortly."

"I can join you, m'lady," one of the men replied. "The king would wish it."

"The king has given me permission to leave unescorted this morning," Ermenilda replied. "You can send someone up to the tower to check, although I doubt he will welcome the interruption. He will not be pleased that you have doubted the queen's word."

The guard hesitated, clearly conflicted, before stepping back to let her through.

"Very well, m'lady," he replied with a curt nod.

Ermenilda strode out of Tamworth without a backward glance, and once again, Wynflaed had to run to keep up with her.

"Milady!" she panted. "You are not yourself this morning . . . what is amiss?"

"Please, Wynflaed. I know you mean well," Ermenilda replied gently, "but I would rather not speak of it."

She did not look Wynflaed's way. Like Aethelthryth, Wynflaed was only concerned for her well-being, but Ermenilda could not bear to see the worry in Wynflaed's eyes.

Instead, Ermenilda kept her gaze firmly focused on the path ahead that led down to where the Tame slid past. After such a heavy downpour, which was showing no signs of letting up, the river had swollen, its edges creeping up the reed-covered banks. Wynflaed, perhaps sensing her mistress's fragility, said nothing more.

They had walked a little way south, following the banks of the Tame. The rain fell steadily, and despite her thick fur mantle, Ermenilda could feel the damp soaking through to her woolen tunic underneath. Soon, they left the walls of Tamworth behind. A small copse of birch appeared to the right of the riverbank, while up ahead, Ermenilda spied a tall, leafy plant growing near the water.

"I shall collect some lovage," she told Wynflaed. "Why don't you see if you can find any fennel in the woods?"

"I'll probably have more luck finding some near the river," Wynflaed replied.

"I think I saw some growing among the trees when we were foraging a few days ago," Ermenilda insisted, waving her maid away. "Go on, I will be here."

With a silent look of reproach, Wynflaed did as bade, turning right into the copse. When her maid had disappeared from sight, Ermenilda let out the trembling breath she had been holding.

It's time.

Wynflaed stopped in the midst of the trees and sighed. She had no idea where Ermenilda had seen fennel growing, but it certainly was not here. The aniseed-flavored herb did not usually grow in woodland anyway, preferring the margins of meadows and hillsides, or the dry edges of riverbanks.

This is futile.

Wynflaed swung her basket around and pushed her sodden woolen cowl off her head. It was soaked through, and she could not get any wetter than she was already.

She scraped her wet hair back from her face and glanced up at the leaden sky above the trees.

It was folly to come out foraging in this weather.

Wynflaed turned on her heel and made her way back through the silver-barked birches toward the river. She knew that she had not spent long searching for fennel, but she was not happy leaving her mistress alone, even for a short while.

Moments later, she emerged from the copse, near where she had left Ermenilda.

Where is she?

Wynflaed's gaze traveled to the tall growth of lovage, its leaves gleaming in the rain. The queen was nowhere to be seen. Wynflaed looked farther up the riverbank to where a large weeping willow draped its branches over the rushing water.

There, on the edge of the bank, was Ermenilda's basket.

Wynflaed's breathing quickened.

"Milady!" she called out.

Only the hiss of the rain and the dull roar of the swollen river answered her.

Wynflaed ran along the bank, her heart hammering in her chest.

"Ermenilda!"

Wynflaed slid down the bank, to where the basket lay on its side. When she looked around her, there was no sign of its owner.

Then, Wynflaed saw it.

Ermenilda's fur cloak, floating down river, no more than ten yards away.

"Ermenilda!"

The cloak had spread out, like a bird opening its wings and about to take flight. Icy panic gripped Wynflaed. Was Ermenilda under that cloak?

Wynflaed could not swim, and so she scrambled back up the bank and tried to follow the cloak, hoping to catch a sign of her mistress. The Tame, usually a lazy flow, moved swiftly this morning.

Within moments, the mantle was lost from sight.

Wynflaed was on the brink of hysteria by the time she reached the Great Tower of Tamworth. Her breath came in short, exhausted gasps, and her lungs felt as if they were on fire. She had long ceased to notice the rain, or the fact that she was soaked through.

Gasping with effort, she sprinted across the yard in front of the Great Tower. She was just a few yards away from the steps when she slipped and fell, facedown, in the mud.

Hot tears trickled down her cheeks as she tried to regain her footing. However, her skirts were sodden and tangled around her legs.

"Wynflaed?"

Strong arms fastened under her armpits and lifted her to her feet. Wynflaed looked up into Elfhere's concerned face, and the last shreds of her self-control dissolved. She began to sob.

"Thunor's hammer, you're soaked through. What's wrong?"

"Lady Ermenilda," Wynflaed gasped the words, barely coherent. "I've lost her."

Chapter Twenty-seven
The Search

Wulfhere ran from the hall, with Mōna at his heels. He descended the steps to the stable yard, taking them three at a time.

His wife's maid had just finished her garbled account of Ermenilda's disappearance, but he did not wait to hear more.

"Saddle your horses!" he roared at his men. "We ride out now!"

Inside the stables, he swung the saddle onto his stallion's back and tightened the girth. Nearby, Elfhere and Werbode did the same, but he barely registered their presence.

I have to find her.

They rode out of Tamworth in a storm of flying hooves.

Wulfhere sent half his men along the western bank of the Tame, while he took the other half across the bridge and rode along the eastern bank, where Wynflaed had seen Ermenilda's cloak. They had brought hounds with them, although the rain would make it difficult to track her scent.

Wulfhere focused entirely on the task. He would not let himself think or feel. He just had to find her. There was no other option.

Yet, he did not find her.

He rode for furlongs, following the course of the Tame as it wound its way south. He waded through the rush-filled water, shouting his wife's name.

"Ermenilda!"

His voice just echoed back at him, cruelly mocking. Never had Wulfhere felt so helpless, and the sensation filled him with rage. If he could, he would have ripped the world apart with his bare hands.

They eventually found Ermenilda's fine rabbit-skin mantle. It had washed up among the reeds on the eastern bank—but there was no sign of the woman who had been wearing it. Still, the rain beat down, ceaseless as if the gods were all weeping.

Wulfhere searched for Ermenilda until dusk fell. With the bad weather, night seemed to come upon them swiftly. One moment, they were riding through the gray gloaming; the next, night's heavy curtain had fallen.

The king and his men made camp above the river, on higher ground in case it burst its banks overnight. They stretched out a hide awning between two oaks and sat upon a leather groundsheet, to protect them from the damp. It was too wet to light a fire, and they had left so quickly that there had been no time to gather provisions.

Wulfhere had no appetite anyway.

He sat at the edge of his men, barely aware of their low conversation, as if they were being careful not to disturb him. Mōna, ever faithful, sat at his feet. In search of comfort, he reached out and stroked her soft ears. Sensing his turmoil, the wolf pressed close to her master.

A long night lay between Wulfhere and his wife. He wanted to take comfort in her being out there somewhere, lost, cold, and alone. But the obvious thought—one that would not have been lost upon his men—was that she had drowned. Wulfhere could not let himself entertain that thought, not for a moment. For the next thought would be that she had deliberately waded into that river and taken her own life.

Wulfhere took a deep, shuddering breath and squeezed his eyes shut.

No, she can't be lost forever. I will find her.

Even though he willed those words to be true—praying to Woden, Thunor, and Freya for it to be so—a leaden weight in the center of his chest warned him otherwise.

They followed the Tame for two more days, before giving up the search. The dogs never picked up Ermenilda's scent, and there was no sign of her body in the river. The Tame eventually cut west, flowing toward the green wooded borderland between Mercia and Powys, a wild land of scattered villages and thick forest.

Wulfhere and his men crossed the river and began their journey home. Along the way, they stopped at villages and asked if anyone had seen a slender, blonde woman with dark-brown eyes. None had.

Wulfhere spoke to no one on the ride home. He withdrew into his own pain, and the sinking realization that the thing he feared most had happened.

Ermenilda had drowned.

She had taken her own life.

She had done it to escape him.

Wulfhere tortured himself with memories of how he had treated her on the night of the victory feast. He had been angry, and he had used her before humiliating her. The stricken look upon her face as she huddled naked upon the furs tormented him. He had gone too far—unleashed the beast within—and wyrd had punished him.

Back in Tamworth, Wulfhere discovered that the second search party had been no luckier than his. The last of his hope shattered—he had been so sure the other party would find her. A somber mood settled over the Great Tower of Tamworth.

Aethelthryth broke down when she saw the king return empty-handed.

"No!" Her wails echoed high into the rafters, grating on Wulfhere's already jagged nerves. "Not my beautiful niece. My pure of heart Ermenilda!"

She turned on Wulfhere, heedless of her own safety.

"This is your fault!" she screamed. "You did not deserve a wife such as Ermenilda. This is punishment for your evil ways!"

Wulfhere turned to his brother, who had risen to his feet on the high seat upon seeing the king enter.

"Keep this woman out of my sight, Aethelred," he ordered, "or I will not be responsible for my actions."

Aethelred nodded before moving across to Aethelthryth. When he reached out to take her arm, she turned on him.

"Maggot spawn!" she screamed, slapping him hard across the face. "Don't you dare touch me!"

Thin lipped, his pale gaze glittering with anger, the prince grabbed her by the arm, twisted it behind her back, and marched her off the high seat. Aethelthryth fought him all the way, kicking and scratching. When his brother finally managed to manhandle her into an alcove, Wulfhere inhaled deeply.

Aethelthryth's shrill voice was still echoing through the hall, but at least he did not have to see the hatred on her face. He already had enough self-loathing to fill the entire world.

Wulfhere stumbled across to the high seat, his limbs leaden with exhaustion.

"Mead!" he croaked. He was not usually a heavy drinker, but today he wished to drown himself in mead until oblivion took him.

His wife's maid, Wynflaed, brought him a large jug of mead and a cup, wordlessly setting it down before him before she took a hasty step back to the edge of the high seat. The young woman's pretty face was red and puffy from crying, her green eyes glistening from unshed tears.

"Milord," she murmured, her voice quivering with grief. "I am so sorry—"

"Leave me," Wulfhere snarled. He had not focused his anger upon Wynflaed, although it would be all too easy to lay the blame for Ermenilda's loss at her feet.

Tears spilled down Wynflaed's cheeks, but she heeded him. Wulfhere ignored her departure, instead pouring a large cup of mead and draining it immediately.

The pain inside him was still there, pulsing like a hot coal, and so he poured another cup. And another. He drank until the sharp edges of the world receded, and he felt wrapped in a cocoon of soft wool. Only even then, he did not forget.

He would never forget.

Chapter Twenty-eight
Hild

Ermenilda awoke to find water dripping on her face from the leaves above. She had slept under a spreading oak, too exhausted to go any farther.

Blinking, she sat up and stretched, groaning at how stiff and sore her limbs were. Yesterday had been endless, a panicked flight from Tamworth that had taken all her strength to endure. She had spent most of the day glancing over her shoulder, sure that at any moment Wulfhere would appear out of the mist on horseback, his wolf running at his side, and drag her back home.

However, the day had stretched out, and night had fallen without any sign of those she knew would be out searching for her.

It's too early for me to relax, she reminded herself, getting to her feet and brushing leaves off her clothing. *I won't be able to do so until I'm far from here.*

Ermenilda glanced around at her surroundings, taking note of where she stood. She had been too tired last night to pay any attention to where she was or to care.

This morning, she realized that she stood in the midst of an oak thicket. The rain had ceased overnight, although a heavy curtain of cloud lay thick over the land, and mist snaked like wood smoke through the trees. The sun had just risen to the east, and Ermenilda tried to guess, as she had done yesterday after leaving the river, which direction was southwest.

Bonehill Abbey lay to the southwest.

Apart from those directions, Seaxwulf had given her little else to go on. She could only hope that she was taking the right path.

Her belly rumbled, reminding Ermenilda that she had not eaten since her two mouthfuls of bread with her broth the previous morning. She had no water either, although she had managed to scoop some out of leaves the night before. She did so again now, just in case she did not come across a waterway during her journey.

After slaking her thirst, she set off through the thicket. She wound her way through the trees till the oaks drew back and she made her way over bare, windswept hills. The clouds were so low here that she could only guess she was traveling in the right direction.

Damp mist swirled around Ermenilda, clinging to her bare arms. She was fortunate to have made her escape in high summer or she would have died of exposure by now, especially without her fur mantle. Even so, the dampness chilled her, and she kept up a brisk pace to ensure she kept warm.

As she walked, Ermenilda's thoughts traveled back to the moment she had made her escape.

She had not wanted to deceive Wynflaed.

The girl was loyal and bighearted, but she would never have let Ermenilda run away without raising the alarm. Even so, Ermenilda had known that Wynflaed would not leave her alone at the river's edge for long, so the moment her handmaid disappeared into the trees, Ermenilda had acted.

She had sprinted up the riverbank and unslung her cloak, before throwing it out into the midst of the Tame. Her mantle billowed in the air before settling upon the swirling water. Then, it began to move downriver.

Ermenilda had dropped her basket at the river's edge and had begun to run. She followed the river for about a furlong, before cutting southwest into woodland—and had not stopped running since.

I hope he does not blame Wynflaed.

The worry, which had surfaced shortly after Ermenilda had made her escape, returned to plague her. Wulfhere's rage would be terrible when he discovered his wife missing. Ermenilda only hoped that he would think she had drowned herself in the river.

If he thinks I have run off, he will never stop hunting me.

The thought made Ermenilda quicken her step even further.

The morning drew out, and Ermenilda's rumbling belly turned into a hard knot of hunger. She started to feel faint and wondered how much farther she would be able to go on. Unused to walking so far, her limbs felt leaden, and her feet now throbbed.

Seaxwulf had told her that Bonehill was a day's journey on horseback from Tamworth. Ermenilda had been traveling on foot since yesterday morning. Surely, she could not be far away from her destination.

It was nearing noon when she came across a small hamlet at the end of a shallow, windswept valley. It was tiny—a scattering of thatched huts around a trickling brook. Sheep grazed on the hillside as she made her way toward the settlement. Their bleating did not travel far on this misty, windless day.

I must be careful, she warned herself. *They must not know who I am. They must not suspect I have run away.*

Ermenilda made her way toward the nearest dwelling, which lay on the farthest edge of the hamlet, apart from the other houses. She could see it was the home of a poor man, with a thatched roof in dire need of repair.

As she approached, a boy emerged from the dwelling. He carried an empty pail, clearly on his way to collect water from the brook. When he saw Ermenilda, he stopped short.

The boy stared, his eyes growing huge. Ermenilda gave him an encouraging smile and was about to greet him when the boy opened his mouth.

"Ma!" he shouted, his gaze never leaving Ermenilda. "There's someone here!"

A woman's voice, slightly irritated, responded. "Who is it, Eglaf?"

"It's a lady," the boy replied. "A stranger."

Ermenilda heard the shuffling of feet from inside the dwelling, and moments later, a young woman, around her own age, emerged. The woman was slender and blonde, like Ermenilda, but the similarities ended there. She was dressed in a worn, shapeless tunic. Her face was gaunt, and her eyes had dark circles under them. Ermenilda could see the woman should have been pretty, but hardship had drained the youth from her face.

The gaze that met Ermenilda's was not friendly.

"What do you want?"

"I'm sorry to trouble you," Ermenilda replied, keeping her voice gentle, "but I'm traveling to Bonehill Abbey and seem to have lost my way. Can you point me in the right direction?"

The woman's mouth thinned, and she looked Ermenilda up and down, as if she was making her mind up about her.

"You're not that lost," she admitted grudgingly. She jerked her head behind her, to where the brook trailed its way west. "The abbey sits at the other end of this valley, around half an afternoon's walk."

Hope rose in Ermenilda's breast. She had feared she had been unwittingly traveling farther and farther from her destination, but instead she was closer than she realized.

"I thank you," she said, smiling. The young woman merely stared back at her, blank faced.

Ermenilda did not want to leave things like that. She could see the woman was unhappy. By the looks of things, she and her boy lived alone, and Ermenilda wanted to help in some way.

"Here . . ." She reached up and removed the amber necklace from around her neck. It was a rich gift, but she would not need wealth where she was going. The necklace, which Wulfhere had given to her as a morning gift, was also a link to her husband. Now that she had escaped, she wished to cast off any reminders of their life together.

Ermenilda stepped forward and offered the woman the pendant.

"Please take this for your kindness."

The woman's eyes went as wide as her boy's had when he had spotted Ermenilda.

"I only gave you directions."

"You've helped me greatly."

The woman took the necklace and tucked it away in her pocket, almost as if she expected its giver to snatch it back.

Ermenilda smiled once more, wishing she could do more to help this woman and her son, and stepped back. She was just about to bid her farewell when the young woman spoke again.

"Are you hungry?"

Ermenilda hesitated before nodding.

"I can give you some bread and boiled eggs to take with you," the young woman said, motioning to her front door. "My name's Myra, by the way. Follow me and I'll get them for you."

Ermenilda did as bade, following the woman into the smoky, dimly lit interior. It was a tiny dwelling and unadorned, yet Ermenilda could see the dirt floor had been swept clean, and the wooden worktable near the fire pit had been scrubbed. The boy followed them inside, his gaze glued to Ermenilda.

"Eglaf, go fetch that water," Myra ordered, ushering him away. "Stop gaping at our guest!"

The boy did as he was told, although not without one more stolen glance at their guest. Ermenilda smothered a smile and watched the woman cut a thick slice off a loaf of coarse bread. Although his mother regarded their guest with curiosity, no doubt wondering over her rich dress and highborn speech, the lad did not bother to hide his fascination.

"It's good to see Eglaf show interest in something," Myra said. "Ever since his father died, he has been so withdrawn. I have worried for him."

The grief on the young woman's face was evident; it was clearly a fresh wound.

"What happened?" The question was out before Ermenilda could prevent it, but Myra did not appear offended.

"He was a king's man," she said quietly, looking down at the slab of bread she had just cut, "and would spend periods away from us. But, he was earning the gold he needed to give me and Eglaf a better life, so I understood."

Ermenilda nodded. It was the unfortunate lot of many lowborn women to keep the home fires burning while her man labored elsewhere.

"It happened while he was riding back from the Kingdom of the Kentish," Myra continued. "It was only an escort, bringing back the king and his betrothed, but they were attacked. Earic died on Saxon lands, and they burned his body there."

Ermenilda stared at the young woman. The air was warm and close inside the dwelling, but a chill settled over her. Earic had been one of Wulfhere's warriors—one of the many who died on that bridge.

"I am sorry, Myra," she managed finally, "for you and Eglaf."

The young woman gave her a tired smile before reaching for a square of linen. She wrapped the bread up with two hard-boiled eggs, still in their shells. She passed the bundle to Ermenilda, along with a bladder of water.

"As am I," she replied. "I loved him very much."

A weighty silence fell, and Ermenilda was at a loss for words. She had no idea what to say, for she did not want to fill the silence with empty, trite platitudes. So, she said nothing.

Myra did not appear to notice or mind. She followed Myra outside into the misty daylight and saw Eglaf toiling toward them with a bucketful of water. He was walking so fast it was sloshing over the side and soaking his breeches. Ermenilda turned to Myra.

"Thank you for the food and drink."

"It should see you through to Bonehill," the woman answered with another brittle smile.

Ermenilda left mother and son and made her way around their cottage before she continued west. She glanced over her shoulder once and saw they stood side by side watching her go. A strange sensation needled her. Was it guilt? Surely not. She was not responsible for Earic's death. But her mother and aunt were . . . and she was kin.

Ermenilda quickened her step and did not look back again.

She reached Bonehill Abbey in the late afternoon.

It had been a much easier walk, especially with a full belly, compared to the morning's march. Knowing that her destination lay ahead made it easier for her to remain focused. She was now far enough away from Tamworth that she had started to relax a little.

As Myra had told her, the abbey sat at the far end of the valley, in the cradle of low hills. A tall palisade surrounded it, and from the hillside above, Ermenilda could see that it was a decent-size structure. There was an older timbered building at the front and two larger wings on either side made of stone farther back. Around the buildings, Ermenilda could make out trees, shrubs, and an extensive garden.

Her vision blurred with tears.

Finally.

Nearly running in her haste, Ermenilda descended the hillside and made her way to the gates. There were no guards here—not in a holy place—just high gates with a hatch where the nuns could greet visitors. A bell hung from a chain next to the gates, and Ermenilda rang it.

She waited awhile for someone to come. While she waited, Ermenilda stole a nervous look around her. It was an exposed valley, despite the encircling mist, and she suddenly felt vulnerable standing out here on her own.

Eventually, she heard footfalls beyond the gate. Moments later, the hatch slowly slid open to reveal a woman's face. She was of middle years, with sharp blue eyes. Her voice, when she spoke, was clipped.

"What is it?"

"I have come to take my vows," Ermenilda replied with as much dignity as she could muster.

The woman frowned, her gaze traveling over Ermenilda before it scanned the area behind her. "Did you travel here on your own?"

Ermenilda nodded. "My husband was a king's thegn. When he died, my family wanted me to remarry, but I refused. They told me that if I wished to become a nun, I would have to travel here on my own."

The woman looked horrified, her sternness dissolving.

"But you have no cloak, no one to protect you!"

Ermenilda gave the woman a pained look. "They are cruel . . . but I was determined to reach you."

Her words had the desired effect, for the woman stepped back, drew the hatch shut, and unbolted the gate—opening it just far enough for Ermenilda to enter.

She stepped into another world. Outside, it was gray, bleak, and shadowy; but inside the walls of Bonehill Abbey, it was lush green and the air smelt of wild herbs. Ermenilda could hear the trickle of water flowing—the brook she had lost sight of earlier resurfaced here. She could also hear the chant of women's voices, the nuns at Vespers. She had stepped into a wide courtyard lined with urns of rosemary, lavender, and thyme. The oldest part of the abbey, the wooden hall, lay before them.

Ermenilda remembered her manners and tore her gaze from the beauty of her surroundings, focusing upon the woman before her. She was roughly the same height as Ermenilda, so it was easy to meet her eye.

The nun wore a gray habit of coarse linen, girded at the waist by a length of rope. Upon her bosom, which even under her shapeless habit was impressive, lay a beautiful rosewood crucifix.

A white veil shrouded her hair from view, similar to the more elaborate headrail that both Ermenilda's mother and aunt wore. Unlike a headrail, which draped across the wearer's shoulders, this nun had tucked her veil into the neck of her habit, so that only her face was visible. Upon her feet, she wore rope sandals.

Perhaps the woman noticed Ermenilda's scrutiny of her, for she smiled.

"I am Abbess Ardwyn of Bonehill," she said pleasantly. "And what is your name, child?"

Ermenilda met her gaze, only pausing for a moment before she made her decision. Her new life would start here, with a new identity.

"Hild," she replied.

Chapter Twenty-nine
Lost

Wynflaed finished winding the wool in her basket onto her distaff. The spindle was full, and she would have to start on another—and another still—when that one was done. It was tedious, repetitive work, but she welcomed it.

She would have worked at her distaff day and night for the rest of her life if it would bring Ermenilda back.

Inhaling deeply, as she struggled not to weep, Wynflaed looked across the hall. Her gaze rested upon the high seat. She had been trying not to look in that direction, but eventually the pull had been too great.

The king was still there, seated upon his carved chair. Dressed in leather breeches and a sweat-stained woolen tunic, his pale hair in disarray, Wulfhere stared vacantly at the scarred top of the oaken table before him. Wynflaed could see the despair etched into his face; the skin had drawn tight across his cheekbones, giving him a wild appearance. His gaze was hooded, dangerous.

I am so sorry.

He had not appreciated her one attempt at apologizing, so Wynflaed resisted the urge to go before the king once more and beg forgiveness. Wisdom told her it was best to keep out of Lord Wulfhere's way for now. Eventually, he would emerge from his fog of pain and would be looking for someone to blame.

She would have her chance to plead for mercy then.

Wynflaed shuddered, suddenly cold despite that she sat next to the fire pit. There was no one else to blame but her, and, sooner or later, the king would realize that.

I need some air.

Wynflaed put her distaff aside and rose to her feet. Highborn women worked nearby at their distaffs or weaving at looms, their whispering and pointed stares following her. Ignoring them, she retrieved her basket and a woolen shawl, and headed toward the door.

"And where do you think you're going?"

One of the women cried out, her shrill voice echoing across the hall. Her name was Burghild; she was a tall, angular woman with lank blonde hair.

"Shirking your duties again are you?"

Wynflaed squared her shoulders and ignored her. She did not fear the wrath of a thegn's wife. It was the king's rage that she dreaded.

Outside, the afternoon was bright and breezy. The air smelled of grass and warm earth, and Wynflaed could hear the squeals of children playing in the streets below.

In other circumstances, such a day would have delighted her, but today Wynflaed barely took it in. Leaving the Great Tower behind, she made her way down through Tamworth's winding streets to the low gate. It was the same route she had taken with Ermenilda three days earlier. Although, the guards did not try to prevent her from going out without an escort this time.

I am merely a servant, she thought, emptiness settling within her. *No one would notice if I walked out of here and never came back.*

Wynflaed did not intend to leave Tamworth.

Where would I go?

Neither could she entertain the thought of taking her own life, as her mistress had evidently done.

Lost in thought, she walked down to the banks of the Tame. The river had slowed since the heavy rain had ceased and almost turned back to its gentle self. Without even realizing she was doing so, Wynflaed found herself retracing her steps along the riverbank, where she and Ermenilda had walked.

When she reached the point where she had spied the queen's cloak, Wynflaed stopped.

How could she have done it?

Wynflaed's mind raced as she tried to grasp just how unhappy Ermenilda must have been to have thrown herself into those swirling waters. She struggled to understand, but she just could not. Ermenilda was too strong, too defiant, to throw her life away. Wynflaed had thought she would fight for longer.

Was marriage to Wulfhere so terrible?

Wynflaed was so engrossed in her thoughts that she did not hear footfalls behind her. She started slightly when a man's voice interrupted her brooding.

"Thinking about how you could have prevented it?"

Wynflaed whirled around to find Elfhere standing a few feet behind her. Clad in light linen breeches and tunic, he looked cool and disturbingly attractive. His golden hair was unbound today, and it flowed over his bare shoulders. His blue eyes—usually laughing or teasing—were clouded with concern.

"I was thinking about how unhappy a soul must be to consider such a thing," she replied.

Elfhere nodded, stepping closer. "I don't understand it either . . . but you mustn't blame yourself."

Bitterness closed Wynflaed's throat. "Mustn't I? The king will."

Elfhere gave her a long, measured look before answering.

"It is himself he will blame . . . not you."

"But I—"

"Listen—you couldn't have stopped her."

"If I had known—"

"You didn't."

They stood there for a moment, their gazes fused, until Wynflaed realized how close they were standing. Elfhere was close enough that she could feel the heat of his body, and she inhaled the masculine musk of his skin. Distracted, she took a step back from him. Elfhere noticed her deliberate attempt to distance herself.

"You cannot run from me forever, Wynflaed," he said gently, his gaze never leaving hers.

Wynflaed gasped. "Hwæt?"

"What are you scared of?"

Heat rose in the center of Wynflaed's chest, flowering outward. She wanted to run now, but her feet felt as if they had driven roots into the soil.

Elfhere took a step toward her, closing the gap between them once more. He reached out and gently stroked her cheek.

"Surely, you know I would never hurt you."

"I know no such thing," she whispered, trembling under his touch.

"I would cherish you."

Wynflaed stopped breathing. His nearness was making her dizzy. She wanted to believe him, but she had seen what happened to girls who trusted in men too easily.

One of her elder sisters had fallen into the arms of a warrior a few years before. One of the king's men, he had been as charming and handsome as Elfhere. It had not prevented him from washing his hands of his lover when her womb quickened with his babe.

Wynflaed had watched her sister's humiliation and despair. She had also seen the way her parents eagerly gave her sister to the only man who wanted her—a tanner in Cantwareburh who had already buried three wives and wanted another to use his fists on. It was then that Wynflaed had decided she would never let a man deceive her with honeyed words and melting looks.

Still, Elfhere tempted her sorely. He was watching now with such longing in his eyes that she felt an answering ache deep within her.

Elfhere smiled. "You are strong and free, Wynflaed," he said gently. "I would never seek to change that—but I would make you mine before another man steals you from me."

"I'm not a piglet some brute can run away with under his arm!" she retorted, although his words made warmth steal through her.

"But would you be mine?"

She heard the sincerity in his voice, the tremor of emotion there as he struggled to maintain his composure. The last walls of resistance crumbled, and Wynflaed nodded.

"I would."

No more words were needed. With a grin of relief, Elfhere stepped forward and gathered her against him. His mouth came down possessively over hers, and he kissed her.

***

Wulfhere stepped inside the garden and closed the wattle gate behind him. It was the first time he had set foot here in months, for he had not visited Ermenilda's garden since early spring. It had been her private place, and he had sensed she had not wanted him to disturb it.

That did not matter now.

Pebbles crunched underfoot as Wulfhere slowly made his way up the path in between beds of kale, comfrey, leeks, and turnips. The garden, now verdant and overflowing with produce, bore no resemblance to the bare rectangle of land he had presented to his wife months earlier.

He remembered the look of joy upon her face, her surprise, when he had brought her here. He had thought that moment had been the turning point—the moment when her feelings toward him would thaw.

They had begun to . . . until he had set out to seek reckoning against her aunt.

Wulfhere sat heavily down upon a narrow stone bench.

He could still feel Ermenilda's presence here. It was like stepping inside a huge tapestry woven by a master weaver. The fruit and vegetables growing around him were all his wife's creations and had thrived under her skilled hand.

A lump lodged in Wulfhere's throat. He felt sick, as if a serpent slithered and coiled itself in the pit of his belly. He could scarcely believe she was gone; the reality of it had not yet sunk in. There was no body to mourn over, no way of knowing if she was really dead. He had scoured that river from one end to the other and sent men out to search the surrounding lands. There had been no sign of Ermenilda anywhere.

She was truly lost.

Wulfhere looked down at his hands before clenching them into fists. She had been his, but ever since coming to live at Tamworth, Ermenilda had slowly slipped through his fingers like sand. He had not been able to hold on to her.

His father had taught him that owning something was all that mattered. One owned men, slaves . . . and a wife. Even sons and daughters were a man's possessions.

Wulfhere was not like his father. He had wanted more than just ownership of Ermenilda; he had wanted her soul. Penda had been fortunate in his choice of wife. He and Cyneswide had been happy together. Cyneswide had accepted who her husband was and loved him despite his flaws. In contrast, Ermenilda had hated who Wulfhere was, and he had done nothing to improve her opinion of him.

Wulfhere exhaled slowly. It hurt to breathe.

He was glad his father was not alive to see the mess he had made of things. Not that Penda would have helped matters. He had not accepted defiance in anyone, least of all women.

A breeze rippled through the garden, lifting the scent off the roses and carrying it to Wulfhere. It smelled like the lotion that Ermenilda used on her face in the evenings. The scent brought back memories of her: seated next to him upon the high seat, bent over sewing next to the fire pit, chatting to Wynflaed as she helped the cooks prepare a special meal, or naked beneath him as he rode her.

Ermenilda may not have loved him, but he did her. Yet, he had never told her—and now he would never have the chance to do so.

This realization bit into him, sharp and cruel, and, finally, Wulfhere could bear it no longer.

He lowered his head into his hands and wept.

PART THREE

Three months later . . .

Chapter Thirty
A Nun's Life

Bonehill Abbey, The Kingdom of Mercia

Ermenilda awoke, heart pounding, drenched in sweat. Breathing hard, she sat up and stared into the darkness.

Jesu, not again.

She had not awoken from a nightmare. Instead, she had just emerged from a wickedly erotic dream. Even though she was now awake, her limbs trembled, her breasts ached, and there was a dull throb between her thighs.

Wulfhere had visited her in her dreams yet again.

She did not want this, did not ask for it, but still he persisted. This dream had been the most vivid so far. They had been in a forest glade at night and both of them were naked, their clothes strewn around them in abandon. Wulfhere had taken her hard, up against a tree trunk, and she had cried out hoarsely each time he thrust within her. The night air had been cold on her skin, the bark rough on her bare back, but she had cared not. Wrapping her legs around his waist, she had drawn him deeper still, crying his name as he ground his hips against hers.

Ermenilda clutched the crucifix about her neck and sat up upon her straw-stuffed sleeping pallet. Around her, the other four novices appeared to be still sleeping. Ermenilda broke out in a cold sweat at the thought that she may have made noises in her sleep. She prayed that she had not.

This has to stop.

How could she prevent these treacherous dreams that struck without warning and unsettled her for days afterward? Perhaps this was her penance, her punishment, for running away from Tamworth, letting everyone think she was dead, and then lying to the abbess about her identity.

Ermenilda listened to the far off howl of a distant wolf and despaired.

Did I really think I could lay my past to rest? He can find me, even here.

The dawn eventually broke, but memories of that dream plagued Ermenilda still. The rumble of his voice in her ear distracted her as she recited her prayers during Prime. The touch of his fingers sliding down the naked skin of her back made her shiver.

It is just the morning's chill, she told herself before attempting to focus upon her prayers. *Nothing more.*

Indeed, the days were growing cooler. Soon, Winterfylleth—the season that marked the change between summer and winter—would be upon them. However, the damp chill that rose from the floor where she knelt had nothing to do with the tremor that ran through her body.

It was a relief when Prime ended and Ermenilda followed the other nuns into the hall where they took their meals. The novices sat at a smaller table—Aeleva, Mildburh, Brynflaed, and Bertana had been Ermenilda's companions since her arrival here. The professed nuns, a group of around twenty, sat at a longer table on the other side of the glowing fire pit.

The food they broke their fast with was simple—meat broth and coarse bread—but it suited Ermenilda well enough. She enjoyed the simplicity of her life here, even if she found herself missing Wynflaed's irreverence and laughter. Life at Bonehill could be very solemn at times.

After their fast had been broken, the nuns all began their daily chores. There was much to be done to keep the abbey running. As one of the novices, Ermenilda worked tirelessly from dawn to dusk. Often, she would stumble onto her pallet at the end of the day, so exhausted that she fell asleep the moment she lay down upon it.

Even her tiredness could not prevent the dreams that stole upon her while she slept.

This morning, Ermenilda helped wash clothes. She and Mildburh scrubbed and lathered habits and undertunics and dried linens outside, next to the babbling brook.

It was hot work, although the overcast sky above and chill wind helped cool the sweat from their brows. Ermenilda had never been idle before coming here—for even highborn women had to keep themselves busy—but the sheer physicality of her chores had strengthened the muscles in her shoulders, back, and arms.

She and Mildburh spoke little as they worked. The young woman was reserved to the point of appearing withdrawn, and Ermenilda found herself missing Wynflaed's easy company once more. Their task took them all morning, although by the time the bell rang for Sext, they had managed to hang the last of the washing on the line at the back of the abbey.

After the noon service, the sisters ate their main meal of the day. Once again, it was simple fare: boiled mutton with turnips served with more coarse bread and washed down with a cup of water. The nuns drank no wine, ale, or mead. The occasional cup of goat's milk was considered a real treat.

Ermenilda preferred the afternoons at Bonehill, for they reminded her of the time she had spent in her garden at Tamworth. During this time, she helped one of the professed nuns, an older woman called Cyneswide, to tend the garden.

The garden at Bonehill was so large that there was plenty to keep them busy, with no two days' work the same. Some afternoons they would tend the bees they kept in hives at the far north of the grounds; other days they would weed the vegetable beds or trim the shrubbery.

This afternoon, they were harvesting vegetables. Summer was ending, and a glut of produce would have to be preserved or stored for the coming winter.

Ermenilda busied herself pulling up leeks while Cyneswide harvested cabbages in the bed beside her. They had been working in companionable silence for a short while when Cyneswide spoke to Ermenilda.

"Sister Hild, you seem distracted today. Is anything amiss?"

Surprised, Ermenilda looked up from her work. She had thought that she had hidden her unease well, but Sister Cyneswide, ever observant, had still seen it.

Ermenilda hesitated a moment, considering whether to deny her observation. However, the older woman's face was guileless, her clear blue eyes filled with concern.

Life could be lonely here at times, even surrounded by other women. The other nuns revealed very little of their lives before coming to Bonehill, and conversation centered on the daily tasks that kept the abbey running. Sometimes, Ermenilda longed for someone to confide in. She did not intend to reveal her identity, for that would have been foolish.

What could it hurt to answer honestly?

"Memories of my past life sometimes trouble me," she admitted. "Of my husband."

Cyneswide nodded, before she gave a sad smile.

"I too am a widow. My husband died over three years ago, but never a day goes by when I don't miss him."

Ermenilda watched the nun curiously. She knew nothing of Sister Cyneswide's life before Bonehill. Judging from her stately bearing, fine manners, and measured speech, she was highborn. Ermenilda guessed she had been an ealdorman's wife, and a high-standing one at that.

"I wish I could forget the past," Ermenilda replied. "A nun is supposed to leave all of her earthly worries behind. I do not wish to remember my husband."

Cyneswide frowned. "Was he cruel to you?"

Ermenilda remembered the scorn on Wulfhere's face after he had taken her that day, the sting of his words. However, that was the only time he had been harsh with her. She could not say he had been cruel, for most of the time he had treated her gently.

She shook her head. "No, but I did not like who he was, how he treated others. He was a godless man."

"My late husband was harsh and cold, but not with me," Cyneswide revealed. "Over years, I often disagreed with his behavior, his actions, but I would never have dared tell him so. I loved him anyway."

Ermenilda yanked a leek out of the ground and brushed soil off its roots.

"That's where we differ, Sister Cyneswide," she replied, suddenly envious of the affection that the nun still clearly bore her dead spouse. "I told my husband every time he displeased me. I did not wed for love."

Cyneswide gave her an arch look.

"And yet, he is in your thoughts."

Ermenilda was introspective and withdrawn for the rest of the day. She recited her prayers woodenly at Vespers and did not join in the conversation at supper about the baking, salting, and drying of food many of the nuns had spent the day doing, in preparation for the long winter.

Instead, she mulled over her conversation with Sister Cyneswide. The older nun's words bothered her.

Irritated, Ermenilda stabbed her fruit knife deep into the flesh of the apple she was coring.

Wulfhere had worked a strange magic upon her—a spell that addled her mind and turned her will to porridge. It appeared that he still wielded that power over her, even though they were no longer together. His memory cast a shadow over her life at Bonehill and prevented her from fully giving herself to god. Abbess Ardwyn would be horrified to discover that one of her charges spent her nights dreaming of the sins of the flesh.

Ermenilda glanced over at the abbess. Seated at the long table, she was deep in conversation with Sister Cyneswide. Everyone here appeared to like Cyneswide, and Ermenilda could see why. She gave you her undivided attention when you spoke—how many people actually did that? Unfortunately, that meant that she saw things you would rather keep hidden, even from yourself.

It will pass in time, Ermenilda reassured herself, stabbing her knife once more into her apple. *He cannot torment me forever.*

Chapter Thirty-one
The Hollow Crown

It was silent in the church, so quiet and still that Wulfhere could hear his own breathing. It was a watchful, expectant silence, and he did not like it.

Wulfhere had stepped inside the cavernous space and walked a few paces across the stone floor when the silence started to bother him. There were a handful of other people here, which surprised him. Seaxwulf had obviously been busy converting the folk of Tamworth to his god. The worshippers knelt near the altar, heads bowed in wordless prayer.

The king stopped, regretting his decision to enter the church. He was about to turn on his heel and leave when Seaxwulf's voice shattered the stillness.

"Lord Wulfhere!"

The priest, clad in a plain brown tunic, girded at the waist with a length of rope, emerged from the shadowed recesses of the church. Wulfhere saw the delight on Seaxwulf's face and realized his mistake.

I should never have come here.

Oblivious of his king's discomfort, Seaxwulf bowed.

"It is a pleasure to welcome you here, milord."

Wulfhere did not respond, and when the silence between them lengthened, the priest filled it.

"After Ēostre, I thought never to see you here again."

Wulfhere frowned. Sometimes, the priest was altogether too frank. Seaxwulf saw his lord's displeasure, and the smile faded from his face.

"I am humbled that you have come."

Wulfhere inhaled deeply and looked around him. He was not sure why he had ventured here. It had been an impulse. He had been thinking about Ermenilda, and his feet had carried him to the church. He missed his wife— and her garden and this church were the only things he had left that reminded him of her.

"Do you wish to pray?" Seaxwulf asked, motioning to the fur upon the stone floor, spread out before the altar, in front of where the other folk knelt. "If you do, I can leave you alone for a while."

Grateful that the priest had finally understood how uncomfortable he felt here, Wulfhere nodded. "Thank you, Seaxwulf."

The priest smiled kindly and with another bow left him.

Wulfhere breathed in the scent of incense and made his way to the altar, stepping around a heavyset man who appeared to be weeping as he prayed.

Things had come full circle, it seemed. He had knelt before the Christian god and allowed himself to be baptized so that he could claim Ermenilda. And here he was, about to kneel before him again now that he had lost her.

Wulfhere grimaced and knelt upon the fur. He glared up at the altar, his gaze fastening upon the iron crucifix perched above him.

Is this my punishment?

Aethelthryth had told him thus, after she learned of Ermenilda's disappearance. He had seen it mirrored silently in her gaze every time their eyes met since.

A god only had power over you if you believed in him. Wulfhere held Woden and his clan close and could not imagine believing in anything else. Ermenilda had been so passionate in her belief, so adamant that he had done something terrible in pretending to believe in the same god in order to wed her. At the time, Wulfhere had dismissed her concerns. What did it matter who he said he believed in? He had what he wanted.

These days, he was not sure he had made the right decision.

Aethelthryth openly blamed him for Ermenilda's death. He could not bring himself to punish her for being so bold—for he too felt he was to blame. He had ignored his wife's wishes, her requests, her pleas, and had done whatever pleased him. He had thought she would just acquiesce and come to accept it after a while.

He was the king. His word was law.

He had not meant to treat her so cruelly the last time he had bedded her, but he had miscalculated just how sensitive and vulnerable his wife was. How he wished he could return in time to that day and unsay those words.

Wulfhere stared up at the crucifix for a moment longer, before dropping his head.

I deserved to lose her.

He had entered new territory, land he was unsure how to cross. He had learned how to be a man and a ruler at his father's knee, but all the things that had once mattered to him seemed empty and meaningless. He had not listened to Ermenilda while she was alive, but he could do so now. He wore a hollow crown, one that bore a bitter reminder of his mistakes.

Wulfhere's gaze focused upon the stone pavers at the foot of the altar.

I will make amends for what I have done.

Wulfhere took a sip of mead, aware that someone was staring at him. He looked up and met Werbode's intense gaze across the table. The warrior had stayed away from him of late, leaving the king to his melancholy while he trained Wulfhere's men and led bands out hunting.

These days, whenever he saw his thegn, Wulfhere sensed Werbode's disdain toward him.

Werbode would never grieve so openly—and so long—over a woman. He had made that clear. He had also made it evident that he considered it a weakness to do so. Wulfhere had ignored him, too entrenched in his misery to care what Werbode thought.

There was little warmth in his thegn's eyes now, just a sharp interest.

"What is it, Werbode?"

"The West Saxons," Werbode replied, his voice a low drawl. "What are you going to do about them?"

Wulfhere held his gaze steadily. He should have expected this conversation was coming. News had arrived two days earlier that the West Saxons were causing problems on Mercia's southwestern border—raiding villages and setting fire to crops. The attacks had been sporadic and would likely die away with the coming of winter, yet Werbode had been incensed.

"I will see if they resume in the spring," Wulfhere replied eventually, before taking another sip of mead. "If they do, we shall deal with it then."

Werbode leaned forward, his dark gaze hardening.

"They must be made an example of." Werbode glanced at Aethelred, as if looking for support, but the prince merely stared back, his expression impassive. Glowering, the thegn fixed his attention on Wulfhere once more. "We should raid their villages, steal their livestock . . . take their children as slaves!"

Wulfhere shook his head. "If the problem worsens, I will act accordingly. But not before."

Werbode made a disgusted sound and sat back, glowering at his king.

Wulfhere watched him, wondering at the man's worsening attitude of late. Their friendship had worn thin, like a rope stretched too tight. Werbode had revered Penda, and when Wulfhere looked set to follow his father's example, the thegn's loyalty had appeared absolute. There was tension between them now—and it grew with each passing month. Wulfhere wondered how much longer he would tolerate Werbode by his side.

Wulfhere tore a chunk off a round of griddle bread and chewed slowly. His visit to the church had made him reflective. Although the fog of sadness had not lifted, he saw the way ahead clearer now. Werbode was merely a distraction, and he would not let the fact that the warrior was spoiling for a fight push him into war with the West Saxons.

Wulfhere had other priorities at this moment.

The king's gaze shifted down the table, past his brother and Elfhere, to the far end where Aethelthryth of Ely sat next to the priest. As always, her posture was prim, her gaze downcast, as she ate. The woman barely suffered her life here and shunned the company of all but Seaxwulf. She attempted to be brave, but Wulfhere could see the unhappiness etched into the lines of her heart-shaped face.

The agony of a proud woman who was being slowly broken.

"You summoned me, milord?"

Aethelthryth stopped before the high seat and dipped her head. In another woman, the gesture would have been respectful, but not in the Lady Aethelthryth of Ely. Her scorn was palpable.

"Yes, Lady Aethelthryth," Wulfhere replied pleasantly, motioning to the seat next to him. "I would speak with you a moment . . . please."

Nearby, Aethelred had taken a seat. The prince had just beaten Werbode at a game of knucklebones. He had left the warrior sulking over a cup of mead at a nearby table. Wulfhere saw the curiosity flare in his brother's eyes.

This was the first time since Ermenilda's disappearance that Wulfhere had spoken directly to Aethelthryth. Usually, he left dealing with the sharp-

tongued and willful widow to his brother—a task
Aethelred had complained loudly over.

Slowly, her body stiff with outrage, Aethelthryth
obeyed him. She stepped up onto the high seat and
perched on the edge of the stool he had offered her.
Wulfhere watched her a moment, noting the way she
stared intently at her clasped hands.

She was an odd female. Full of passion and intensity,
but not the sort of woman that would bring a man any
joy. Was it any wonder that Ermenilda's beliefs had been
so strong, with an aunt such as this?

"Are you well, Aethelthryth?" he asked finally.

"Yes, milord."

"Have we made you comfortable here?"

"Yes."

"And, I trust my brother has not been a brute toward
you?"

Aethelthryth looked up sharply, while Aethelred
made a choked sound behind her.

"You left me in charge of a shrew, brother," Aethelred
muttered.

Wulfhere ignored him, focusing instead on
Aethelthryth.

"He has the manners of a goat," she said coldly, "but
he has not mistreated me."

"Good." Wulfhere steepled his fingers in front of him
and regarded her. "I would not like to hear that you were
mistreated here."

Aethelthryth's finely arched brows shot upward.

"I have decided," Wulfhere said slowly, "that your
time here as my hostage has come to an end."

She stared at him, clearly not believing what she was
hearing. Wulfhere smiled slightly, an expression so rare
these days that it strained his facial muscles.

"I am not playing with you, Lady Aethelthryth.
Tradition dictates that a hostage is only kept as long as a
king desires. Tomorrow, I will organize an escort to

accompany you back to Ely. I will provide you with enough gold to rebuild your church and your town."

Aethelthryth clutched her hands together tightly. Wulfhere could see she was shaking.

"But why?" she whispered.

"The reason does not matter," he replied quietly, "but I will say that I am sorry for the pain you have suffered on my account. My wife begged me not to have my reckoning, and I ignored her at my peril. I cannot undo what has been done, but I will not keep you here against your will any longer."

Wulfhere looked over at Aethelred. "My brother will accompany you, to ensure your safe return to Ely."

His brother's face went slack with shock.

"Hwæt! Can't you send Werbode—or Elfhere?"

Wulfhere shook his head. He held his brother's gaze steadily, aware that others around them—including Werbode—were now listening to their conversation.

"I trust no one more than you, Aethelred."

They were strong words, and Wulfhere meant them. He had grown up distrusting both his brothers— something their father had always encouraged. Penda had enjoyed pitting them against each other. When he had claimed the throne, Wulfhere had expected Aethelred to start plotting against him. It surprised him that the opposite had happened. His younger brother had been sly as a youth, but events of late had matured him.

Satisfied that Aethelred would not give him any more trouble, Wulfhere turned his attention back to Aethelthryth. There were tears in her eyes, but her face was solemn. He would never have this woman's love, but then nor did he expect to. Her response when it came surprised him all the same.

Her voice was barely above a whisper, yet he heard the sincerity in it.

"Thank you," she said.

Chapter Thirty-two
Moving Forward

The next morning it rained. It was not torrential, like the day Ermenilda disappeared, but a thick, wet mist that descended over the world and soaked everything under it.

Aethelred was in a foul mood as he followed his brother out of the hall.

"What did I ever do to you to deserve this?" he muttered.

"This is an honor," Wulfhere replied, pretending to ignore his brother's ill humor. "I did Lady Aethelthryth wrong and am attempting to make amends."

They stepped outside, and Aethelred cursed, pulling his fur cloak up around his ears.

"Guilt over Ermenilda has addled your brains," he muttered.

Wulfhere shrugged. "Perhaps it has . . . or maybe I am seeing clearly for the first time."

Aethelred gave him a hard look, his pale-blue eyes questioning.

"You are truly sorry, aren't you?"

Wulfhere gave a bitter smile. Aethelred would never know just how sorry he was.

Together, the brothers descended the steps into the muddy yard below. The king's men had prepared the horses for the journey, and slaves had strapped on saddlebags filled with provisions. The horses did not like the rain. They carried their heads low and flattened their ears back. Likewise, many of the warriors who would escort Aethelthryth back to Ely wore scowls, while others muttered oaths under their breaths.

They had almost reached Aethelred's horse, when Wulfhere turned to his brother.

"I think I will visit mother while you're gone."

Aethelred inclined his head, smiling.

"She will like that."

Aethelred had visited their mother a few times already at Bonehill Abbey, where she had gone to live as a nun three years earlier. Wulfhere had kept meaning to pay her a visit, but his wedding to Ermenilda, followed by his journey to Ely and the events that unfolded afterward, had drawn his attention. Now, the visit was well overdue.

He had found himself thinking often of his mother of late. Perhaps it was guilt, but he needed to see her.

At that moment, Aethelthryth emerged from the Great Tower. A small figure, clad head to toe in fur, she glided down the steps and wove her way around puddles and horse dung, to where her palfrey waited.

Aethelred dragged a hand through his short blond hair, now wet from the rain, causing it to stand up in hedgehoglike spikes.

"I swear this is cruel revenge for some wrong I've done you."

Wulfhere laughed softly and slapped his brother on the back.

"You'll be fine. Just get her to Ely safely and your job is done."

"Aye," Aethelred grumbled, "if the witch doesn't scratch my eyes out in my sleep on the way there."

He said that loud enough for Aethelthryth to hear. The widow threw him a venomous look before turning her back on him.

Wulfhere turned his attention from his brother and Aethelthryth, his gaze traveling over the assembled escort. Elfhere was also accompanying Aethelred. He was saddling his horse a few feet away, unaware that a young woman approached him.

It was Wynflaed, Ermenilda's handmaid.

The sight of her pained Wulfhere. The young woman had been a permanent fixture at his wife's side. She had been the last person to see Ermcnilda alive. The girl had tried to apologize, but Wulfhere had not wanted to hear it. Now, months on, he did not blame Wynflaed for his wife's death. Even so, he wished she had returned to her kin in Cantwareburh.

Instead, she had found a reason to stay on in Tamworth.

"Elfhere!"

The warrior turned to the girl, his face splitting into a grin. He kissed her passionately, not caring who saw.

An ache twisted deep in Wulfhere's chest, and he looked away. The love between Elfhere and Wynflaed had been the talk of the Great Hall for several months. Although he did not wish either of them ill, the sight pained him.

Such natural, uncomplicated affection held a cruel mirror up to what Wulfhere had shared with Ermenilda. There had been no easy kisses, no smiles between them. Apart from the passion they had shared in the furs, their rapport had been stiff and awkward from the moment they met, till the day Ermenilda disappeared.

***

Ermenilda looked up at the sky and frowned. The air smelled fresh and rich, but the misty rain was heavy enough to wet her face in moments.

There would be no gardening in this weather. Disappointed, she blinked water out of her eyes and wiped her dripping face with the hem of her sleeve. Then, with a sigh, Ermenilda retreated indoors.

Inside, all the nuns were busy. They were forever industrious; not a moment was spent idle at Bonehill. Ermenilda could smell cooking—the pungent aroma of boiling cabbage, turnips, and carrots for the evening pottage—coming from the kitchens. The smell blended with the more pleasant scent of baking bread.

Ermenilda's belly rumbled. Meals were frugal here at Bonehill, and she worked so hard that she often felt faint with hunger by the time mealtimes arrived. Owing to the rain, this afternoon would be less arduous than most.

Later on, Ermenilda would join the other novices for a lesson on reading and writing. Every two days, Abbess Ardwyn took it upon herself to instruct the novices; in just over three months, Ermenilda could now read and write simple sentences.

Until her lesson, she would have to occupy herself with weaving. As highborn women, she and Sister Cyneswide had been given a complex tapestry to work on—a large hanging that depicted Christ crucified on the cross. The tapestry would take them another ten months, at least, to finish.

Ermenilda retrieved her pickup stick, a long pointed length of hardwood that she used to insert warp threads into the tapestry. As she did so, she noticed how red and sore her hands looked. Once, she had the pale, delicate hands of a lady, despite the time she spent in her garden at Tamworth. Hard physical labor at Bonehill had given her the hands of a farmer's wife. She would have liked some lard to rub on them, to soften the skin, but such luxuries were forbidden in the abbey.

Turning her attention to the task at hand, Ermenilda started to weave. She and Cyneswide worked companionably, side by side, for a while before Ermenilda became bored with the silence.

It was always so silent here. Not like the noise and confusion of the Great Tower of Tamworth.

"Why did you take the veil?" she asked finally, careful to keep her voice low lest one of the other nuns overhear.

Sister Cyneswide glanced at her, surprised, before answering.

"I came here because my husband died, and there was no place for me in my old life."

Ermenilda frowned. "Your family didn't want you?"

Sister Cyneswide shook her head and picked up her tapestry beater. "It was not as simple as that."

Ermenilda sensed her companion did not want to divulge more, although her words had piqued her curiosity.

"I thought women came here because they wanted to," she said quietly.

"Most do," Cyneswide replied. "Certainly, no one forced me either. It's just that the choices of women are sometimes few."

They certainly are.

"What of you, Sister Hild?" Sister Cyneswide asked, turning the conversation away from herself.

"It was always my dream to become a nun," Ermenilda admitted.

"It was?"

Ermenilda smiled at the older woman's incredulity. "Aye, all the women in my family are pious."

One of the other nuns passed by carrying a basket of wool over to where two of the novices were winding wool onto distaffs. Ermenilda remained silent until she was out of earshot.

"Are you happy here, Sister Cyneswide?" she asked, curiosity getting the better of her.

Cyneswide gave a pensive, enigmatic smile.

"Being happy does not come into it," she replied, with a shake of her head. Ermenilda heard the faint rebuke in the older woman's voice and realized that she had overstepped the mark. Cyneswide may have been a warm and gentle-natured woman, but she was also an intensely private one.

"I accept my life here," Cyneswide concluded, her gaze meeting Ermenilda's, "as will you."

Chapter Thirty-three
The Visitor

Wulfhere swung down from his stallion and passed the reins to Werbode.

"Make camp here," he instructed his retainer. "I will rejoin you in the morning."

Werbode frowned. "You're going to sleep inside the abbey?"

"I'm the king," Wulfhere replied. "I sleep where I want."

Werbode chuckled. "Aye, perhaps one of the nuns will offer to share her bed."

Wulfhere gave the thegn a cool look but did not respond to the deliberate provocation. Instead, he turned to Mōna, who sat expectantly at his feet, and stroked her ears.

"You wait here, girl."

Wulfhere left the party of twenty men he had brought with him from Tamworth and strode across the rippling grass to Bonehill Abbey's gates. It was a bleak spot, here at the end of a windswept valley, and he wondered how his mother had fared. It would be an altogether different life from the comfort of the Great Tower of Tamworth.

The shadows were lengthening; it was getting late in the afternoon. Wulfhere and his men had left Tamworth just after breaking their fast and had made good time. Still, he knew that nuns kept to strict routines, and he hoped he had not arrived too late in the day.

Wulfhere rang the bell, listening to its mournful sound echo across the valley. He glanced back at his warriors. Werbode had done as bade and was organizing the men. There were few trees in the exposed valley, so he had sent out a party to gather wood for a fire and to cut branches for tents.

Hearing the scuff of footsteps beyond, Wulfhere turned back to the gate. The hatch, just level with his neck, slid open, and a woman's face peered out.

"Wes þū hāl," she greeted him hesitantly, her sharp blue eyes silently assessing him.

"Wes hāl," he answered, his gaze meeting hers. "I am King Wulfhere of Mercia. I am here to see my mother."

The nun closed the hatch without another word and opened the gate to admit him.

"I am Abbess Ardwyn," she said, dipping her head in respect. "Welcome to Bonehill Abbey, milord."

Wulfhere nodded and let his gaze travel around his surroundings. There was an atmosphere of peace inside the abbey, and the scent of herbs and flowers made him relax. The tranquility reminded him of Ermenilda's garden, although it pained him to think of that special place.

"You have made this a beautiful spot," he said, turning back to the abbess.

She smiled, and he could see that his comment had pleased her.

"Thank you, milord. We have worked long and hard to make it what it is." She dipped her head once more. "Come, I will take you to see your mother."

Sister Cyneswide was waiting for her son when he entered the garden. Seated upon a low stone bench, she sat as still as the shrubs and flowers surrounding her.

Wulfhere barely recognized her, clad in a shapeless gray habit, her hair shrouded by a white veil; she bore no resemblance to Penda's golden queen. However, the deep blue of her eyes, when her gaze lifted to meet his, was unmistakable. As was the gentleness on her face.

Wulfhere's throat unexpectedly tightened—a reaction that surprised him. Although he was fond of his mother, he had neglected her over the past few years. He had focused on other matters, like taking back the throne, finding a wife, and exacting vengeance. It was only now that he realized how much he missed her smile, her reassuring presence.

"Wulfhere," she said softly, her face radiant. "How handsome you have become."

She rose to her feet and embraced him. Wulfhere hugged his mother close, overwhelmed by his reaction to seeing her. She still smelled the same: the faint scent of lye soap and lavender.

Wulfhere cleared his throat and struggled to compose himself.

"I apologize for not coming sooner, Mōder."

"You have had much to occupy your thoughts," she replied.

She was making excuses for him, as she had once done for his father.

"I still should have come sooner," he answered with a shake of his head.

They sat down, side by side, upon the bench, surrounded by birdsong and the sigh of a light wind that stirred the leaves. At the far end of the garden, Wulfhere spied the ghostly shapes of nuns, as they went about their work.

"I last saw Aethelred in the spring," Cyneswide said softly. "He told me of how you had taken back the throne, and of your marriage to a Kentish princess. I am proud of you, Wulfhere, as would your father be."

Wulfhere stared back at her, something deep inside his chest twisting. His mother must have seen the look of anguish on his face, for she frowned.

"What is wrong?"

He shook his head. "I have made a mess of things. You would not be so proud, if you knew the truth."

Cyneswide's frown deepened. "What has happened?"

Wulfhere looked away from her, staring down at the grass beneath his boots.

"My wife is dead. Three months ago, during heavy rains. I believe she threw herself into the Tame and drowned, although her body has never been found."

His mother did not respond to this news, and when the silence grew uncomfortable, Wulfhere glanced across at her. Cyneswide was watching him, her eyes glittering with unshed tears.

"She did not want to wed me," he told her. "She hated me before we even met, but my actions did not improve matters."

He saw the confusion in his mother's eyes, and so he began the tale from the beginning. He told her of his exile, of his winter visit to Cantwareburh. He explained how he had sworn to take back the Mercian throne and renounce the old gods if King Eorcenberht would agree to the match. He told her of the attack, during their journey home, and of who was to blame. He told her of Ermenilda's garden and of how things had softened between them for a short while, before his decision to take vengeance upon her aunt shattered their fragile rapport.

He told the story plainly, without any emotion or embellishment, although when he finished it, he felt raw on the inside, as if he had reopened a wound that was just beginning to heal.

"Wulfhere," Cyneswide breathed, brushing away a tear that had escaped and was trickling down her cheek. "You should not blame yourself."

Anger flared deep within Wulfhere.

"I *am* to blame, Mōder. If I could return in time, I would do things differently."

Cyneswide observed him, and Wulfhere could see she was thinking.

"You are not like him at all," she said, finally.

"Like who?"

"Your father."

Wulfhere gave a bitter laugh. "All I ever wanted was to follow in his footsteps, but I've failed there too."

His mother gave a faint smile. "It wasn't a criticism. I am glad you are not like him."

Wulfhere held her gaze, surprised. "You are?"

"Penda lacked humanity. Even I, who loved him the most, never saw a hint of vulnerability in all the years we were together. Paeda had his cruelty . . . but you and Aethelred are kinder."

"I still managed to make a mess of things," he replied, gazing out across the lush garden. "What I would give for a second chance."

It was then that he saw one of the nuns walk across the garden. She had her back to him and carried a wicker basket under one arm. Even in her loose robes, the woman walked with regal elegance, her posture straight and shoulders back.

She reached an apple tree at the rear of the garden and began to pick fruit from the lower branches. As she worked, the nun turned slightly, revealing her profile to him.

The world stood still.

Wulfhere was vaguely aware of his mother asking him something, but he could not tear his gaze away from the nun at the bottom of the garden.

"Wulfhere, what is it?"

Heart pounding, he turned to his mother.

"That nun." He finally spoke, although his mouth felt as though it were full of wool. "Who is she?"

Cyneswide frowned, her gaze shifting to where the nun was stretching up to retrieve an apple from a high branch.

"That's Sister Hild," she replied, frowning.

"How long . . . how long has she been here?"

"Since midsummer," his mother replied. "She arrived here around three months ago, after her husband died . . ."

Cyneswide's voice died away. Realization dawned, and her face paled as she stared at the nun.

"Oh . . ."

Wulfhere rose to his feet, his pulse thundering in his ears.

"Her name is not Hild," he rasped. "That woman is Ermenilda . . . my wife."

Chapter Thirty-four
Ghosts

Ermenilda plucked the apple from the branch and deposited it into her basket. A breeze feathered her cheeks, and she glanced up at the sky, noting that the light was starting to fade. Vespers were nearing; soon she would have to retreat indoors.

Behind her, a man's voice intruded.

"Ermenilda."

She froze. A chill swept over her, followed by a wave of fire. She knew that voice, recognized its deep pitch.

For the love of Mother Mary and all the saints . . . no . . .

Slowly, as if she were swimming in deep water, Ermenilda turned.

He was standing a few feet behind her.

Wulfhere was staring at her as if he looked upon a demon. The king was an imposing and intimidating sight, dressed all in black, with a gray squirrel cloak about his shoulders.

Wulfhere's face was rigid with shock, his pale eyes frozen wide. Ermenilda saw a muscle in his clenched jaw flicker, the only sign of his inner turmoil.

Taking a deep, shuddering breath, she clutched her basket to her breast and took a step backward. She was dumbstruck. Her tongue felt glued to the roof of her mouth. There were no words, no excuses, which could extricate her from this moment. Behind Wulfhere, she spied Sister Cyneswide approaching.

The older woman's face was ashen and taut, her gaze full of reproach.

Ermenilda's gaze returned to Wulfhere. What connection did he have with Sister Cyneswide?

Wulfhere must have seen the confusion in her eyes, for his mouth twisted.

"I'm here to see my mother," he said softly. "Only, I did not expect to set eyes on my wife's ghost."

His mother?

The pieces of the puzzle fell into place, and all of the things Cyneswide had revealed to her in their conversations took on a new meaning.

The man that Cyneswide had never stopped loving was Penda of Mercia.

Ermenilda moved, pivoting away from him, and attempted to flee back inside the abbey. Wulfhere intercepted her, his hand closing over her forearm.

Ermenilda gasped, her basket dropping from nerveless fingers. The apples rolled out onto the ground at her feet.

"Not a ghost then." Wulfhere squeezed gently, as if proving to himself that she was real. "But flesh and bone."

She could not bear the look in his eyes, the accusation and pain she saw there. He had thought her dead, only to discover that she had merely run away from him.

She had never meant him to know.

"Why?" he demanded, his voice raw.

"You know why," she finally managed, the words barely above a whisper.

His hand dropped away from her, leaving an imprint of heat on her forearm. Hostility and pain pulsed between them like a living thing.

"I grieved for you, Ermenilda," he ground out, his eyes glittering, "and all the while you've been here, laughing at my expense."

Ermenilda shook her head and wrapped her arms about herself. It was a mild evening, but she felt chilled to the bone.

"I did this to save us both."

Wulfhere's gaze narrowed further still. "You did it for yourself, no one else."

Ermenilda ran, and this time Wulfhere did not try to stop her. She picked up her skirts and fled across the grass, under a stone arch and into the stone building beyond.

Only the whispering wind followed her.

Ermenilda sat upon her straw-filled pallet, staring sightlessly at the wall, when Sister Cyneswide entered the novice's dormitory.

She heard the nun's soft footsteps, the scuff of her sandals on stone, and felt the pallet shift as the older woman sat down next to her. Ermenilda did not look her way; she was too humiliated to do so. She had shared intimate details with Cyneswide—information she could use against her if she so chose.

Cyneswide did not speak. Instead, she sat next to Ermenilda in gentle silence. Outside, the bell was ringing for Vespers, but both women ignored it. This afternoon, neither of them would adhere to Bonehill's strict routine.

Eventually, Ermenilda broke the silence.

"So, you were queen."

"Aye, I was."

Ermenilda glanced across at the nun, studying her as if for the first time. Now that she was looking for it, she could see the family resemblance. Wulfhere had the same cheekbones, the same nose.

"You never guessed who I was?"

Cyneswide gave a wry smile and shook her head. "Time stands still here at Bonehill. The goings-on in the world outside cease to matter. I knew my son had married a Kentish princess, but nothing else."

Ermenilda nodded, before glancing down at her hands clasped upon her lap. She wanted to stay seated here forever, to pretend she had never seen Wulfhere. She had felt restless at Bonehill of late, but now that her peace had been shattered, she was desperate to remain here.

"He cannot make me leave," she whispered.

Cyneswide did not reply immediately. When she did, her voice was firm.

"Wulfhere blames himself."

"That's not the impression he gave me," Ermenilda replied, her tone sharpening. "He thinks me selfish and cruel."

Cyneswide shook her head. "He is in shock. Before he saw you in the garden, Wulfhere told me everything. He would have done anything to go back and change the past. I've never seen a man sorrier."

Ermenilda clasped her hands tightly together. She did not believe Cyneswide. It was all too easy for a mother to see the good in her son. After all, she had loved Penda of Mercia, one of the most hated men in Britain.

"I will not go from here," she said, fear rising within her at the thought of returning to Tamworth. "He cannot force me."

Cyneswide sighed, impatience creeping into her voice. "He is the King of Mercia. If he wishes to take you away from here, no one—not even the abbess—will be able to prevent him."

Wulfhere waited alone in the chapter house, the space where the abbess and other nuns or visiting monks and bishops would meet to discuss matters. The room had a high vaulted ceiling, and richly detailed tapestries covered the walls. Low stone benches, where the nuns would sit for their meetings, lined the edge of the room.

Wulfhere did not sit down upon any of them. Instead, he paced the room.

Betrayed. Insulted. Wounded.

Anger snaked through him and made him want to lash out. He felt like tearing this room apart with his bare hands, ripping down the walls—stone by stone. Yet, underneath the anger, there was a rising sense of relief, of burgeoning joy.

Ermenilda is alive.

He was furious and hurt, but to know his wife had survived had lifted a heavy mantle from his shoulders.

Wulfhere heard the sound of footsteps and whirled to face the three women who silently entered the chapter house. His mother, her blue eyes clouded with worry, led the way, followed by the stern-faced abbess. Ermenilda—pale and tense—entered last.

"Lord Wulfhere." Abbess Ardwyn bowed her head respectfully, although her mouth had drawn up as if she had just taken a sip of vinegar. "Your mother has informed me of all."

The abbess turned to Ermenilda, her disapproval palpable.

"So, your name is not Hild but Ermenilda."

The young woman nodded, her brown eyes huge on her pale face.

"You lied to me about your identity." The abbess's voice lashed like a whip. "That was a wicked thing to do."

Ermenilda looked down at the flagstone floor.

"I am sorry, abbess."

Abbess Ardwyn made a noise of disgust and turned back to Wulfhere.

"She is your wife, milord. Take her away with you when you leave here."

"No! I must stay!" Ermenilda's face had gone taut. Her slender body trembled. Looking upon her, Wulfhere could see her abject horror at the thought of leaving with him. If she had struck him across the face, it would have hurt less.

Ermenilda's outburst had not impressed the abbess. The older woman's brows had knotted together in disapproval beneath penetrating blue eyes.

"Excuse me?"

"Forgive me, abbess," Ermenilda gasped, clearly struggling to rein in her emotions, "but this is my home now. I do not wish to leave."

"What you wish does not concern me," the abbess sniffed. "You are a liar and had no place coming here without your husband's permission."

Abbess Ardwyn turned back to Wulfhere.

"Take her with you in the morning. I will make sure she is ready."

Wulfhere said nothing. Instead, he looked across at his wife. Ermenilda was staring at the floor and was clearly struggling not to weep. His mother had wisely remained silent since entering the chapter house. However, Wulfhere could see the concern etched across her face.

"My wife thinks me a beast," he said finally. The words hurt him, but he forced them out. "She would be happier here."

The abbess glared at him. "I cannot abide lying. This woman came here with a tale of how she was recently widowed. She told me her kin had ridiculed her wishes to become a nun, so she had traveled here on her own. We all praised her for her devotion, but everything she told us was false."

"I had to lie," Ermenilda burst out, tears streaming down her face. "You would not have taken me in otherwise!"

Abbess Ardwyn gave the younger woman a cold look before she turned back to Wulfhere.

"Your wife is no longer welcome here," she told him, her voice clipped with barely restrained anger. "If you do not take her with you, I will cast her out."

Chapter Thirty-five
Insults

The looks on his men's faces when Wulfhere led Ermenilda out of Bonehill the next morning were almost comical.

Under other circumstances, Wulfhere might have found their dumbstruck expressions amusing. This morning, their reactions just added to Ermenilda's humiliation of him.

Some of them paled as if they had just seen a wraith, while others muttered oaths under their breaths.

Werbode just stared. It was rare to see the thegn lose his composure, but the sight of Ermenilda—alive and well—flummoxed him.

Ermenilda had removed her veil, revealing that she had braided her blonde hair tightly around her head. A woolen cloak hung from her shoulders, although underneath, she still wore the coarsely woven gray tunic—the last remnant of her life at Bonehill Abbey.

The sun had just risen over the edge of the valley to the east, and the sky was clear, promising a bright day ahead. Wulfhere led Ermenilda up the incline, his hand gently guiding her elbow. They halted about five feet from the king's men. Mōna approached, tail wagging, but Wulfhere stilled her with a gesture.

He greeted his men. "No, your eyes do not deceive you." The words were bald, and Wulfhere could hear the flatness in his own voice. There was no way to soften the news. "Queen Ermenilda lives. It appears she did not drown in the river but instead fled to Bonehill to start a new life as a nun. Had I not visited my mother, I would never have known."

The men stared, their silence the only response Wulfhere needed. Werbode was the first to find his tongue.

"You will take her back?" he asked, incredulous.

"I would prefer she remain at Bonehill," Wulfhere admitted, "but the abbess has cast her out."

"Leave her to the wolves then," Werbode replied. He watched Ermenilda, his lip curling.

Wulfhere shook his head. "She is my wife. I cannot treat her thus."

"She let you think she was dead. You owe her nothing."

Wulfhere understood Werbode's anger, but the warrior asked the impossible. He would never leave his wife out here to die. Instead, he led her across to his stallion and helped her mount.

He swung up behind her, ignoring his men's shocked faces.

Ermenilda stared ahead, barely taking in her surroundings, as Wulfhere turned his stallion northeast.

Back to Tamworth.

It hardly seemed real. She felt as if she were moving through fog, as if none of this was happening to her. She had seen the astonishment and anger on the faces of Wulfhere's men—and the rage upon Werbode's—but none of it had touched her.

She had spent the night weeping in despair, feeling hollow inside.

Wulfhere sat close behind her; the heat of his body enveloped her back, and she could feel the strength of his arms on either side of her torso as he guided the stallion up the hill, away from Bonehill. His presence was oddly reassuring. Without his protection, she was doomed.

Ermenilda glanced back at the place that had been her home for the past three months. From here, the abbey appeared a sanctuary of green in a bleak, empty valley.

Cyneswide was still there and would remain so. Ermenilda had watched her say good-bye to Wulfhere at the gates just after dawn. Wordlessly, she had embraced her son, before cupping his cheek with her palm. Wulfhere had said nothing. Theirs had been a silent farewell.

Ermenilda turned her gaze from Bonehill Abbey and closed her eyes. To think she had chafed under the austerity and restrictions of daily life in the abbey. Now, she would give anything to return there.

The irony was that Wulfhere did not even want her back. It was only out of some sense of decency that he did not leave her to the wolves.

Wulfhere did not speak as they rode, and she was grateful for his silence. He understood the gravity of the situation. He would have to explain her deceit once more to his hall once they reached Tamworth—something that would humiliate him more than it would her.

At midday, they stopped for a meal of bread, cheese, and apples. Bonehill, and its lonely valley, now lay many furlongs behind them, and the party halted amid woodland. The trees were changing their coats, turning from shades of green to red and gold, and the air was crisp with the promise of autumn. The king's party stopped next to a small stream. The trickling of water and the murmur of the wind through the trees were the only sounds in the peaceful spot.

Ermenilda let Wulfhere help her down from his horse, although she carefully averted her gaze. She could not bear to look at his face. She had preferred anger, not the wounded look in his eyes this morning.

Moving as if in a dream, Ermenilda sat down upon a tree stump. She was vaguely aware of the men moving around, unbuckling saddlebags and unstoppering water bladders. She paid them no mind, instead staring down at the apple she held but did not eat.

Mōna came to see her, nudging up against her leg. The wolf's behavior surprised her. In all the months Ermenilda spent at Tamworth, Mōna had largely ignored her. She was loyal to Wulfhere only and tracked him like a shadow.

Not so today. The she-wolf gazed at her with soft eyes and licked her hand. Ermenilda placed a tentative hand on the wolf's head. Her pelt was plush, and her ears soft.

"Hello," she murmured, her misery lifting for a moment. "You are a beauty, aren't you?"

Werbode's voice, aggressive and rough with malice, intruded.

"That wolf will be the only one to acknowledge you, once we reach Tamworth."

Ermenilda looked up to find him looming over her. The warrior had a wild, dangerous look in his eye.

"You will be shunned, treated like the devious witch you are."

He was standing too close, and Mōna let out a growl, low in her throat. Werbode ignored the wolf, his dark gaze burning into Ermenilda.

"I knew from the first you were trouble, but Wulfhere couldn't see beyond your pretty face."

Ermenilda eventually found her tongue. Werbode had always unnerved her, but now he was frightening.

"Get away from me."

The warrior leered at her. "Afraid? You should be."

Wulfhere stepped in between them, forcing the warrior to take a step back.

"Werbode, that's enough."

The warrior spat on the ground in response. "You still defend her?"

"She is the Queen of Mercia, and you will address her as such," Wulfhere replied, his voice emotionless.

Werbode shook his head and drew his seax from its sheath at his waist.

"The sight of her turns my stomach, as does your weakness," he snarled.

A deathly hush settled over the glade.

Wulfhere watched his thegn, giving no sign of offence, surprise, or fear. Mōna's growling grew louder. Ermenilda saw the hackles rise on the back of the wolf's neck, and her body coiled, ready to spring.

"What are you doing, Werbode?" Wulfhere asked gently.

"Showing the others who you really are."

"And who's that?"

Around them, his men shifted uncomfortably, their gazes darting between the king and his thegn.

"Weak. A man who lets a woman make a fool of him."

Wulfhere appeared unmoved by Werbode's insult, although the thegn's words chilled Ermenilda.

Is that what they all think?

"Do you really want to fight me?" Wulfhere asked.

Werbode smiled at him, showing him his teeth. "I want to gut you."

Wulfhere drew his own seax, a short fighting dagger with an ornately carved wooden handle.

"One of us is going to die here," he told the thegn.

Werbode's smile widened. He backed away from the king, shrugged off his cloak, and tossed his seax with an arrogant flick of his wrist. "It's time to meet your precious god."

Ermenilda watched the scene unfold with growing horror. Yet she could not help but be impressed by Wulfhere's reaction to his thegn's threats. If they concerned him, he did not show it.

Instead, Wulfhere turned his head to Ermenilda, their gazes meeting for the first time since dawn.

"If I should fall, Mōna will guard you," he told her. His gaze shifted to the wolf. Mōna stared back at him, her yellow eyes glowing.

"Àmundae," he commanded softly.

Protect.

Ermenilda wanted to speak, to tell Wulfhere to halt this madness, but her throat had constricted.

Wulfhere took off his fur cloak and dropped it to the ground. He stepped away from her and Mōna, walking out in the clearing where Werbode awaited him.

"Wulfhere, stop!" The words finally burst from Ermenilda. "You don't have to do this. Ignore him!"

Wulfhere glanced back at her, a bitter smile curving his lips. "Some things cannot be ignored. He insults us both."

"But I don't care if he insults me. They're only words!"

"Words have more power than you realize." Wulfhere looked away from her. "You may not care, but I do—and Werbode will answer for it."

Chapter Thirty-six
Blood and Honor

"Still explaining yourself to your fishwife?" Werbode mocked as Wulfhere approached him. "I wouldn't be surprised if she cut off your balls on your wedding night."

Wulfhere smiled at him, and the expression chilled Ermenilda to the bone. It was a killer's smile.

"You talk too much," Wulfhere told Werbode quietly. "It's always been a failing of yours."

In response, the warrior spat once more on the ground. However, Ermenilda could see his arrogance had ebbed slightly.

A hush had settled over the clearing as the king's men watched and waited for the fight to begin. To Ermenilda's untrained eye, both men looked like equal opponents. They were both tall, muscular, and in their prime. Yet, in looks they were the opposite—one as dark as a raven's wing, the other as pale as a summer's dawn.

The two men circled each other. Werbode grinned, tossing his knife from hand to hand as if he was toying with the king. In contrast, Wulfhere appeared watchful, his body coiled and ready. Neither man bore shields. They both carried their weapons in their right hands.

Werbode attacked first, with a suddenness that made Ermenilda start. He closed in on the king fast in short, shuffling steps that brought him hard up against his opponent.

Wulfhere was ready for him. His left hand snapped up, grasping Werbode's right wrist, and he struck at him with his own weapon. The blade scored the edge of the thegn's leather jerkin. Werbode twisted away and danced back a few steps.

They circled each other once more, before Werbode attacked again, slashing at Wulfhere's face. The king brought his seax up to deflect it, and the two men drew apart.

It was like watching a deadly dance. They circled—gazes fused—before attacking, withdrawing, and attacking again. Ermenilda saw they had different fighting styles; Werbode was showy and aggressive while Wulfhere was watchful and minimal in his movements, as if conserving his energy.

Werbode drew first blood, in a downward slice that slipped under Wulfhere's defense and cut into his left thigh.

Ermenilda heard Wulfhere's hiss of pain. A dark patch soaked through the leg of his breeches, but he paid it no mind. A moment later, he lunged forward, catching Werbode by surprise, and struck out at his face.

The edge of Wulfhere's blade left a ribbon of scarlet across the thegn's cheek.

"Your mother was a dirty whore!" Werbode cursed him as they circled once more. "I had her. All your father's men had her."

Werbode meant his words to inflame, to incite Wulfhere into anger so he would do something rash and foolish.

Wulfhere did not rise to the bait.

Angered, Werbode attacked again, his blade cutting into Wulfhere's leather wrist brace. Ermenilda saw blood trickling down her husband's bare arm, but like the injury to his thigh, he paid it no mind. His attention did not waver from his opponent.

They continued to fight, and more blood flowed. Wulfhere sustained another cut to his leg, although he managed to slash Werbode deeply across the front of his right thigh and above his left hand. The hand wound bled copiously, dripping onto the grass.

Ermenilda watched the fight, nausea creeping up her throat as she did so. She had risen from the tree stump but felt as if her feet were made of stone—she could not move. Mōna stood next to her, the beast's muscular body pressed against hers. The wolf continued to growl low in her throat, her gaze fixed upon the two men circling and slashing at each other just a few yards away.

The fight ended as quickly—and violently—as it had begun.

Werbode leaped high into the air, aiming a killing thrust at Wulfhere's throat. The king ducked beneath him and brought his own seax up under Werbode's rib cage, burying it to the hilt.

Werbode's grunt of agony ripped through the glade. He collapsed to the ground, still slashing at his opponent. Wulfhere moved fast. He yanked the blade free and knelt on Werbode's chest, pinning him down. He stared down at him with pitiless eyes. Without uttering another word, he cut Werbode's throat.

Werbode lay twitching under him, his blood soaking into the dirt.

Wulfhere eventually climbed to his feet. Ermenilda saw the fire in his eyes. Battle lust still consumed him. However, he did not look at her, but at his men.

"Does anyone else question my honor?" he asked them, his voice a low growl.

Heart pounding, Ermenilda studied their faces. She searched for a sign that another sought to challenge him. None came. Werbode had acted alone.

"Does anyone else wish to insult the queen?" Wulfhere demanded, his voice hardening.

Only silence greeted him.

Ermenilda approached Wulfhere cautiously, as one would a wounded animal. He was standing alone, by his horse, and was attempting to staunch the flow of blood from the cut on his thigh with a leather strap. She noticed he was pale and guessed it was from pain and loss of blood.

"Wulfhere," she greeted him softly. "Will you let me take a look at those wounds?"

The king turned to her, his expression enigmatic.

"I am fine. They can wait till Tamworth."

Ermenilda held Wulfhere's gaze steadily.

"Please . . . you're still bleeding."

The king exhaled sharply, irritated, but Ermenilda remained before him. Finally, he nodded. They stood a few yards away from where Wulfhere's men finished their noon meal. They had dragged Werbode's corpse away into the trees, where scavengers would most likely find him, and returned to their meal as if nothing had happened. Their nonchalance shocked Ermenilda, but then she remembered that these were all hardened warriors, used to the blood and gore of a shield wall.

The death of one man—and one who had not been well liked—meant little to them.

Wulfhere and Ermenilda walked over to the stream. First, making sure she avoided eye contact with him, Ermenilda undid the leather brace on Wulfhere's wrist and looked at the wound. It was not deep, but it was still bleeding heavily. She tore strips of linen from her undertunic and wet one of them in the stream, before washing the wound. Then, she bound it with a dry strip of cloth.

All the while, Wulfhere said nothing. He merely watched her under hooded lids.

When Ermenilda had tended to his arm, he undid his breeches and pushed them down to his ankles so she could examine the two wounds on his left thigh. Ermenilda gritted her teeth when she saw how serious one of the cuts was. Werbode's seax blade had sliced deep into the flesh, cutting into muscle.

"This will need stitching," she told him, "but I will bind it as best I can for now."

Wulfhere nodded, although she could see he was sweating from the pain. As she tended to him, Ermenilda was aware that Mōna sat nearby watching them calmly with warm amber eyes.

"My wolf seems to have taken a liking to you," Wulfhere observed.

"Aye," Ermenilda agreed, not taking her gaze from her task. "I cannot think why, though. Everyone else here hates me."

"I do not," he replied.

"You should," she said stiffly. "After what I've done."

Wulfhere's mouth twisted.

"So you agree with Werbode. I should have cast you out into the wilderness?"

She looked back down at the leg she had just bound. Despite her best efforts, blood had started to seep through the bandage.

"It's what I deserve," she replied.

Wulfhere gave a soft laugh, causing her to look up and meet his gaze for the first time since they had stopped by the stream.

"I think you'd like that . . . Saint Ermenilda, the martyr."

There was no malice in his voice, just weariness. Even so, the words held a sting. Ermenilda finished binding his wounds in silence.

***

They entered Tamworth as the sun slid gently beyond the western horizon.

Ermenilda rode alongside Wulfhere upon a bay gelding that had been Werbode's, and they led the party up to the high gate. Her skin prickled under the stares and whispers that greeted them. Many of the townsfolk cried out her name and pointed.

Beside her, Wulfhere stared ahead, as if he had not seen them. Ermenilda clenched her jaw and attempted to do the same, although it was hard to maintain her composure as the crowd swelled in size.

The news of her return raced ahead of them like the plague, and by the time they rode under the high gate, all those who lived inside the Great Tower of Tamworth had spilled out into the yard to greet them.

At the back of the group, standing on the stone steps leading down from the tower, Ermenilda spied Wynflaed.

The young woman stood frozen to the spot as she stared at Ermenilda. Her thick auburn hair tumbled about her shoulders, and her green eyes were enormous on her pale face. The maid's expression was not unlike the one Wulfhere had worn when he had discovered her in Bonehill's garden. Wynflaed looked at her as if she had risen from the dead.

Ermenilda slid down off her horse and glanced over at Wulfhere. He was pale, his face all sharp angles, although she could not tell whether the austerity on his face was due to pain or anger. He handed his horse over to a stable boy and crossed to her, limping slightly. Ermenilda glanced down and saw that the linen she had bound his leg with was now bright scarlet.

"Come," he said, taking a firm hold of her elbow. "Best you wait upstairs and allow me to explain what has happened."

Ermenilda swallowed hard. Nerves had twisted her belly in knots, yet she could not let him face his hall alone. She had never planned to return to Tamworth, but now that she had, it would be cowardly to hide up in the King's Loft.

If she had been prepared to run away, she also had to be prepared to deal with the consequences.

"I should stay with you," she replied. "Otherwise I shall only give everyone more of a reason to hate me."

Wulfhere's gaze met hers, and she saw his surprise, before he eventually nodded.

"Very well, let's go in and face them."

Chapter Thirty-seven
Seeking Forgiveness

Wulfhere's chest heaved in agony. He lay with a blade clenched between his teeth while Glaedwine finished stitching his wounds. The cunning man had poured strong wine over the wound, before stitching it with a hemp thread—a process that had nearly caused the king to pass out from pain. They sat alone in an alcove, out of sight from the rest of the hall.

"You were fortunate, milord," Glaedwine said as he straightened up and reached for a basin of warm water. "Any deeper and Werbode would have severed an artery."

Wulfhere unclenched his jaw and removed the seax blade. His left leg pulsed; it felt as if it was on fire.

"I still bled like a stuck pig."

"Aye, but you could have bled to death then and there."

The cunning man wet a scrap of linen and washed away the blood from the king's leg. Glaedwine was a tall, spare man with limbs that appeared too long for him. He had been a healer at Tamworth for many years, and had served Penda faithfully. His skills were renowned. Still, the man reminded Wulfhere of a sly crow. He spoke little and saw much.

Glaedwine, like the other residents of the Great Hall, had stood and listened, while Wulfhere explained how and why Queen Ermenilda had returned to them.

Wulfhere closed his eyes and tried to ignore his throbbing leg. His thoughts returned to his people's reaction to the news—their shock and anger.

Would they ever forgive her?

Will I?

Not that his forgiveness mattered. He was far from blameless in this mess. They had been a poor match as man and wife, and things were ruined beyond repair now. It was enough that Ermenilda was alive. He would not have to live with her death on his conscience.

Still, Wulfhere was not sure how it would be with Ermenilda back in Tamworth. Oddly, things had changed between them. Ermenilda was now an aloof stranger. She had despaired at leaving Bonehill, but she no longer gazed upon him with scorn. Instead, her loathing appeared to have turned inward.

"I will need to watch your wounds carefully."

Glaedwine interrupted his brooding. Wulfhere opened his eyes and pulled himself upright on the furs. The water in the basin next to the healer was now deep red.

"Will they fester?" he asked, frowning.

The cunning man hesitated. Watching him, Wulfhere felt a pang of misgiving. He had sustained injuries before, but Glaedwine had always assured him that he would heal.

This time, Wulfhere saw doubt in the healer's eyes.

"Only time will tell," Glaedwine replied softly.

Ermenilda was sitting on the edge of the furs, dressed in an undertunic, when Wulfhere climbed up to the King's Loft. Beneath them, she could hear the rise and fall of voices, as folk chatted around the fire pit before retiring for the night.

As soon as Wulfhere had made his explanations to his hall, she had retired upstairs. She had not even gone to greet Wynflaed—or her aunt, whom she had not even seen yet. After the shock of her return, she decided it was better she lie low for the rest of the evening.

"Milord," she greeted him nervously.

"Why are you not asleep, Ermenilda?" Wulfhere replied, limping across to the furs and sitting down heavily on the edge of them. "It's late."

He sounded tired and in ill humor. Ermenilda did not blame him. This had been the worst day of her life, and she imagined he felt the same. Ermenilda climbed under the furs and pulled them up under her chin.

"I wanted to speak to you," she said quietly.

Wulfhere glanced up from where he was taking off his quilted vest.

"Can't it wait till morning?"

"I would like to clear the air between us."

Wulfhere raised a blond eyebrow, and Ermenilda's nervousness increased. She had been working up to this all evening, and he was not making this an easy task.

"I wish to apologize," she finally managed.

Wulfhere sighed. "Ermenilda . . ."

"For all of it," she interrupted him. "For running away, for letting you think I was dead. For being the reason you're injured."

Wulfhere watched her, his expression veiled. "Are you not just sorry you were found out?"

Ermenilda swallowed. "I know it's difficult to believe."

Wulfhere sighed, his shoulders bowing slightly. "Then I should apologize for making your life so unbearable that you had to run from me."

He lay down on top of the furs and turned away from her, still clad in a sleeveless tunic and breeches, although his feet were bare.

"Go to sleep, Ermenilda," he said softly.

Ermenilda lay back on the furs and listened to the gentle rise and fall of her husband's breathing. A single clay cresset still burned nearby, casting their quarters in a soft light. The pile of furs they lay upon was wide enough so that they could sleep easily apart; there was at least a span of three feet between them. Even so, Ermenilda could not relax.

These furs brought back memories, all of them unsettling, and Wulfhere's behavior toward her unbalanced Ermenilda further still. She had preferred his anger and coldness to this bitterness and resignation. Most men would have killed her for what she had done. Yet, he had fought Werbode to defend her honor and had taken her back into his hall.

Tonight, despite everything that had happened, there had been an odd camaraderie between them. Wulfhere appeared the only person in the Great Hall who wished her to remain here.

Ermenilda slept fitfully and awoke in the early dawn. She lay in the darkness, her thoughts returning once again to the events of the day before. Her throat closed with dread at the thought of having to face folk once more, although she knew that hiding from them would just make matters worse.

In the hall below, she heard the first of the slaves stir and the crackling of the fire pits as they roused the embers and added wood. Shortly after, the scent of wood smoke filled the King's Loft, followed by the aroma of baking griddle bread.

Ermenilda rolled onto her side, facing the wall of Wulfhere's back. He had not moved all night and still slept soundly. She was grateful he had kept his distance physically from her, although it came as no surprise. He no longer looked at her with need in his eyes, as he had before she ran away. His hurt and bitterness had obliterated lust.

Above them, the pale dawn light streamed in through the high, narrow window, alerting Ermenilda that she would soon have to rise from her furs and face the day.

Beside her, Wulfhere groaned in his sleep and rolled over onto his back. In the half-light, Ermenilda propped herself up onto her elbows and observed him. His face gleamed and his white-blond hair clung to his scalp.

Tentatively, careful not to wake him, Ermenilda reached across and placed the back of her hand on his forehead. The skin was damp and hot.

Wulfhere's eyes snapped open.

Ermenilda withdrew her hand sharply, as if burned.

"What are you doing?" His voice, still heavy with sleep, rasped slightly.

"You have a fever," Ermenilda said, frowning to mask her discomfort. She sat up and reached for her woolen overdress. "We will need to call for Glaedwine again this morning."

They broke their fast together, alone upon the high seat. Ermenilda noted that Wulfhere's cheekbones were flushed, his eyes unnaturally bright. He ate little and sipped listlessly at his cup of broth.

Ermenilda sat silently beside him, her own appetite also deserting her. She looked about her, noting once again that she had not seen her aunt. Nor had she seen Prince Aethelred since their arrival the day before. It also appeared as if some of the king's retainers, Elfhere among them, were absent.

"Where is Aethelthryth?" she asked Wulfhere.

"I sent her back to Ely," Wulfhere replied. "My brother is accompanying her."

Ermenilda stared at him, caught off guard by his admission.

"She is no longer your hostage?"

"Lady Aethelthryth is free," he replied, before taking a sip of broth. "It no longer pleased me to keep her here. She has enough gold to rebuild her church and the town, if she so wishes."

Wulfhere looked at her. "I wanted to make amends. In honor of your memory."

Lost for words, Ermenilda looked away. She noted that many observed them. Some of the women who resided in the Great Hall were giving her cold and disdainful looks. They were the wives of ealdormen and thegns, women who had once liked her. She had spent many a morning working alongside them at her loom or distaff. After what she had done, it would be foolish to think they would be friends now.

Ermenilda glanced over at where Wynflaed was helping a slave girl make bread. Her maid did not look the queen's way as she pummeled the dough with her fists. Ermenilda could see the tension in her shoulders, the grim set of her lips.

Life here would be bleak indeed without Wynflaed's friendship.

Ermenilda spotted Glaedwine. The healer had just entered the hall and was making his way across the rush-strewn floor toward the high seat. Ermenilda had sent out a slave to fetch him, as soon as she had come downstairs. The cunning man bowed before Wulfhere, his sharp gaze silently assessing the king.

"You are unwell, milord?"

Wulfhere made an impatient gesture. "My wife seems to think so . . . a fever, nothing more."

Glaedwine stepped up onto the high seat, his expression darkening.

"A fever is not lightly dismissed." He gestured to the alcove where he had tended Wulfhere the day before. "Come, I should take another look at those wounds."

Ermenilda watched Wulfhere rise and limp his way over to the alcove, with the healer following him. They left her alone upon the high seat, and moments after the king and cunning man had disappeared, Ermenilda felt the unfriendly stares around her magnify, cutting into her like boning knives.

Rising from her seat, she went to retrieve her distaff and basket of wool. It would be a long morning, and she needed work to take her mind off everything. On her way to retrieve her distaff, Ermenilda passed by a group of women who sat together sewing. Their hate-filled whispers followed her.

Deceitful, pious bitch.

He should have wrung your neck.

Heart pounding, Ermenilda pretended not to hear them. She picked up her basket and spindle, clutching them to her, and hastened back to the relative safety of the high seat. Sitting there once more, Ermenilda had just begun winding wool onto the wooden spindle when she heard someone approach.

She looked up to see Wynflaed before her.

Ermenilda gave the handmaid a tentative smile.

"Wynflaed! It is good to see you."

"How is the king?" the young woman asked coolly, ignoring Ermenilda's greeting.

"He has a fever," Ermenilda replied, glancing over at the hanging that screened Wulfhere and Glaedwine from view. "Werbode cut him deeply on the thigh yesterday . . . the wound may fester."

Wynflaed did not reply to this comment. She only watched Ermenilda, her emerald gaze reproachful. When the silence became too uncomfortable to bear, Wynflaed finally spoke. Her voice was flat, accusing.

"You let me think you'd drowned. I thought it was my fault—that you were lost because of me."

Ermenilda put down her distaff, remorse sweeping over her.

"I'm so sorry, Wynflaed," she whispered, although the words seemed hollow and inadequate. "I could not risk involving you."

Wynflaed's eyes flashed, and her pretty mouth thinned.

"You did involve me. The king could have slain me for losing you, but fortunately for me he blamed himself."

"I realize that, and I am sorry."

Her apology appeared to have little effect on Wynflaed. The young woman folded her arms across her chest.

"How could you do such a thing?"

Ermenilda inhaled deeply. She could not weep here, in front of everyone. If she started crying, she would not stop.

"I was desperately unhappy," she finally admitted. "I thought if I ran away I could make a fresh start."

Wynflaed watched her but said nothing. Her silence was damning.

"It was a mistake," Ermenilda concluded, the words choking her. "I realize now that there are some things you can never outrun."

Chapter Thirty-eight
Protection

Wulfhere's fever steadily worsened as the day progressed.

Glaedwine had been forced to cut away the stitches he had made a day earlier and clean out the wound, which had swollen and filled with pus. The agony, when the healer poured strong wine into the wound, caused Wulfhere to pass out. When he awoke, the cunning man had completed his task, although Glaedwine's face was even grimmer than earlier.

"I will need to do that every day," he had told him, "or you risk losing your leg, or worse."

This news put Wulfhere in a bleak mood. Weak with fever, he sat upon his carved wooden throne and watched the activity in his hall with a glazed stare. Mōna came to see him, although he could barely summon the energy to stroke her plush pelt. The wolf sniffed at the fresh bandage on his thigh and gave a low whine.

"Aye, Mōna," Wulfhere murmured. "It's bad."

On the other side of the hall, he spied Ermenilda. She was taking a drink from a water barrel. Dressed in a plain blue woolen tunic, which left her arms bare, she was lovely to behold. A heavy belt girded her hips, drawing attention to her lithe frame. Her silky blonde hair hung down her back in a long braid, although wisps had come free and framed her face.

She was so beautiful it pained him, yet he could not tear his gaze away. Even after her deceit, he still wanted her. He always would.

Ermenilda moved away from the water barrel, circuiting a group of gossiping women and returning to the large loom she had been working upon. The women's cold stares followed her.

Watching them, Wulfhere frowned.

It was a chill evening, despite the two roaring fire pits inside the Great Hall. A biting north wind buffeted the tower, forcing its way inside through gaps, cracks and openings.

The evening meal was pottage and bread—simple fare, but Ermenilda enjoyed it. She had gotten used to eating modestly in Bonehill, and the pottage the slaves in her hall prepared was superior to the one the nuns served up, day after day.

Next to her, Wulfhere did not touch his meal.

Ermenilda cast him a sidelong glance. They had spoken little all day, although her gaze had often returned to him. She could see he was getting sicker. His eyes had that glazed, faraway look that those fighting a strong fever acquired. He sat slumped in his chair, as if he lacked the energy to even hold himself upright.

She was not surprised when he made a mumbled excuse to her and Seaxwulf and limped off to bed.

The priest watched him go.

"I worry for him," Seaxwulf said, when the king was out of earshot. "Such an injury can kill a man."

Ermenilda gave a cautious nod. The fact had not been lost on her either. Guilt needled her, for Wulfhere had sustained that injury defending her honor.

The priest was watching her under veiled lids. They had barely spoken since her return to Tamworth. She had sensed his disapproval of her, as she did now.

Ermenilda held his gaze. "Speak freely, Brother Seaxwulf. You have every right to be angry with me."

Seaxwulf's mouth thinned, but he said nothing. After a few moments, he looked away, his gaze settling upon the trencher of half-eaten pottage before him.

"My opinion does not matter," he said, finally. "I expect the abbess would have told you how the church views such deceit."

Ermenilda nodded. She still felt the sting of Abbess Ardwyn's shrill words.

"She was incensed," Ermenilda admitted.

Seaxwulf's mouth twisted into a wry smile. "The abbess is not a woman lightly crossed."

Ermenilda did not reply. Instead, she took a sip of watered-down wine from her cup, her gaze taking in the long tables where folk ate, drank, and chatted over their pottage. After the sternness and silence of Bonehill, the noise inside the hall almost overwhelmed her.

"So, Wulfhere has forgiven you?" Seaxwulf asked. Ermenilda's attention shifted back to the priest, and she frowned.

"No . . . I think not."

"Yet, he has taken you back, as his queen."

Ermenilda nodded, wary of where this conversation was heading.

"What is it you wish to say, Brother Seaxwulf?"

"It is not easy to wear the crown," the priest replied gently. "Wulfhere has come to realize that with power comes great responsibility."

Seaxwulf paused, as if measuring his words, before concluding.

"He is still finding his way, but he needs you at his side to guide him."

Ermenilda retired to the King's Loft, in a tense and pensive mood.

Seaxwulf's words had bothered her more than she liked to admit. The priest had left her to work at her distaff, as soon as the meal ended, and she had been relieved to see him go.

Ermenilda stepped up onto the platform that ringed the edge of the hall and stopped to pat Mōna. The wolf silently guarded her master from below. Ermenilda climbed the ladder to the loft. No one paid the queen any mind as she left the main hall, or bid her good night, but Ermenilda did not care. She preferred they ignored her than reviled her.

Upstairs, Wulfhere lay clad only in his breeches on his side of the furs. The sight of him half-naked caused an odd flutter in Ermenilda's chest. She paused at the top of the ladder, discomforted. Even from this distance, she could see a sheen of sweat covered his naked skin. Quietly, Ermenilda stepped onto the platform and made her way over the furs.

His eyes opened as she approached him.

"Good eve, Ermenilda," he rasped.

She nodded in response before deftly removing her woolen overdress, so that she was clad only in a thin linen tunic, and sliding into the furs beside him.

"How are you feeling?" she asked.

"Terrible," he replied and attempted a smile. "Like I've been clubbed repeatedly before being dunked in scalding water."

Ermenilda winced at the description. "Surely, Glaedwine will be able to heal you. I hear his skill is famed throughout Mercia."

"He worries that Werbode's seax blade carried a taint, which has poisoned my blood," Wulfhere replied. "If that's the case, there's little he can do."

Ermenilda did not reply. Wulfhere spoke in such a matter-of-fact fashion that she wondered if he cared what happened to him.

Silence stretched out between them for a few moments, before Wulfhere broke it.

"If I die, you will be in danger."

"You won't die," Ermenilda replied quickly. Too quickly, for his fever-glazed eyes widened. "You don't need to worry about me," she concluded, looking away from him.

"I've seen the way folk here now look at you," Wulfhere answered. "Without my protection, you risk harm."

Ermenilda met his gaze once more. The intensity in his voice worried her, and this time she did not deny the danger she was in. Eventually, she nodded.

"What should I do?"

Wulfhere reached to the right of the bed, where his fighting dagger lay sheathed in its leather scabbard. He handed it to her. "Take my seax. Wear it strapped around your waist at all times."

Ermenilda took it wordlessly, fear fluttering in the pit of her belly.

"I'm not sure I'll be able to use it," she murmured.

Wulfhere ignored her protest. Instead, he kept his gaze fixed upon her face.

"Mōna will protect you. From tomorrow onward, wear the seax and take my wolf everywhere with you."

When Ermenilda remained silent, he reached out and placed a hand on her forearm. She stifled a gasp of surprise. His skin burned as if lit by a furnace within.

"Promise me," Wulfhere rasped.

"Very well," Ermenilda agreed.

This conversation had put her on edge. She found it awkward that Wulfhere focused so entirely upon her, when he was the one lying there with an infected leg and a fever raging through his body.

She was the last thing he should be worrying over.

The next morning, Ermenilda awoke to find Wulfhere's condition had deteriorated further. He could not even summon the energy to rise from the furs, so Ermenilda went downstairs to break her fast alone.

As he had asked, she strapped the seax around her waist before doing so.

Ermenilda sent for Glaedwine and sat alone upon the high seat. She ate a light meal of fresh bread, washed down with a cup of milk. Afterward, she retrieved a bowl of water and a clean square of cloth, and climbed back up the ladder to the King's Loft.

"What are you doing back here?" Wulfhere greeted her. His tone was surly. He was not taking well to being ill and bedridden.

"The healer will be here soon," she replied, ignoring his brusqueness. She placed the bowl of water and cloth on the floor, near the furs, and crossed to a small table, where a clay jug and cup rested. Wordlessly, she poured the king a cup of water before crossing to him and kneeling.

"You must drink something."

"I'm not a child," he grumbled.

"No, but you're ill, and you need water," Ermenilda replied.

Wulfhere raised himself up on his elbows, groaning from the effort, and let her raise the cup to his lips. He took two gulps before sinking back down into the furs with a groan.

"I feel like an old man."

Ermenilda wet the cloth she had brought upstairs and bathed his forehead. Wulfhere let out a soft sigh and closed his eyes.

"You have gentle hands," he murmured.

Ermenilda smiled at that but said nothing. She was wringing out the cloth and about to wipe Wulfhere's face with it when she heard the clunk of booted feet upon the ladder leading up to the loft. She swiveled to see Glaedwine step up onto the platform, his robes swishing around him. He clutched a basket of his herbs, tinctures, and remedies by his side.

"How fares the king this morning?" he asked.

"Worse," Ermenilda replied, rising to her feet. She looked down at Wulfhere. He had opened his eyes and was watching her. Usually, the cunning man attended to Wulfhere on his own, but she thought she might stay to assist.

"Would you like me to remain, and help Glaedwine?" she asked.

Wulfhere shook his head. "You don't need to see this, Ermenilda. Leave us for a while."

Ermenilda nodded and, without another word, left the platform. She knew that the healer would have to clean and dress Wulfhere's infected leg, something that would cause the king great pain. She did not blame him for not wanting others to witness it.

She descended the ladder, but the moment she stepped down from it, Ermenilda felt hostile stares digging into her flesh. Word that the king's condition had worsened had obviously spread around the hall. She could see the accusations in their stares.

Nearby, she spied two women, Aeaba and Burghild, who sat together sewing. Before her departure, they had been friendly toward her, although Ermenilda had found their delight in gossip wearisome. Now, they viewed her like an imposter. Their hate-filled stares pinned her to the spot.

Wulfhere had spoken true. If he died, they would surely stone her to death.

Ermenilda suppressed a shudder and decided it was time she removed herself from the hall for a while. She had not visited her garden since returning to Tamworth and suddenly longed for it.

"Come, Mōna," she commanded. The wolf, which had been sitting at the foot of the ladder, smoothly rose to her feet and trotted to Ermenilda. Mōna glanced back at the ladder expectantly.

Ermenilda reached down and stroked the wolf's pelt. In answer, Mōna gave a low whine and nudged Ermenilda's leg with her muzzle.

"He's not joining us today," she murmured. "Sorry, girl."

Ignoring Aeaba and Burghild—who continued to glare at her—Ermenilda led the way out of the Great Hall, with the wolf trotting at her side.

Chapter Thirty-nine
Friends Again

The moment that Ermenilda stepped beyond the wattle gate into her garden, the gloom that had dogged her steps for the past few days lifted. Weeds had started to choke some of the vegetables, but the peace of her surroundings welcomed her.

Tears blurred Ermenilda's vision as she walked up the path between the vegetable beds.

I should have come here earlier.

At the center of the garden, there were signs that someone had been working here recently—a pile of weeds, freshly pulled from the damp soil. Ermenilda smiled. Wynflaed had not abandoned the garden in her absence.

Mōna sat down nearby, watching her.

"We'll stay here awhile, girl," Ermenilda told her, before retrieving a basket and a small wooden trowel. "I have some work to do."

Relieved to be alone, Ermenilda knelt at the edge of one of the beds and began to weed.

Her return to Tamworth had been even harder than she had anticipated. Wulfhere's fight with Werbode and now his sickness had thrown her into turmoil. Guilt was now her companion. Wulfhere grew increasingly ill, while the atmosphere in the hall itself crackled with tension, like heavy air before a storm.

It was a cool, overcast morning, perfect for gardening. Ermenilda worked hard, losing track of time. The sun had reached its zenith in the sky before she eventually took a break.

Wiping the sweat off her brow, she sat upon the stone bench at the heart of the garden and took a gulp of water from the bladder she had brought with her. Nearby, Mōna had stretched out on the pebbly ground and fallen asleep.

Ermenilda knew she should probably return to the hall and join the king's retainers for the noon meal. Indeed, her belly rumbled—but she could not face them all so soon. The silence and solitude of her garden embraced her like an old friend, and she did not want to leave it.

She rested upon the bench for a few moments more, before returning to her work. The wind had got up, fanning Ermenilda's heated cheeks. She was in the midst of pulling up some cabbages, which had gone to seed, when she heard the gate creak open.

Ermenilda tensed and turned to the sound. Likewise, Mōna sat up, instantly alert.

Wynflaed had entered the garden, bearing a basket. The young woman stopped just inside the gate, her gaze going to Mōna. Like many inside the hall, Wynflaed was wary of the king's white wolf.

Ermenilda rose to her feet, brushing dirt off her hands. After their conversation the day before, she was worried what Wynflaed might say to her.

"Good day," Ermenilda greeted her hesitantly.

Wynflaed nodded, her gaze never leaving Mōna.

"It is safe for me to enter?"

Ermenilda smiled. "Of course, Mōna won't hurt you."

Unconvinced, Wynflaed moved slowly up the path.

"The wolf always ignored you before. What has changed?"

Ermenilda shrugged. "She has become protective of me since my return."

Wynflaed stopped a few feet away and held out the basket.

"You weren't at the noon meal, so I brought you something to eat."

Ermenilda smiled once more, gratitude washing over her.

"That is kind, Wynflaed. Thank you."

She approached the maid and took the basket from her, before seating herself upon the bench. Ermenilda peeked inside and saw there was bread, cheese, slices of cold mutton. and some small sweet onions. Her mouth watered in anticipation.

"There's enough for two, would you like some?"

The girl shook her head. "I have already eaten."

Ermenilda helped herself to some bread and a slice of mutton and began to eat. After the second mouthful, she motioned to a spot on the bench beside her.

"Please, it's difficult to eat while being watched. Why don't you sit down?"

Wynflaed did as bade, although Ermenilda could feel the tension emanating off her. Eventually, the maid broke the silence between them.

"They say the king is worse."

"He is," Ermenilda confirmed.

"What will you do if he dies?"

Ermenilda's stomach twisted painfully at the thought. "I don't know."

Life as a nun at Bonehill was not an option. In fact, she wondered if any nunnery would take her after what she had done. She could go to her aunt in Ely, or return to her parents in Cantwareburh, but neither of those options tempted. She still missed her mother and sister, but the last few months had changed her—she knew she could not return to her old life.

Still, the thought of remaining in Tamworth, reviled by all, did not appeal either.

Ermenilda finished her meal and brushed the crumbs off her skirts. She glanced across at Wynflaed to find her staring morosely at the ground.

"I missed you, Wynflaed," she admitted. "Yet, I remember you used to smile more. Have I angered you so much?"

Wynflaed sighed and glanced up. "It was a shock, seeing you again, milady, but I am glad you are alive," she began, her voice subdued. "Much changed after you disappeared—life here changed. I no longer had you as my companion. Now, with Elfhere gone, accompanying Aethelred to Ely, I feel isolated."

"Elfhere?" Ermenilda lifted a questioning eyebrow. "I thought you were ignoring him."

Wynflaed blushed prettily and picked at a loose thread on her tunic.

"Not anymore . . ."

Genuine pleasure flooded through Ermenilda at this news. Her own life was a mess, but it was a relief to see that love and joy existed elsewhere.

"I am happy for you both," Ermenilda said, reaching across and placing a hand on Wynflaed's forearm. "You are well suited, and I've seen the way he looks at you. Elfhere will treat you well."

Wynflaed smiled, and the expression lit up the cloudy day.

"Thank you," she replied, her gaze softening. "I missed you as well . . . and I am sorry your garden is so overgrown. I have so many chores inside the Great Tower these days that I have neglected it."

Ermenilda waved off her apology and rose to her feet.

"There is nothing to be sorry for. You have done well to manage what you have. Come, work with me awhile. I'd welcome your company."

***

By the end of the first day after Wulfhere had taken to his bed, he slipped into unconsciousness.

The following morning, Ermenilda assisted Glaedwine as he treated Wulfhere's wounds. The king lay upon the furs, unaware of their presence as they worked. The fire that consumed him glowed like a smith's forge.

"This is the worst fever I have ever tended," the cunning man admitted. "If it rises any further, it will damage his mind."

Ermenilda frowned at this news. Glaedwine was a man of few words. If he declared that a patient was ill, then the situation was serious indeed.

The deeper of the two cuts on Wulfhere's thigh was swollen and wept pus. Ermenilda looked on as Glaedwine removed the stitches, cleaned the oozing wound, and added a poultice of mashed garlic, onion, and wine.

"How will that help?" Ermenilda asked. The stench of the festering wound, mixed with that of the poultice, made her bile rise. Still, she held the bowl full of the foul-smelling ointment for Glaedwine as he worked.

"This should help draw out the taint," Glaedwine told her. His gaunt face was stern, and Ermenilda could not tell if he believed the treatment would work.

"Will it heal him?"

"If he is strong enough to fight the fever off."

Ermenilda looked down at Wulfhere's face. She had returned from her garden, late afternoon the day before, to find his condition had deteriorated. He had spent most of the night groaning in his sleep, fighting demons only he could see. Now, he muttered nonsense and writhed as he fought the fire within him.

After applying the poultice, Glaedwine left the loft, promising to return later in the day. Ermenilda remained at Wulfhere's side and wiped his brow with a cold, wet cloth. She would not go to her garden today. With Wulfhere this ill, she could not leave him.

Wynflaed brought some bread and cheese up to her mistress at noon, her green eyes filled with concern as they rested on the man who lay unconscious upon the furs.

"He is worse?"

Ermenilda nodded, before handing her the bowl she had emptied of water.

"Please refill this, Wynflaed."

The young woman took the bowl and, with another worried look in Wulfhere's direction, descended the ladder to do her mistress's bidding. Once she had gone, Ermenilda turned back to her husband. The flesh had started to melt away from his strong frame, and his mane of white-blond hair stuck listlessly to his scalp.

Fight, Wulfhere. You must fight.

It dawned on her that she was beginning to worry for him. It was a terrible thing to watch such a vital, powerful man sicken.

Ermenilda winced as something clenched deep in her chest.

The irony of the situation was not lost on her. She had resisted Wulfhere of Mercia from the first moment they met, and now here she was willing him to live.

Chapter Forty
The Prince Returns

A biting wind was blowing in from the northeast when Aethelred led his men across the bridge leading into Tamworth.

The lazy waters of the River Tame sparkled in the late afternoon sun. It was one of those bright autumn days, when every detail stands out in vivid relief. Even the Great Tower of Tamworth, rising high above the thatched roofs like a grim stone god, looked attractive in such weather. The afternoon light was so pure that Aethelred could pick out every detail on its lichen-encrusted, pitted surface.

Leaves wheeled and skittered over the earth, and billowy clouds raced across the pastel sky. His stallion's hooves clip-clopped hollowly on the dirt road as he urged it into a canter.

A smile stretched across Aethelred's face. It was good to be home.

He led his company under the low gate and up the tangle of streets toward the Great Tower. It had been an exhausting journey, and never had he been so relieved to ride into Tamworth. Aethelred was looking forward to downing a cup of frothing ale, putting his feet up next to the fire pit, and catching up with his brother.

However, when he reached the high gate, one look at the expression of the spearman guarding it caused his good mood to sour.

Even before the warrior spoke, Aethelred knew something was wrong.

Ermenilda was mopping Wulfhere's fevered brow when Prince Aethelred appeared at the top of the ladder. His face was grim, his pale gaze hard, as he stepped out onto the platform and moved toward her. Ermenilda's throat closed at the sight of him. The prince looked incensed.

Trembling, she rose to meet him.

"Lord Aethelred."

He ignored her, instead stopping before the furs and gazing down upon his brother's fever-racked body. Tense moments passed, and Ermenilda saw the anger, grief, and disbelief on his face.

"How long has he been like this?" he finally demanded.

"Werbode injured him five days ago," Ermenilda replied softly, "but he has not been awake for over a day now, and his condition worsens."

Aethelred's gaze shifted from Wulfhere and pinned her to the spot.

"This is your doing."

Ermenilda nodded. There was little point in denying the obvious.

"He was cursed the day he met you," Aethelred ground out. His crystalline gaze, so like his brother's, was as hard as flint. "You have brought him nothing but suffering."

Ermenilda flinched, but she could not deny his words.

"I'm sorry for it, Aethelred. If I could undo what has been done, I would."

The prince's gaze widened. He had clearly not expected her to acknowledge the truth. Another tense silence stretched between them before Ermenilda eventually broke it.

"My aunt," she began hesitantly. "How is she?"

Aethelred's gaze shifted away from hers, back to where Wulfhere lay.

"She's well," he replied gruffly, "or she was when I left her at Ely. Her tongue is still sharp enough to flay the flesh off a man."

Ermenilda gave a small smile. "Aethelthryth has a forceful character."

The prince snorted at that, before kneeling down at the edge of the furs next to his brother. He reached out and laid a hand on Wulfhere's arm, before inhaling sharply.

"He is burning alive. Fetch Glaedwine—we need him now!"

"The healer has been tending to him. He says that Werbode's knife has poisoned the king's blood. There is nothing more he can do."

Ermenilda watched Aethelred a moment, before she sidled away toward the ladder. It was clear that the prince wished to be alone with his brother for a while.

"I will return shortly," she said. "I need to fetch some fresh water and cloths."

Aethelred nodded but did not look her way.

Alone in the loft with Wulfhere, the prince struggled with the grief that gripped his throat.

His brother was seriously ill; he did not need to be a healer to understand that. Wulfhere's skin, drawn sharply across the bones of his face, was flushed and mottled. The healer had cut away the left leg of his breeches, allowing the wounds access to the air. An evil-smelling poultice covered the cuts, leaving Aethelred wondering if the stench was due to the ointment that Glaedwine had used or the infection. Wulfhere's leg had swollen to twice its size. At least there were no livid streaks radiating down his leg from the wound. That was a sure sign a man would either lose his leg or die.

Even so, he could see his brother was gravely ill.

With Wulfhere gone, he would become king. Their father had brought his sons up to be rulers, and to fight each other for the prize if they had to.

If it had been Paeda lying there, Aethelred may have felt differently. Their eldest brother had been a difficult man to like. Growing up, he had bullied his younger brothers mercilessly, something Aethelred had never forgiven him for. Over the years, the two of them, Wulfhere and Aethelred, had drawn close in response to Paeda's cruelty. Yet, it was not the only reason that Aethelred was upset now.

Without Wulfhere, he would be alone—the last member of a once mighty dynasty.

"There's only us now, Brother," he murmured, reaching out and gripping Wulfhere's fevered hand. "Fæder, Paeda—they're both gone—we're all that's left of the Iclingas."

Aethelred squeezed Wulfhere's hand tighter still. "Don't abandon us. Don't abandon me."

Ermenilda did not dine alone upon the high seat that evening. Aethelred joined her, as did Elfhere, Seaxwulf, and Glaedwine. Slaves brought them trenchers of hare stew while Wynflaed circled their table, filling their cups with sloe wine.

Ermenilda took a sip of the strong wine and sighed as its heat settled in the pit of her belly. The past few days had been exhausting, and now with Aethelred's return, she found herself on the defensive once more. This evening, her nerves felt stretched as taut as a drum, and her back and shoulders ached as if she carried a great weight upon them. The tension inside the Great Hall was taking its toll on her.

The hare stew was rich and delicious but she ate sparingly. Across the table, the prince said little. He appeared to have withdrawn into his own thoughts.

Wynflaed leaned over Elfhere, filling his cup with wine. Ermenilda watched their gazes meet. Elfhere, his sea-blue eyes filled with warmth, smiled at the young woman. She returned the expression, her hand brushing his as she pulled away.

Ermenilda could see the attraction between them, the invisible thread that pulled them close. She witnessed the unabashed affection and desire on their faces and felt a pang of envy.

That's how it should be between a man and a woman.

After the evening meal, Ermenilda returned upstairs to tend Wulfhere. His breathing was now labored, and he had grown deathly still.

Glaedwine paid his patient a visit shortly after, with Aethelred and Seaxwulf close behind him. An ominous silence filled the loft as they watched the cunning man attend the king. Eventually, Glaedwine sat back on his heels, his expression bleak.

"His wounds are slightly better than yesterday, but his fever is not," he told them. "He's stopped fighting . . ."

"Is he dying?" Aethelred rasped.

The healer turned to Aethelred, pity in his eyes.

"It will be decided tonight," he replied. "If the king lives to see the dawn, then he might survive, otherwise the fever will take him . . ."

Glaedwine's voice trailed off.

Seaxwulf cleared his throat, his gentle gaze settling upon Ermenilda.

"May I bless him, milady?"

Ermenilda nodded, not trusting herself to speak.

***

Night settled over Tamworth. Outside, the wind howled, hurling itself against the tower's stone walls and pummeling the roof and shutters. Nature had whipped itself up into a fury, almost as if it raged against what was happening within.

Ermenilda sat at her husband's side and listened to the wind. Wulfhere had gone pale and still. Her eyes burned with fatigue and her body ached, but she would not sleep tonight.

Even so, she felt in need of some fresh air. She had been at Wulfhere's side for a long while and wished to feel the wind's fury upon her face before she took her place at the king's side for the remainder of the night.

Moving slowly, her limbs heavy and clumsy, Ermenilda crossed the platform and climbed down to the hall below. As always, Mōna lay curled up at the foot of the ladder. The wolf opened one glowing eye as Ermenilda stepped past her.

"Stay there, girl," Ermenilda commanded softly. It was late, and she would not be going far. She would not need Mōna's protection. Most of the inhabitants of the Great Hall had either retired to their alcoves, which lined the sides of the wide space, or had stretched out upon the rushes to sleep.

Only Aethelred was awake. He sat by one of the fire pits, cradling a cup of mead in his hands. The prince did not appear to notice her. Instead, he gazed sightlessly into the flames. His face was drawn, his eyes hard. Shortly after Glaedwine had delivered his news, Aethelred had stormed away, leaving the priest to bless his dying brother.

Ermenilda eyed him as she picked her way across the hall, weaving in between the prone bodies of men, women, children, and dogs. The depth of his grief over his brother surprised her; she had thought that rivalry between Penda's sons would have hardened them against each other. Did he not covet the crown?

She left the hall behind, silently passing through the entrance hall toward the doors. Stepping outside, Ermenilda braced herself against the wind. It hit her like angry fists, pummeling her skin and clawing at her clothing. She had not brought her cloak with her, and the chill air bit at her skin. She welcomed its fury.

Ermenilda stood on the wide stone ledge, above the steps leading down to the yard below, and closed her eyes. She inhaled deeply. The wind slapped at her face and whipped her hair around, but it was what she needed. Its ferocity gave her strength for what was to come.

She lingered there awhile, on the edge of the darkness, until the cold started to drill into her bones. Reluctantly, Ermenilda pushed her way back through the doors.

The entranceway was a shadowy space, lit only by two pitch torches on each wall. Passages led off either side to store rooms. Ermenilda was halfway across it when two figures stepped out of the shadows.

Instantly, she recognized Aeaba and Burghild, two of the women whose hostile stares had dogged her steps since her return to Tamworth. Their husbands were thegns, and both women had a high standing in the Great Tower. Aeaba was plump with thick walnut-colored tresses that she wore braided around her head. Her friend, Burghild, was tall and thin with pale blonde hair.

Both women stalked her, their narrowed gazes glinting in the torchlight.

"Christ-worshipping witch," Burghild whispered. "Did you think we would never get you alone?"

"You can't take that wolf everywhere with you," Aeaba chimed in. "Sooner or later, we were going to corner you."

Ermenilda backed up toward the door she had just entered, her heart hammering. The biting wind had sharpened her senses, and she was aware how vulnerable she was here without Mōna to protect her.

"What do you want?" Ermenilda gasped out the words, fear turning her limbs weak.

"You should be punished," Aeaba replied, her voice rising. "The king is too sick to do it, so we must."

"A pretty face is wasted on you," Burghild added. "You need some scars."

Terror pulsed through Ermenilda. Clumsily, she drew Wulfhere's seax. It was a wicked-looking blade, and it caused both women to check their step.

Burghild recovered first. "Do you think that scares us?"

"You don't have the stomach to use it?" Aeaba mocked.

"Don't come a step closer!" Ermenilda gasped, holding the knife low as she had seen Wulfhere do when he and Werbode fought. Now that she held a weapon, her paralyzing fear had ebbed slightly. In its place, she could feel anger building.

Aeaba made a grab for her.

Without thinking, Ermenilda slashed the dagger at her and felt the blade bite flesh.

Aeaba squealed and fell back clutching her arm.

"Hōre! You cut me!"

"I warned you," Ermenilda said between gritted teeth. Her husband was upstairs dying, and these two were preventing her from returning to him. "Keep away from me."

Chapter Forty-one
The Long Night

Silence filled the entrance hall.

Ermenilda's attackers glared at her, deciding upon their next move. Strangely, the last of her fear had dissolved now, and she readied herself to fight.

"Come on then," she taunted the women. "But, don't think I'm going to make it easy for you."

A moment later, a man's voice echoed through the hall.

"I'd heed her if I were you."

Ermenilda's gaze shifted behind Aeaba and Burghild to where a figure leaned against the doors leading into the hall. The man detached himself from the shadows and stepped into the light.

Aethelred viewed the trio with a hooded gaze.

"Aeaba . . . Burghild. Do your husbands know what you're up to?"

Ermenilda saw both women blanch, although Aeaba was the first to recover. She was a bold, pugnacious woman, and her self-righteousness was too strong to be leashed for long.

"Our husbands would applaud our actions, milord," she replied, drawing herself up as she faced him. "This woman has brought shame upon her own husband, upon your family. She must be punished."

"You take a lot upon yourself, Aeaba," Aethelred said softly. Ermenilda knew that tone. Wulfhere used it when he was angry. "That is for the king to decide, not you."

Aeaba's confidence appeared to falter slightly. She glanced at her accomplice, but Burghild seemed to have developed a sudden fascination with the wooden floor beneath her feet.

"Go to bed," Aethelred ordered, his tone brooking no argument, "and let no more be said of this. If I ever catch you threatening the queen again, I will deal with both of you harshly."

Aeaba and Burghild slunk away like beaten dogs, taking their bitterness and resentment with them. The door to the main hall whispered shut behind the women, leaving Aethelred and Ermenilda alone.

"Did they hurt you?" Aethelred asked.

Ermenilda shook her head and sheathed the seax, noting that her hands were trembling.

"Thank you," she murmured. "I don't know what would have happened had you not intervened."

Aethelred gave a soft, humorless laugh. "You looked to have the situation in hand, to me. I just thought I had better step in before those two stupid geese got their throats cut."

Ermenilda tried to smile but failed. The whole incident was yet another reminder of all the mistakes she had made.

"I had better return to Wulfhere," she replied quietly.

The light from the cressets lining the walls flickered across Wulfhere's ashen skin. He was breathing so shallowly now that Ermenilda could barely make out the rise and fall of his chest.

Glaedwine was right: Wulfhere was giving up the fight.

Ermenilda sank down on the furs next to her husband, her limbs still quivering from her brush with Aeaba and Burghild. She knelt upon the floor before her husband and, clasping her hands together, murmured a heartfelt prayer.

"Please Lord, spare this man. Don't take him from this world . . . not now."

Finishing her prayer, Ermenilda climbed onto the furs. She stretched out next to Wulfhere and lay on her side, facing him. She reached out and took his limp, heated hand in hers.

"Fight, Wulfhere," she whispered, her voice catching. "Don't let Werbode take you with him."

Her husband did not respond. He just lay there, sinking further and further into darkness. Ermenilda watched him for a few moments before grief splintered inside her.

"I'm so sorry," she whispered. Tears slid down her cheeks, scalding them. "The truth is that I never wanted us to be happy together. I made up my mind about you before we ever wed. I wanted to hate you, to feel superior to you. I learned at my mother's knee—her bitterness and resentment became my own—and it poisoned everything between us."

Her husband was a warlord, but he was not the monster she had portrayed him to be. She accepted that now, although she had known from the first. His quest for revenge had sickened her, but it was no worse than the motivations that had spurred her own mother and aunt to plot an attack on him. Wulfhere was not responsible for his father's actions, but Aethelthryth and Seaxburh had wanted reckoning at any cost.

"We're all flawed," she told him, her voice quavering, "and me more than most. If you would only live, Wulfhere, I would show you just how sorry I am. Live and I will love you—I promise!"

There were no more words, for her weeping now turned to silent sobs. She shifted closer to him and laid her head upon his chest. His skin was dry and scorching, as if too close to a fire pit.

Ermenilda's tears rained down, soaking them both.

She wept for a long while, an outpouring of pent-up emotion she had been suppressing for months.

Ermenilda let it all go.

When she finished crying, she fell asleep where she lay, upon Wulfhere's bare chest.

She awoke to the rumble of voices and the aroma of baking bread.

Below, the Great Hall was coming to life, as its inhabitants stirred. Ermenilda listened for a few moments, letting the fog of sleep clear. For a short spell, she forgot where she was. All she knew was that it was dawn and time to rise.

Then, she remembered Wulfhere.

She still lay upon his chest; she had not shifted all night. The skin against her cheek no longer burned, but was quite cool.

Ermenilda's heart leaped and the last remnants of sleep dissolved. She sat up, pushing the hair that had come free of its braid from her eyes.

Her gaze went to Wulfhere's face. He was still and pale. Dread rose within her, and she placed a hand on his forehead, confirming that the fever was gone.

Is he dead?

She leaned back over his chest, this time placing her ear over his heart.

Ermenilda held her breath, and then she heard it.

The slow, reassuring thud of his heart. She felt the gentle rise and fall of his breathing beneath her.

Relief swept over her in a giddying wave.

He's alive!

Ermenilda scrambled to her feet and flew across the platform toward the ladder. She needed to fetch Glaedwine.

The healer placed his hand on Wulfhere's forehead and gave a grunt of approval.

"Good."

He checked for swellings over the king's body—prodding under his arms and in his groin, and gave another grunt when he found nothing to concern him. Lastly, he cleaned the wounds on Wulfhere's thigh and examined them.

"There is no pus this morning," he announced. He looked up, his gaze meeting Ermenilda's across the furs. "I think your husband will live, milady."

Ermenilda smiled back at him, speechless with relief.

"He will wake up soon enough," Glaedwine concluded. "Make sure he has something to eat and drink when he does."

Ermenilda nodded. "Thank you, Glaedwine."

Prince Aethelred stood next to the cunning man. The tension appeared to leave his body at Glaedwine's judgment. He was now watching Ermenilda, surprise etched on his face. She met his gaze, and he frowned.

"I thought you cared little for my brother. Yet, here you are rejoicing that he will live."

They were blunt words. Ermenilda did not blame Aethelred for his reaction but, this morning, nothing could dampen her joy. Wulfhere would live, and that was all that mattered.

She gave Aethelred a small, enigmatic smile.

"A long night changes many things."

Aethelred snorted and cast Glaedwine an exasperated look. "God's bones, I'll never understand women."

The healer laughed before casting a shrewd look in Ermenilda's direction. "You're not alone, Aethelred—neither do most men."

***

Wulfhere awoke slowly. First, he was aware of the faint murmur of voices. He felt warm air caress his skin and breathed in the aroma of roasting meat . . . mutton.

His body felt weak but blessedly cool. The furnace that had roared within him and the aching in his joints had both disappeared.

Wulfhere's eyes flickered open. It was day, for pale light filtered in from the high windows above him. He swallowed before wincing. His throat felt like a dry piece of wood.

"Water," he croaked weakly.

"Here." A woman's soft voice greeted him. "Drink slowly or you'll choke."

It was then that he realized his head was resting upon someone's lap. He caught the faint scent of rose water and lavender.

Ermenilda.

He drank from the cup she raised to his lips, taking three swallows although he wished to drain the whole cup. He rested back against her with a groan.

He felt as weak as a newborn lamb.

"What happened?" he rasped. "Did I sleep?"

"The fever almost claimed you," Ermenilda replied, "but you fought back."

It was all returning to him now. The knife fight with Werbode, his injuries—and the fever that followed.

"My leg . . . will I lose it?"

"Glaedwine says it will heal, now you are over the worst."

She shifted from under him, removing her softness and scent. Instead, she placed a rolled up fur under his head as a pillow and came to sit by him.

Wulfhere drank her in. Dressed in a simple, sleeveless tunic the same color as her eyes—walnut brown—she was a welcome sight. However, he noted the tiredness etched upon her delicate face and the lines of tension about her eyes and mouth.

"You worried us all," she said, before favoring him with a smile.

The expression made his breathing still. There was a softness in her eyes when she smiled at him that he had never seen before.

"Even you?" he asked. He cursed his raspy voice. It sounded as if he had just swallowed a cup of sand.

She nodded. He saw her blush, and her eyes glittered unnaturally bright.

"When you found me at Bonehill, you could have punished me," she began, her voice low and steady, "but, instead you protected me from Werbode, and even when you were ill, you worried for my safety."

Ermenilda broke eye contact with him, developing a sudden fascination with her hands clasped upon her lap.

"I never had a chance to thank you," she whispered.

"Thank me?" Wulfhere eventually found his tongue. "All I have ever done is hurt you."

Her gaze shifted back to him.

"I am hardly blameless," she replied firmly. "Both of us had a part to play."

Silence fell. Wulfhere watched her. A veil had lifted revealing them both to each other for the first time. He reached out and took her hand, clasping his fingers around hers.

"Can we start again?"

It took everything he had to ask the question. His chest constricted as he waited for her answer. It suddenly hurt to breathe.

Wordlessly, Ermenilda squeezed his hand. Then, she nodded.

Chapter Forty-two
Healing

"You win again!"

Aethelred flung the knucklebones down on the table in disgust. Glowering, he reached for the jug of ale and refilled his cup.

"If I hadn't been watching you like a hawk, I'd think you were cheating."

Wulfhere gave a soft laugh and raised an eyebrow.

"Poor loser."

The brothers sat upon the high seat. It was late morning, and the cooks had almost finished preparing the noon meal. The aroma of rabbit and leek pie wafted through the hall, causing Wulfhere's stomach to growl. In the five days since he had awoken from the fever, he had been constantly hungry. He was still weak, and his leg pained him, but Glaedwine assured him the wounds to his thigh were now healing well. They had scabbed over, and the swelling had now completely gone.

"Another game?" he asked Aethelred.

"Not likely," his brother grumbled.

Wulfhere regarded the prince a moment, smiling at Aethelred's inability to lose gracefully.

"I haven't asked you how the trip to Ely went," he said, changing the subject. "Did the widow behave herself?"

Aethelred's expression darkened further.

"We fought from the moment we left Tamworth till when I left her among the ruins of Ely," he admitted.

"I am sorry to have burdened you with such a shrew," Wulfhere replied, forcing himself not to grin. "Surely, it was not too much of an ordeal."

Aethelred snorted, before he grinned wolfishly. "I did see her once without her headrail during the journey," he admitted. "Did you know she has long, dark hair . . . beautiful."

Wulfhere sat back in his chair. Aethelthryth, even without her nunlike veil, had not appeared the sort of woman to tempt a man. His brother's admission surprised him.

Aethelred poured himself some ale and took a deep draft.

"So have you and Ermenilda mended things?"

Wulfhere smiled, his gaze moving to the other side of the hall where his wife worked upon a tapestry.

"Things are better," he admitted, "although it will take time. We never really knew each other before."

Aethelred nodded, and he returned his brother's smile. "At least you are no longer at war with each other," he replied.

***

Ermenilda glanced across at Wulfhere.

"Are you tired? Shall we return to the hall?"

"I'm not a feeble old man," Wulfhere grumbled. "I think I can manage a short walk."

Ermenilda glanced down, hiding a smile. Now that he was healing, Wulfhere was proving to be an irascible patient. His energy was returning, but he chafed at not being able to ride, hunt, and fight as he had before. He still walked with a limp, although it lessened with each passing day. Wulfhere had little patience with his healing body.

They walked down an incline, in between rows of timbered houses, after paying Seaxwulf a short visit at his church. It was a windy afternoon, and gusts caught at the fur cloak that Ermenilda wore about her shoulders. The nights were drawing in, and the days were getting colder. As always, Mōna loped after them. She was ever their shadow these days, and Ermenilda had grown fond of the wolf.

"Shall we visit my garden?" she asked him.

"Aye," Wulfhere replied, casting her an apologetic look. He knew that he was being grumpy. "It is a while since I saw it."

He reached out and took her arm, tucking it through his. It was a protective gesture, and Ermenilda welcomed it. Many days had passed since Wulfhere had awoken from his fever, and they were still circling each other warily. Wulfhere kept a respectful distance from her, and although they slept in the same furs at night, he had not touched her. There was an unspoken pact between them that they would find their way forward slowly.

They passed many townsfolk on the way down the hill. Children were playing in the dirt after the day's chores had been done. Women were bringing in washing, while men carted wood indoors for the fire.

Folk called out to them, hailing their king and queen. Wulfhere raised a hand to acknowledge them, and Ermenilda was relieved to see that outside the Great Tower at least, folk did not hate her.

They entered the garden, with Mōna at their heels, and walked to its heart. Ermenilda watched Wulfhere look around taking it all in. She had spent many afternoons out here since her return, and Ermenilda was proud of how the garden was looking. The last of the roses had dropped from the bushes lining the space, and some of the other plants were going to ground for the winter, but there were still some of the hardier herbs and vegetables growing.

"After you disappeared, I used to come to the garden," Wulfhere said finally, turning to her. "I felt your presence here."

Ermenilda looked down, suddenly self-conscious. "It was a thoughtful gift for a new bride. If I hadn't been so full of prejudice, I would have appreciated it more."

"Other highborn women wish for furs and jewels, but all you wanted was a garden."

Ermenilda glanced up and saw he was smiling.

"Aye, I'm not like other women. That was why I wished to take the veil."

Wulfhere's smile faded. He reached out and gently stroked her cheek. Ermenilda swallowed, a blade of need arrowing through her. They had deliberately avoided touching each other over the last few days, although the feel of his fingers on her skin reminded her of what they had shared in the past.

"Do you miss Bonehill?" he asked. "Do you still wish for that life?"

Ermenilda shook her head, surprising herself that this was the truth.

"I learned that I like the world beyond the convent walls, with all its dirt and barbarity, more than I realized." she admitted.

Wulfhere gave a soft laugh, his pale gaze twinkling. "I am glad."

The king and queen entered the Great Hall just before sunset, still walking arm in arm. They crossed the rush-strewn floor, past where slaves were making the finishing touches to the evening's pottage, and made their way toward the high seat.

Elfhere was waiting for them, with Wynflaed at his side.

The warrior's face was serious, his body tense. Next to him, Wynflaed's cheeks were flushed, and she fidgeted nervously.

"Elfhere, Wynflaed," Ermenilda greeted them first. "Is something amiss?"

"No, milady?" Elfhere replied, although the tension in his body appeared to coil tighter as the king and queen stopped before them.

Elfhere's gaze went to Wulfhere, and he bowed his head.

"Lord Wulfhere, I come to ask permission to wed Wynflaed."

The king held his thegn's gaze for a few moments. Wulfhere saw anxiety in the man's eyes and knew that he was the cause.

"You look so worried, Elfhere. Do you really think I would deny you?"

Wynflaed stepped forward, ignoring the look of warning that Elfhere cast her. She bowed her head, and when she spoke, her voice trembled.

"Milord, I still blame myself for letting the queen out of my sight. I understand if you feel the same way."

Wulfhere shook his head thinking he should have dealt with this sooner. It was clear Wynflaed had struggled under a mantle of guilt since Ermenilda's disappearance—one she had not yet shed.

"I never blamed you, Wynflaed," he said quietly. "I raged upon myself, and you were a reminder of what I had lost."

He paused, then waited for her to look up and meet his gaze. When she did, he saw that her eyes glistened.

"I know you have served Ermenilda loyally," he told her. "I give both you and Elfhere my blessing."

Wynflaed stared at him for a moment. Her body sagged and she burst into tears. Elfhere reached out and pulled Wynflaed against him. His gaze met Wulfhere's, and he smiled, the tension leaving him.

"Thank you, milord."

Chapter Forty-three
The Handfasting

Elfhere and Wynflaed wed on a sunny afternoon, outside the walls of Tamworth. The ceremony took place upon the wide meadows beyond the east gate. To the north, the barrows of Mercian kings looked on as the warrior and his young bride faced each other before Seaxwulf and pledged their lives to each other.

To the left of the priest, Ermenilda stood at Wulfhere's side. She found herself struggling not to cry as she watched the lovers make their oaths. The priest finished blessing them. Then, he unwound the ribbon that tied their hands together, so that they could drink from the same cup and share a honey seedcake.

Crowds of people surrounded them. All of Tamworth had turned out for the celebration, and Wulfhere had ensured that a great feast was prepared for them. Wild boar, mutton, and venison all roasted on spits behind the crowd, and the wood for a bonfire had been laid in the center of the meadows, ready to be lit for the dancing and reveling that would follow after dusk.

When Elfhere and Wynflaed had both pledged their gifts to each other, Seaxwulf solemnly pronounced them wed. Without hesitation, Elfhere pulled Wynflaed into his arms, his lips claiming hers for a passionate kiss.

A roar went up in the crowd. Some of the men hooted, whistled, and called out ribald comments. When the clamor died away, all gazes went to the king.

Ermenilda also looked at her husband healed and strong. Just the sight of him caused her breathing to quicken. He was dressed in a quilted vest and leather breeches embossed with fine patterns. His gold and silver arm rings glinted in the setting sun, as did the circlet he wore upon his head. His pale hair glowed as if lit by moonlight, and a plush ermine cloak hung from his shoulders.

Ermenilda ached to touch him. Despite that they had grown ever closer over the past days, they still kept their distance physically. She wondered how much longer Wulfhere would restrain from touching her. Perhaps he no longer desired her. Disappointment tightened in the pit of Ermenilda's belly as she considered this possibility.

Wulfhere's gaze traveled across the crowd. When he spoke, his voice echoed over the meadows.

"Let the celebrations begin!"

Night's long shadow crept over Tamworth, chasing away the rosy blush of the setting sun. The bonfire in the center of the meadows roared to life. Men rolled out barrels of mead, ale, and sloe wine, and slaves passed around platters of roast meat, tureens of braised onions, and baskets of griddle bread.

Back from the fire, three musicians stood upon a platform, playing a lively tune upon a bone whistle, lyre, and drum. Wulfhere sat at the head of a long table, with Ermenilda at his side. They shared a platter of food, and Wulfhere watched his wife help herself to pieces of meat, before unselfconsciously licking grease from her fingers.

The sight filled him with a hunger that had nothing to do with food.

For weeks now, he had avoided touching her, but he was not sure how much longer he could continue to do so. She was radiant this evening, clad in a long-sleeved plum-red gown that hugged her lissome form. A plush red-squirrel cloak hung from her shoulders, and a slender circlet studded with tiny stones sat upon her head. She wore her hair unbound this evening, and it rippled over her shoulders like sunlight.

It was torture watching her, spending days and nights by her side and not being able to touch her. After everything that had happened, and after the last time they had lain together, Wulfhere was wary of ruining the fragile happiness they had found.

Every night, he lay listening to his wife's gentle breathing, the warmth of her body reaching out to him, and wondered how he would continue to endure it.

What if she shrank away from his touch?

Once the feasting ended, the revelers moved away from the tables toward the fire. The music rose high into the night sky, and the roaring fire gave off a glow that lit up the meadow for a furlong in every direction.

Wulfhere and Ermenilda remained seated at the table, watching Elfhere and Wynflaed take the first dance.

"They make a handsome couple," Ermenilda observed, raising her cup of wine to her lips. "Elfhere noticed Wynflaed on the journey from Cantwareburh, but she resisted him for a while."

"Aye, she made him work for her affections," Wulfhere agreed.

Their gazes met and held. Suddenly, it was as if they were alone. The raucous, excited crowd swirling around them had disappeared.

Wulfhere's gaze devoured her. Ermenilda's skin looked creamy and burnished with gold in the firelight, her brown eyes dark and luminous. Her lips parted slightly as she held his gaze. Desire clawed up Wulfhere's throat, threatening to choke him.

Wordlessly, he reached out and cupped her chin, running his thumb along her bottom lip.

He did not want to talk about Elfhere and Wynflaed, to skirt around the subject they had been avoiding for days. He wanted to talk about them.

"You are so beautiful that it hurts me to look upon you," he murmured. "I'm dying with need for you, Ermenilda."

Her gaze widened, and he saw her pupils dilate. His words affected her. Not saying another word, he leaned in for a kiss. His lips gently touched Ermenilda's, and he heard a sigh escape her. He ran the tip of his tongue along her lower lip and she groaned.

Oblivious to any onlookers, he pulled Ermenilda against him, his hands cupping the back of her head as he kissed her. Ermenilda's mouth opened under his, and, for the first time, she kissed him back, her tongue darting tentatively into his mouth—testing, tasting, and teasing.

Wulfhere eventually pulled away, his heart slamming against his ribs. He would have her tonight or he would die.

"Will you come with me?" he asked.

She nodded, and Wulfhere saw the same desire that thrummed through him reflected in her eyes. Wordlessly, he rose to his feet, took her hand, and led her away through the revelers.

Ermenilda's pulse raced as she followed Wulfhere across the meadows. His hand gripped hers firmly. The heat of his skin caused shivers of excitement to ripple through her.

He did not lead her back to Tamworth, as she had expected, but east, toward the woodland. The line of trees rose up in a dark shadow against the deep indigo sky, and the light from the bonfire illuminated the gnarled trunks of the first of them.

Mōna padded after her master and mistress, only stopping when they reached the trees. Here, Wulfhere turned and met the wolf's gaze.

"Stay here, Mōna, and keep watch."

Obediently, the wolf sank down upon her haunches and remained where she was as Wulfhere and Ermenilda disappeared into the trees.

Wulfhere did not lead her far. About ten yards in, they came across a small glade ringed with ash and beech. Here, Wulfhere turned and fell upon her.

Ermenilda was ready for him. Her arms locked around his neck, and she raised herself on tiptoe to face him, her mouth savaging his. Wulfhere's hands tore at her clothing, and she fumbled at his. Their fur cloaks dropped to the leaf-strewn ground, and the rest of their clothing followed moments later.

Ermenilda was barely aware of Wulfhere tearing her gown and undertunic off her. All that mattered was the feel of his lips, his tongue—and the hunger for him that pulsed at her core. She grasped at his vest, her fingers tangling in the laces as she struggled to pull it from him.

Panting, she released him and let Wulfhere shrug off the vest and unlace his breeches. She watched the moonlight play across the muscular lines of his chest and belly, and the breadth of his shoulders. Her gaze went to his shaft, and she moaned. It was hard, swollen, and straining toward her.

Wulfhere gathered her up and pushed her back against the trunk of the nearest tree. The feel of his naked flesh on hers and the coolness of the night's air on her bare breasts made her gasp. She writhed against him, wanting him closer still.

Wulfhere bent down and suckled each breast, while his hands moved down the length of her body. Her nipples ached, her breasts sensitive to every touch. When he parted her legs and stroked her between them, Ermenilda shuddered, pleasure radiating out from his fingers.

She gasped his name, collapsing against him as he continued to suckle and stroke her.

"Please," she panted, reaching down and stroking the length of his pulsing erection. "Waited . . . too long. I need you . . ."

Wulfhere answered her with a low growl.

He parted her legs wide and thrust inside her in one smooth movement, burying himself deeply. Ermenilda's cry echoed through the clearing. She heard herself pleading with him.

He ground into her, pinning her against the tree trunk. Then, he began to move inside her, in long deep strokes. Her pleas turned to cries. Wave after wave of throbbing pleasure crested inside her. Ermenilda dug her fingers into his shoulders and wrapped her legs around his hips, drawing him deeper still.

Wulfhere's hoarse cries rose above hers. His body shuddered as he drove into her. A moment later, his body convulsed, and he spilled his seed deep in her womb. Ermenilda clung to him, as if he was a rock in the midst of a raging sea.

Slowly, she became aware of her surroundings: the moonlight filtering through the trees, the faint sound of music, and revelry to the west. She felt the heat from Wulfhere's body and the steady drum of his heartbeat against her breasts.

This is from my dream.

She remembered it now; she had dreamed of this many times while at Bonehill Abbey, to awake aching and tormented after Wulfhere had taken her. Only, now it was real.

Wulfhere's lips trailed the length of her neck, and she shivered under the light touch.

"My Ermenilda," he whispered. "I love you . . . never doubt it."

Epilogue

Collecting Rosemary

Two months later . . .

The snow was falling gently as Ermenilda entered her garden.

The chill air, laced with wood smoke, smelled dank. Delicate snowflakes fluttered down from a colorless sky. It was getting late in the day, and beyond the swirling snow, daylight was fading.

Ermenilda moved through the garden, her rabbit-skin boots sinking into the pristine crust of fresh snow. Basket under her arm, she made her way over to the large bush of rosemary. It grew against the wattle fence that encircled the perimeter. Unlike some of the other herbs, this hardy one would grow all winter.

Working quickly, for the cold air numbed her fingers, Ermenilda snipped off a large branch of rosemary and placed it in her basket.

"I knew I'd find you here."

Ermenilda turned to see Wulfhere behind her. He wore a squirrel cloak about his shoulders. Snowflakes settled upon his hair and eyelashes like tiny jewels.

Ermenilda met his gaze and smiled. She turned and showed him her basket.

"You can't have lamb without rosemary."

Inside the hall, the cooks were roasting two whole lambs over a spit. Ermenilda had insisted they needed to season the meat.

Wulfhere rolled his eyes. "Aye, and thanks to that lamb, the whole tower is filled with greasy smoke."

Ermenilda grimaced. It was true—and another reason why she had been eager to venture outdoors, despite the chill. She was loath to return inside the Great Tower. The cold weather kept everyone indoors, and the odor of stale sweat, together with the smoke from the roasting lamb, made the air in her garden seem perfumed in comparison.

"Come." Wulfhere held out his arm to her. "We will both freeze if we remain out here much longer."

Arm in arm, Wulfhere and Ermenilda left the garden and trudged slowly through the snow back toward the Great Tower.

"I didn't realize you were so fond of rosemary," Wulfhere commented, casting a look in Ermenilda's basket.

Ermenilda shrugged. "Not usually, but I have a yearning for its flavor this evening."

She gave her husband a sidelong glance. She had initially wanted to share her news with him tonight, once they had retired to their loft. Since they were alone now, she thought that perhaps this was the right moment.

"Glaedwine says that a woman can crave odd foods once her womb quickens."

Wulfhere abruptly halted and turned to her. The look of shock on his face made her smile.

"You're with child?"

Ermenilda nodded, smiling hesitantly. "Glaedwine confirmed it this afternoon. The babe will be born late summer."

The joy on her husband's face made Ermenilda's breath catch. Wulfhere was a self-contained man; few besides her saw behind the iron shield he presented to the world. Yet she now knew that he felt things as deeply, if not more so, than other men. In a world where only warriors survived, Wulfhere was careful whom he revealed his soul to, but the happiness in his eyes now brought tears to hers.

"You are pleased then?"

Wulfhere laughed, the sound echoing across the empty yard where they stood. He picked her up and swung her around, as if she weighed nothing. When he set her down, his eyes were shining.

"Pleased? There is no happier man in the whole of Britannia."

He kissed her, a long, sensual kiss that melted her limbs and made Ermenilda wish they were lying naked in the furs together. When the embrace ended, they were both breathless.

Ermenilda met her husband's gaze and, reaching up, stroked his cheek.

"And there is no happier woman either," she replied softly.

The End.

Historical Note

All those who have read my previous books will know that all my novels are based around real historical events and figures. This novel is no exception.

Wulfhere was Penda of Mercia's second son, who ruled from 658–676 AD. He was married to Ermenilda, a Kentish princess, and was the first Christian king of Mercia. After Wulfhere's death, Ermenilda was said to have taken the veil and become abbess of Ely. After her death, she was sainted. Her feast day is February 13.

There is quite a bit of evidence to suggest that their marriage was one of opposites—the wolf and the lamb. This gave me the idea for this story. However, the story recorded by history paints Wulfhere out in a very poor light.

Here is one version of the story (very different from mine!) from *Virgin Saints of the Benedictine Order* (pp. 59–64, Forgotten Books):

Wulfhere was married to the saintly and beautiful Ermenilda, daughter to Erconbert, King of Kent, and of Sexburga his wife. The latter was the daughter of the King Annas, of holy memory, who was slain by Penda. Wulfhere and Ermenilda were strangely matched, for if Wulfhere had inherited his father's courage and military prowess, he had likewise inherited his violent and cruel temper. We wonder how St. Sexburga could have entrusted her gentle young daughter to a man of such character, and, above all, to a pagan; yet she may have foreseen that Ermenilda's influence would at length prevail, and that the leaven of her virtues would gradually impregnate the whole country over which she would one day be queen.

Besides, it was not the first time in history that the "leopard was to lie down with the kid, and the wolf with the lamb" (Isaias xi. 6); a Patricius and a Monica, a Clovis and a Clotilde come readily to mind.

Wulfhere and Ermenilda had four children. Werburgh was the eldest and the only girl; the boys were Ulfald, Rufifin, and Kenred: the last seems to have been much younger than the others. Wulfhere probably did not interfere with the religion of his daughter, since she was baptized and allowed openly to profess her faith. He no doubt thought Christianity good enough for women: but with his sons it was a very different matter. He wished them to be fond of war, to shed blood without scruple, and to shrink from no means so long as they attained their end. Ermenilda was therefore obliged to use her influence with the utmost tact, and to instil Christian principles into them without allowing their father to suspect what she was doing. Fortunately the children all inherited their mother's temperament and virtues; and she did not cease to water and tend with the utmost care the tender plants entrusted to her, endeavoring to enkindle within their hearts the undying flame of charity, and to impress on their minds the imperishable truths which lead to life eternal.

Werburgh must very soon have noticed the contrast between the violent nature of her pagan father and the gentle sweetness of her Christian mother, since we read of her that she had a serious thoughtfulness beyond her years, and took no pleasure in the usual enjoyments of a child. . . .

At that time St. Chad, afterwards Bishop of Lichfield, was living as a hermit in closest union with God in a neighboring forest. St. Ermenilda desired very much that her sons should have him for their master in the spiritual life now that they were growing into man's estate; yet she dreaded her husband's violence if he should come to know of her plan, and endeavored to carry it out with the greatest secrecy. It was therefore agreed that the two elder boys should go out on pretence of hunting expeditions, and that in the course of the chase they should slip away and seek out the hermit's cell. This happened several times, no one apparently suspecting anything; and their young hearts being inflamed by St. Chad's instructions, they begged him not to defer their Baptism. At length the Saint acceded to their request, and, pouring upon their heads the regenerating water, washed their souls white in the Blood of the Lamb.

In the meanwhile Werburgh had reached a marriageable age, and on account of her striking beauty and sweet ways, she was eagerly sought after by suitors for her hand. . . .

However, she had bound her virginity by vow to Christ, and with angelic purity repulsed all suitors, God himself dwelling in her as sole master of all her affections.

Among those who sought her in marriage was a powerful nobleman named Werebode. Wulfhere was greatly indebted to this man, and was anxious to keep on good terms with him from motives of policy as well as of gratitude. He therefore readily agreed to give him his daughter, provided she herself would agree to the union. Werebode was a headstrong, haughty man, unaccustomed to be thwarted, and with a very exalted idea of his own attractions. When, therefore, Werburgh turned a deaf ear to his proposals, he was stung to the quick, and being mad with passion, his love speedily turned into hate. He understood that it was her religion which had raised a barrier between them, and he determined to be revenged both on Werburgh and her faith. He had noticed the mysterious disappearance of the two young princes in the forest, and had secretly watched their interviews with St. Chad. He therefore formed the diabolical plan of compassing their ruin.

He sought out their father and poured out a story full of slander and cunning about the deceit of his sons, telling him how they had deserted the gods of their ancestors, Odin and Thor, and had embraced the religion of the Crucified, and how they were plotting to seize their father's crown and kingdom to make it Christian too. It was easy enough to rouse Wulfhere's passionate nature, and Werebode so worked upon his feelings that he became beside himself with rage. "Come," said Werebode, "and I will give you proof of my story"; and with that the two rode off into the forest. It happened that at the moment they reached the hermit's cell the two boys were kneeling in the rude chapel, having but now received holy Baptism from the hands of St. Chad. . . . The King was exasperated, and, breaking in violently upon them, demanded angrily of them to renounce their superstition and give up their foolery. But no threats could move them, and the father in his fury bade Werebode murder his own sons. Werebode had attained his end, but his triumph was to be shortlived, for soon after he perished miserably.

We can well imagine [Ermenilda's] grief . . . at the terrible crime committed by her husband, and at the loss of two who were dearer to her than life, yet joy and gratitude for the martyrs' death, which had won for her sons an immortal crown. Taking Werburgh with her, Ermenilda set out for the hermitage, and there found St. Chad keeping vigil by the precious relics. Ulfald and Ruffin lay locked in each other's embrace, apparently wrapped in a deep sleep, for no trace remained on their countenances to tell of the violence of their death; rather the smile, which lingered there betokened the souls' awakening to gaze for ever on the Master for whom their lives had been sacrificed. Tenderly and reverently St. Chad, assisted by Ermenilda and

Werburgh, laid them in their last resting-place, which was soon to become so favourite a place of pilgrimage. Then the mother and daughter retraced their steps homewards with heavy hearts, not knowing what to expect, scarce knowing what to hope for. But the dying prayer of the sons for their father had not been in vain; the blood which they had shed cried for mercy and not for vengeance, and even Wulfhere's hard nature could not withstand the flood of grace which the little martyrs obtained for him. Remorse, keen and deep, had taken possession of him, and he bitterly deplored the fearful result of his passion. Humbled and crushed, he listened the more readily to the words of hope spoken to him by Ermenilda and Werburgh, and consented to go to St. Chad to confess his sin and be instructed by him in the faith for which his sons had died. Finally, he embraced Christianity, and with the sacred waters of Baptism expiated his crime.

I've also used an excerpt from the epic Anglo-Saxon poem *Beowulf* (1384–1389) as the scop's song in chapter twenty-five.

About the Author

Award-winning author Jayne Castel writes Historical Romance set in Dark Ages Britain and Scotland, and Epic Fantasy Romance. Her vibrant characters, richly researched historical settings and action-packed adventure romance transport readers to forgotten times and imaginary worlds.

Jayne lives in New Zealand's South Island, although you can frequently find her in Europe and the UK researching her books! When she's not writing, Jayne is reading (and re-reading) her favorite authors, learning French, cooking Italian, and taking her dog, Juno, for walks.

Jayne won the 2017 RWNZ Koru Award (Short, Sexy Category) for her novel, ITALIAN UNDERCOVER AFFAIR.

www.jaynecastel.com

CPSIA information can be obtained
at www.ICGtesting.com
Printed in the USA
LVHW101459091122
732745LV00009B/48

9 781537 121086